BERYL BLUE, TIME COP

JANET RAYE STEVENS

Janet Raye Stevens
☺

GREAT BROOK PUBLISHING

ACKNOWLEDGMENTS

A big shout out to all the writers and readers who have helped me make this first story in Beryl Blue's adventures shine like the brass buttons on her boyfriend Sully's dress uniform. Suzanne Tierney, Tracy Brody, Brenda Lowder, Christine Gunderson, Ruth McCarty, Miranda Darrow, Cori Deyoe, Kari Lemor, and especially Lea Kirk and the many writing contest judges who've given me your feedback, time, and advice – you all have my undying gratitude.

Thanks also to Elizabeth Turner Stokes for creating such a kickass cover, and to producer/director Irwin Allen, whose cheesy-fun TV series, *The Time Tunnel,* hooked me as a kid and inspired a life-long love of all things time travel.

To my husband who keeps me sane and to my kids who work diligently toward the opposite result

1

"**B**eryl Blue, Time Cop," I shouted. "*Stop!*"

The guy I chased didn't. Didn't even slow down. Which put me in A Mood, as Grandma Blue had called my teenaged temperament. But who could blame me for getting annoyed? My ankle still bitched from last week's not-so-fun run in 1599, when I took down that woman stalking Shakespeare. The trip through the temporal gate today had been its usual shake-and-bake fun. And now here I was in 1977, running after an overdue time tourist on a steamy hot July afternoon.

While wearing a policewoman's uniform with a worsted wool jacket and skirt.

And pantyhose.

What's more, the time-perp I pursued zipped along on roller skates. Sprinting after him made my ankle throb like hell.

"Come on, man," I called. "Stop!"

The guy pumped his chalky legs harder, picking up

speed. His skate wheels rumbled as he zigzagged around pedestrians. He was cruising for a close encounter with my Cack .28, and I was going to oblige. Time Scope Excursions had a whole list of rules for time tourists, but number one was to come home when your vacation in the past had ended. No exceptions.

That's where I came in. My job was to find and extract overdue time tourists any way necessary.

I slipped the weapon out of its holster and armed it. My quarry skated into the clear. I aimed. The guy fell. Not from the Cack's invisible burst of scorching juice. From a crack. In the sidewalk. Flew ass over teakettle and landed flat on his squishy butt. To my relief, and to the delight of Hampton Beach's feathery-hairdo crowd, who cheered his triple-gainer wipeout.

I holstered the Cack and limped over to him. He grimaced up at me. Would've been comical if he didn't look so pathetic, splayed like a starfish in his disco roller boogie outfit, his short shorts riding up high enough for all 1977 to get a good look at his package.

I averted my eyes. I'm dainty that way.

"You wouldn't have caught me if I didn't trip," he said, sitting up and wincing in pain.

"Seriously? I would've killed you." I tapped my holster for emphasis. Time Scope didn't fool around. Better to take out a rogue time tourist than have them upset the timeline by running wild in the past.

I helped the guy to stand. He wobbled like a newborn colt until he got his balance.

"Please, ma'am, don't bring me back," he said. Begged, really.

"Ma'am?" Yikes. I was twenty-four, still got carded everywhere I went. This guy was pushing forty. "Do I look like your grandmother?"

"I'm sorry, ma'am, uh, officer. But, please, don't take me back. I don't *belong* in 2130."

Oh, crap. He was one of *them*. A runner. He hadn't stepped through one of Time Scope's temporal gates to go on an expensive vacation, or even with a nefarious plan to loot the treasures of the past. He'd intended his time trip to be only one way. He'd intended to disappear into history.

"That's what they all say," I muttered, avoiding his pleading eyes, because—irony alert—I didn't belong in 2130 either. Six months ago, I was a happy wannabe librarian living my life in the early 21st century. Well, sort of happy. Okay, pretty miserable if truth be told. But the thing was, I could never, ever go back to that time. "And, seriously, 1977? I mean, *Star Wars* comes out, I get that. But of all the time periods in all of history, why run here? Why now?"

"I love the music. And..." He sniffed the air. "You smell that? What is it? It's heavenly."

I'd caught the smell too, had packed on five pounds just from the aroma. "Fried dough."

His milky blue eyes lit up. "Fried dough," he said with reverence, then his voice cracked with sudden panic. "Please don't take me back. Say you killed me. Say anything. *Please* let me stay."

This guy hit new levels of pathetic, going straight for my heart. Guess he didn't get the memo. I used to let emotions guide me. Not anymore. Glo Reid, Time Scope and a lying guy named Jake Tyson had seen to that. Now I was nothing but a cold-hearted company goon.

At least, that's what I kept telling myself.

"Look, disco man," I said, harsher than I intended. I would *not* let this pathetic puppy get to me. "You *can't* stay. A skate down the sidewalk in 1977 won't change anything, but if you disappear into the past? The future. Is. Screwed. So, no way I'm leaving you here, *capiche*?"

My bad ass act seemed to scare him more than threatening him with the Cack. He came along quietly when I suggested we find a spot where we could disappear without witnesses. I towed him away from the beach toward the bustling downtown, looking for an alley. He gazed wistfully at the boat-sized cars clogging the street, the people dressed in colors that would make Joseph's *Technicolor Dreamcoat* look subdued, and the stores advertising wares still made in the USA.

"Wait." I stopped, spotting a sale sign in a store window. I felt a smile coming on. I hadn't smiled in a while. It felt good. "A quick stop, then back home and off to the cage with you."

"That's contraband," my prisoner cried when he saw where we were headed. "I'll tell unless you let me go."

"No, you won't." I patted my holster again and he shut up. But to be on the safe side, I decided to invest in a big piece of fried dough for his enjoyment before we went back to the future.

"You bucking for Time Cop of the year, Beryl?" Carmine slapped the buzzer and the holding cage door clanged sideways. "That's the third temporal ex-pat you brung in this month."

I shrugged. "It's an epidemic."

Carmine scratched his salt-and-pepper mustache then dug into his ear for good measure. "I don't get why anyone would run to an earlier time. We got everything you could ever want here."

"I know, right?" I said, adjusting the package in the brown paper bag tucked under my arm. Not *every*thing.

I signaled to my disco friend to wipe fried dough crumbs off his face then pushed him into the cell. He rolled across the tile, and I held my breath as he tripped-fell onto a bench. The guy had been through enough without the added indignity of face planting in front of Time Scope's second shift. The cell door slid shut and I turned away from his sad blue eyes.

Poor guy. He'd be off to rehab in the morning. Not the kind of rehab anyone from my 21st century home would recognize. No twelve steps, no daily affirmations. It was a quick fix that involved some kind of laser lobotomy. The guy would be all happy-happy, joy-joy and would never want to roller boogie in another time period again.

I pushed the guy's brain-scrambling fate out of my mind. What he'd done was dangerous. I cringed to think what could've happened to the historical timeline if I hadn't caught him.

After what seemed like weeks of paperwork, I returned my '70s cop uniform to wardrobe and changed into jeans and a windbreaker. I tucked my contraband into my backpack and took a Metro-Slide home in the fading daylight of an April afternoon. The lights in my high-rise studio apartment popped on as I entered. Jenjen, my monstrous Maine coon, met me at the door. I took off my jacket and hefted my backpack onto the kitchen counter, pushing aside a stack of books. Jenjen leapt up with impressive agility for such a fat cat and stuck his face into the backpack as I unzipped it.

"That's not for you." I pushed him away and pulled out a six-pack of Budweiser.

I'd broken one of Time Scope's many rules: no souvenirs. But it wasn't like the powers that signed my paycheck dared to squawk. After everything I'd gone through on the company's behalf, they owed me. Big time.

I slipped my finger through the ring-tab on one of the beer cans and popped the top. The beer was foamy from the time trip, but still cold.

"Can't get beer like this here in 2130," I said, taking a sip and scratching behind Jenjen's ear. "Not without a prescription, anyway."

He twitched his tail, a signal in any century that said, "Not interested. Feed me."

A bowl of kitty chow later, he washed his paws contentedly as I settled into my chair and started on my own dinner, the second can of my contraband six pack.

"Entertainment Communications Interface," I said, resting my sore ankle on a footstool. A portion of my apartment's west wall dissolved at my command to reveal a giant TV screen. Several function icons popped up. "Music." The icons faded, except for the G-clef, which blossomed in size. "World War Two mix. Random."

The aching, melancholy "I'll Be Seeing You," sung by Rosemary Clooney, softly filled the air. My heart wrenched as the memories rushed in like a flood tide. I thought of the roller boogie disco man and the music he loved. Music that made him give up everything to flee to another time. I didn't get his passion for the thumping '70s disco beat, but I got where the passion came from. I'd risk everything, too, if I could go back to that one moment, forget about the timeline, and just go.

Go to *him*.

Before I could stop myself, I had the photograph in my hand. I'd never uploaded it to the Interface. I didn't want anyone else to get access to it, whether by accident or design. I wanted it where only I could see it, only I could hold it. I'd tucked the photo into a drawer in my bedside table, promising myself I'd only look at it once a month.

Yesterday. I'd made that promise yesterday.

"What can I say, Sully?" I murmured, gazing at the photo. "I'm weak."

There they were, in glorious four-by-five black-and-white. Four GIs crowded around a small table littered with beer bottles and shot glasses, looking like the cast of a John Wayne World War II movie. Marco, Griff, Stan...

And Sully.

I slid my thumb over Sully's face. I longed to stroke that impossibly strong jaw for real. To touch that Grand Canyon-deep chin cleft. Run my fingers through his thick, copper-red hair. A cigarette dangled from his lips, as usual. Smoke coiled around his eyes, making him squint. He was smiling. The one honest, happy moment before he shipped out. Before places like Normandy and Bastogne.

I was in the picture, perched on Sully's lap. I looked pretty. I was smiling too. Really smiling. I was so soft then. Not my body. I'd always been a solid size fourteen. My heart was soft. Sully had his arm around my waist, his free hand rested on my leg. I could almost feel his touch, his hand on my thigh, his fingers gently massaging. The ache in my heart doubled.

I had to stop doing this, had to stop pining for a memory and longing for a past I couldn't share.

I reached for another can and popped the top on my third beer, hoping the buzz beginning to cloud my brain would help me forget.

Forget, for just a little while.

2

I picked up a stack of recently returned books from the cart, heaved a self-pitying sigh, and headed to the bookshelves. The tall, metal behemoths ranged across the attic floor in a row, like soldiers at attention.

Shelving. *Ugh*. My least favorite part of my job.

I'd wanted to be a librarian since I was a kid and had first discovered the wonderful world of books. An odd career choice in this digital age, but for me, it made sense. Books helped make me the snarky know-it-all I am today. They got me through the trauma of losing my parents at six, losing my grandmother and only remaining relative at fifteen, and two long years in the cold bosom of the Massachusetts state foster care system.

But I had yet to reach my goal. At the moment, I toiled for minimum wage as a wannabe librarian in my hometown library. Up to my eyebrows in student loans and only a year into my multi-year plan to earn my master's in Library and Information Sciences. As a wannabe, I got stuck with all the mundane chores the real librarians

9

fervently avoided. And the most mundane of mundane chores was shelving.

I sneezed. Especially shelving in the musty, dusty attic of a 150-year-old building.

I got to work, moving fast to outrun the dust, wedging each book into its spot back on the shelf. Before long, I reached the last book on my cart, *World War II for Dummies*. I looked up, way up, to the top of one of the stacks, at the space where the book lived. Then I looked at the ladder, a creaky old thing the word *rickety* had been coined for.

I considered ditching *Dummies* and heading to Dunkins for a pumpkin spice donut and a mid-morning shot of caffeine. Except, no way was I giving the prickly library director, George Spencer, the chance to accuse me of falling down on the job. Not when I had an evaluation coming up. So, I tucked the book under one arm and started to climb. The ladder moaned and groaned and I trembled—heights and I had long ago agreed to disagree —but I made it to the top unscathed.

For a second, anyway.

I reached over to shove the book into place when the world tipped. No, correct that—*I* tipped. And fell. Face down like a skydiver with no parachute. I should've hit the floor with a spectacular thud, maybe smacked my head on the metal stepstool poking out from under the shelf, but something cushioned my fall.

Not something. *Someone.*

I would've cursed, in a whisper, of course—I'm a (wannabe) librarian after all—but the impact *oofed* the wind out of me. The small woman under me didn't say anything, didn't move either and I thought I'd killed her. Entirely possible, with me landing on her like that. She should've been pancaked into the floorboards. But no, she wasn't dead and proved it by shoving me off her and scrambling up.

Then she held out a hand. Dumbly, I reached up to shake, as if she were saying, "Nice to meet ya," before I realized she meant to help me up. I let her, and damn she was strong for someone so small. She lifted me like I was made of paper.

"Are you injured?" she asked, watching me dust myself off.

Uh, shouldn't I ask *her* that question? With follow-ups like *who are you* and *where'd you come from?* The library was closed on Mondays, the doors locked up tight. Even if she had somehow slipped inside, the attic entrance was in the other direction. She could've come from only one place.

Through the wall.

I took a breath. "I think I may have hit my head."

She looked concerned.

"On account of I think I'm seeing things," I added, staring at the wall where it met the pitched ceiling. It leaked there. Water seeped through the wood panels like pooling blood in even the slightest rainstorm, but it was solid. And four stories up. How could somebody just walk through it? Well, run. I'd seen only a fast-moving blur as I fell, as if tiny her had been rushing to catch not-so-tiny me.

I swung back to her. She looked kind of like the actress Halle Berry, only younger, around thirty, but with the same petite build, awesome bone structure, and toned body. And wearing, weirdly, a blue gingham dress like Dorothy in *The Wizard of Oz*. No ruby slippers or Toto, but she did have a big messenger bag slung bandolier-style across her front.

"And the fact that I'm hallucinating," I added. Like Dorothy, I'd conked my noggin, and had fallen into a dream-delusion, with no hope of help. My boss George and the head librarian, Ida Pellerin were four stories below. I could be stuck up here for hours with Halle Berry's clone and, hey, if I had to imagine a one-on-one with a celebrity, why couldn't she be a he? Say, a Hemsworth? Any Hemsworth would do. I wasn't picky.

I reached for a chair near the dust-speckled, antique rolltop desk. "I think I need to sit for a minute."

"You do that. You had a scare." She waited a beat. No, half a beat. "Rested? Good. My name's Glo Reid. I'm here because I need your help."

It struck me that she might not be a head trauma-induced delusion after all. Except for the flying through the wall thing, she seemed pretty real. She breathed. Sweat beaded her forehead. She also wore some god-awful perfume. Smelled like a Walmart ninety-nine-cent special, heated with a blowtorch.

"O-kay," I said warily. "You need my help. With what?"

"Saving the world."

Maybe *she* was the one hallucinating. "Sure. You can't ask me to find some overdue books. I have to save the world."

"You're the only one who can."

"Why? Somebody messing with the Dewey Decimal System?"

Glo shot me a *wise-ass* scowl. "Worse. *Much* worse. I'm security director for Time Scope Excursions in the year 2130. One of my team's gone rogue. Into the past. Specifically, 1943. He's bent on destroying the historical timeline. I need *you* to help us stop him."

Yeah, she *definitely* was hallucinating. "Uh-huh."

She reached into her bag and pulled out a tablet in a blush-colored case. "Here are my credentials." She tapped the screen and the light popped on.

"Really? You expect me to believe people are still using tablets a hundred years from now—"

I swallowed my snark as a rainbow of pixels swirled up from the screen, settling like dust into a 3-D hologram of Glo in a drab gray uniform and a don't-screw-with-me frown. Text scrolled under the image, displaying her name and everything she had just told me. She'd clearly gone all in to try to convince me her delusion was real, including getting her hands on some amazing tech.

"*Now* will you help me with this mission?" she demanded.

Mission? Off. Her. Rocker. How long had she been like this? Maybe crashing through walls was her hobby and it'd done a number on her brain.

"Depends." On whether she had a weapon in that bag. "Why don't you tell me about this...mission? Then I'll decide."

I adopted an attentive expression as she poured out her story. Now, call me cynical. Getting kicked in the teeth by fate and the foster care system for two years wasn't exactly a recipe for *Pollyanna*. Pardon me if I had trouble swallowing Glo's tale. Rogue time cop from 2130 out to kill GI Joe in 1943? Me, Beryl Blue, the only person in all of time who could stop him? *Please*. Something about my DNA being unmapped, but I didn't really pay attention. I only paid attention to how insane her story sounded. Plus, a total rip-off. That time traveling madman bent on changing history thing had been done to death.

But I humored her, letting her talk, as I scrambled for a way to get to the book cart—and my phone—so I could call 911.

"You're not listening," she said.

"I am. Madman wants to kill John Sullivan for some nefarious purpose. I have to stop him. See? I'm listening."

"No, *Tom* Sullivan." Big sigh. "I *knew* this wouldn't work. I told h—" She cut off. "I'll just show you." She began tapping on the tablet's screen. "Don't move."

Note to self—when an alleged time traveler tells you not to move, you move. And fast. Because I didn't and a second later, I was trapped. A blue tornado whipped up inside the attic, followed by a NASCAR-level *vroom*. The stench of sulfur, mixed with Glo's perfume, stung my nostrils. The bookshelves and walls wavered and shimmied and began to melt like a Dali painting. Electricity shivered over my skin. *Under* my skin. My feet left the ground and I gaped down in terrified awe as my toes hovered a foot above the floor.

Glo tapped the screen again. It was like she flicked the *on* switch to a giant vacuum cleaner. The library dissolved and my body was sucked into an undulating vortex with a sickening *s-p-p-p-lurch.*

Now I believed. Every damn word Glo had said.

I screamed. I'm dramatic like that. Who wouldn't be, when your atoms were being scrambled into a million pieces? When your stomach felt as if it was being ripped out through your navel? When you're flipped end over end like an out-of-control ride at Six Flags and certain death was imminent?

Then...*pop!* And nothing. Except some birds chirping and a distant rumble, like thunder on the horizon. And me lying dazed and confused in the middle of a dirt road. Still screaming.

"Please shut up."

I opened my eyes to see Glo frowning down at me, crisp blue sky above her. Her gaze shifted and her expression suddenly scrunched like a constipated goose.

"Move!" she cried.

I looked left. Not thunder—the rumble of an Army truck. Headed right for us. Fast. The driver leaned on the horn. I scuttled like a frantic crab out of its path. Wind whipped my hair as the vehicle roared by, just missing my toes.

I collapsed onto the grass and curled into a fetal ball. *"Ohmigawdohmigawdohmigawd..."*

Glo plopped down next to me. "Stop whining. He missed you by a country kilometer."

"Wh-what was that...tornado ride you took me on?" I cried. "Felt like you were cutting out my kidneys with a spoon."

"Welcome to the temporal skip. It's a little rough on

re-entry."

"A *little* rough?" I unspooled from the fetal position and sat up. "Where are we?"

"Outside your hometown of Ballard Springs, on the road to Camp Davis. October, 1943."

I should've been all, *yeah right*, but I'd just been sliced-and-diced in a temporal food-processor. Almost flattened by a truck that looked like it drove straight out of *Saving Private Ryan*. I was a believer.

I scowled. "I want to go home. *Now*."

She got what Grandma Blue called a mulish set to her jaw. "No, Beryl. You're here to do a job and you're going to do it."

"Why am *I* the only fool who can do this job?"

A long pause. "*I'd* do it, but I might not be welcomed by the soldiers in this era. The American military is still segregated."

"Yeah. I know that history," I said, softening. And I knew my World War II history in particular, thanks to Grandma Blue. She thought the era she'd grown up in was the bee's knees and made sure to tell me all about it. I might not win big playing 1940s *Jeopardy*, but I knew enough about the period not to embarrass myself.

I eyed Glo, still doubtful. "Tell me again what this so-called mission's all about."

She sighed. "It's about a man named Jake Tyson. In the next forty-eight hours, somewhere between the Army camp—" She gestured up the road where the truck had gone. "And the town, Ballard Springs—" She pointed the other way. "Jake's going to kill Sergeant Tom Sullivan."

"And he's going to kill him because...?"

"I told you, we don't know why. We just know he *is*. Look, it's not that important."

She flicked the tablet screen again and a 3-D image of Jake crystallized. And what an image. Late-twenties, tall, lean, black hair, chiseled cheekbones, stunning blue eyes, almost a young Jake Gyllenhaal clone. A genuine clone, for all I knew. With these future people able to travel in time, there may be a clone-your-favorite-celebrity machine on every corner too.

"All you need to know is that Jake's gone rogue. He stole one of these devices." She shook the tablet and Jake's hologram did a little dance. "It's a Temporal Displacement Catalyzer, what we call a Kicker. He used it to go on an unauthorized time-trip. We tracked his temporal DNA here, where he intends to kill *this* guy in the next two days."

More tapping and Jake melted into the screen like the Wicked Witch, replaced by a broad-shouldered guy in a sergeant's uniform. The image was blurry, but I saw enough to be able to pick him out of a police line-up.

"If Jake gets to him, it'll irrevocably change history," Glo went on. "We have to stop him."

"*We?*"

"Okay. *You.*"

"Because all time trippers in your era get their DNA mapped. Which can be tracked with that Kicker thingy. But, since you don't have my DNA on record, Jake won't see me coming."

"Hey, you *were* listening."

I'd heard it, just didn't believe it. Still couldn't. "How do you know I won't freak and run away?"

"I don't. But I've been watching you a while. I have confidence you won't run."

"You've been watching me?" She hadn't mentioned this bit of intel in the library. "What're you, Clarence the angel from *It's a Wonderful Life*? How long have you been watching me?"

"Long enough to know you're right for the job."

"Why? Why me?"

Glo regarded me soberly. "Because of your life. What you've been through."

"Really? Life throwing shit at me was training for this mission?"

"It made you tough. You lost a lot. Your grandmother, your parents." She let that hang a moment. "It was an accident, right?"

I gazed toward the field across the road, bordered by a stone boundary wall. Neat rows of apple trees cut across the field's center. The fruit had already been picked, but the scent of apples still floated on the autumn breeze. My mother loved the fall, and apple picking. One of my earliest memories, a memory I hung on to.

"Yeah," I murmured. "My parents died when I was six." A car fire I'd barely escaped, another of my earliest memories. One I did my best to forget. "I lived with my grandmother after that, until...cancer. After that, foster home roulette." I gazed at Glo. "But I'm guessing you know all that."

She nodded. "That's why we chose you. You're strong. You survive."

"I suppose I should be flattered. But, simple fact, I had no choice."

She patted my knee and stood. "Come on, you've got a job to do."

"Right. The job. And what is that exactly? You've been slim on details. How do I stop this Jake guy from destroying the world?"

"First, you have to dress like you belong here." She put down the Kicker and dug some clothes and a pair of shoes out of her apparently bottomless bag. "Put these on."

"You think of everything." I got up and sifted through the pile she handed me. Blue wool skirt, cream-colored sweater set, a fortress of undergarments, ugly-ass Mary Jane shoes. "Seriously? I have to wear these?"

"You can't run around in *that*," she said as if my jeans and *Doctor Who* tee shirt personally offended her. "You need to fit in. The world's at war. Everyone's suspicious. The slightest hint you don't belong, a single word of where and when you're from and you could end up in jail. Or worse."

My shoulders sagged. Why argue? I was already in 1943, so...

I ducked into the lilac bushes. Reasonably sure no one could see me through the droopy leaves, I changed. The skirt and sweater set went over silk stockings with honest-to-goodness garters, a slip, and silk boxers under a belly-flattening girdle. Here I was doing crunches every damn day when all I had to do was squeeze myself into an official GI Jane girdle. Not to mention the industrial strength bra that lifted and separated better than any boob job ever could. No wonder all those Greatest Generation pin-up babes looked like they were 38-double-Ds.

"I'm not much into cosplay," I said when I emerged from the bushes. "But dang, this outfit sings." Except the shoes. They'd be ugly in any era.

Glo stuffed my twenty-first century clothing into her bag and looked me over. "You'll do. Everything seems to fit."

"Perfectly. It's almost like you knew my measurements — *Oh*." These people were incredible, and not in a good way.

"There's a suitcase over there, under that bush," Glo said, pointing. "It should have everything you need for the weekend. Sergeant Sullivan will be along soon, headed to that gas station down the road. He's got leave. I suggest you hitch a ride with him."

"Wait, I thought I was after Jake Tyson, not the other guy."

She gave me a patient look. "You are. But where the sergeant goes, Jake's sure to follow."

"What if this Tom Sullivan doesn't want me hanging around?"

Her lips wiggled like a worm on the sidewalk. Her version of a smile, I guess. "Beryl, what soldier on leave wouldn't want a beautiful brunette like you around?"

"Uh, did you just call me beautiful?"

"If the shoe fits, as your Grandma Blue would say."

It hit me. Grandma Blue would be about ten years old now, living not too far from Ballard Springs. "Glo, if I can stop this Jake guy, doesn't that mean I can...you know, maybe, save my parents?"

My throat went tight. Beryl Blue, selfish twit. Shouldn't I ask for the chance to go after Hitler, or one of history's other monsters? For the greater good. Instead, I thought only of myself and my own pain.

Glo looked me straight in the eye. "Beryl, history *can't* be changed. If you save your parents, it causes ripples that turn into waves that end up impacting every moment of time from that point forward until..." She ground her teeth. "Chaos is a mild way to describe it. That's why Jake *has* to be stopped. If he succeeds, he screws up *everything*."

Well, she'd stomped on my hope blossom quite thoroughly.

She softened a fraction. "I know. It sucks, as you'd say. Nobody knows it better than me. I have to deal with this every day. And now Jake and his insane..." She held up both hands. "Let's move on, okay?" She took a long silver rectangle out of her bag and handed it to me. "Here. It's a Cack .28. It'll do the job."

I took it, staring at the thing in confusion. Metal, cool, smooth to the touch. Like a TV remote, it had control buttons. Unlike a remote, the buttons were marked arm, stun, and kill. That third directive gave me chills.

"It's self-explanatory," Glo said. "Press *arm* and it's ready to fire for thirty seconds. Aim carefully and get close. The weapon's range is only six-point-five meters. Understand?"

I had no idea what that distance translated to in American math, but I nodded dumbly, too overwhelmed to comprehend any of it.

"Good. Only shoot when you're sure of your target. We don't want you to accidentally kill a bystander. The only one we want you to kill is Jake."

The world screeched to a halt.

"*Kill?* I thought I was supposed to bring him in, like a cop. I think I can take him down. I'm a black belt." Third-degree black belt, in fact. I'd started karate on the state's nickel back in my foster kid days, thanks to my court-appointed therapist. She thought it'd be a good way to channel my hostility, specifically away from her.

"Beryl, this can't be fixed with a kick to the gonads. Jake's broken temporal law. He's trying to rewrite history. That's a capital crime, punishable by death." She nodded at the Cack. "Go on, try it out."

"No way. Sorry, Glo, but mission declined."

I held out the weapon. She went all *not it* and stuck her hands behind her back.

"What's to keep Jake from killing me first?" I asked before thinking the question through. *Gah.* What if he tried to kill me first? I wanted to go fetal again. "Glo, take me home. Now!"

Her face closed up and she started tapping the Kicker screen again.

I took that as a no. "I can't kill Jake. I'm *not* killing him, or you, or anybody." I could barely breathe.

"Beryl, you *have* to." She pinned me in her gaze. She'd gone stone cold, emotionless. Hard as nails and twice as unforgiving. "Jake won't, *can't* be brought in, or taken down. He has to be dead. *You* have to kill him. It's the only way."

I struggled to stay upright. "Why? Why do *I* have to do it?"

"Because, if you don't, you won't live to see tomorrow."

And then she vanished in a tornado of blue wind.

3

ou won't live to see tomorrow.

A bald-faced threat, right out of a cheesy movie. Or a bad dream. I dropped down on the grass, mainly because my legs wouldn't hold me up. This couldn't be happening. A madwoman from the future bopping around in time? Trying to convince me she'd whisked me to 1943 and I had to kill a guy with a TV remote before she would take me home? Threatening me with death if I didn't do what she asked?

This *had* to be a dream. A nightmare.

Except... The leaves fluttering on the trees were peak fall—vibrant red, yellow, and orange. That looked real. Birds chirped like crazy. That sounded real. The apple scent in the air and the exhaust belched by a passing Humphrey Bogart movie car smelled real. Really real.

Another vehicle drove by, this time a jeep that kicked up gravel as it bounced down the road. Five men in uniform were crammed into the seats. The guy riding shotgun stared straight ahead, his hat pushed back at a rakish angle, as if he dared the wind to grab it. I recognized him from the hologram Glo had shown me.

Sgt. Tom Sullivan.

He was real. And right on time. And I was supposed to save him.

I gulped. *Okay, 1943, I'm stuck with you, now what?* I could sit here in a cocoon of denial. Give in to the mother of all panic attacks. I could run away, my default setting when I got scared. Or... I could shove the fear into the deepest compartment in my brain and get on with it. Do the job as best I could. So I could go home.

Not like I had a choice, anyway. Glo had flown away like Glinda in her bubble, leaving Dorothy to face the unknown on her own. Dorothy had improvised and I could too. Maybe I could figure a way out of that tricky *kill* option, talk Jake into giving up or something.

Everything might...no, everything *would* work out. It had to.

Feeling a bit less terrified and a fraction more confident, I got up and dragged the suitcase Glo had mentioned out from under the bush. Old school, like the kind Grandma Blue carried long ago when she went on her mysterious weekends away. Leather, with a braided handle and silver snaps, the brand name stamped on the lid read *Amelia Earhart*, which would've seemed ironic in a lost luggage kind of way, if I had time to think about it.

I snapped the suitcase open and tossed the Cack on top of the colorful things inside. I closed the cover, hoping never to see that strange weapon again. Then I set out, hurrying along the road's dirt shoulder.

I aimed for the filling station ahead. I grimaced when

I realized where Glo had dropped me. If Camp Davis was nearby, this had to be Rand Road. That picture-postcard apple orchard would become the concrete eyesore known as the Rand Farm Mall in my time. I got caught shoplifting a scented candle from *Spencer's Gifts* there at the precocious age of twelve. Didn't want the candle, it smelled like sweaty socks dipped in oatmeal, as I recall. I just wanted to see if I could do it. I could *not*, and Grandma Blue went ballistic when she'd gotten the call from mall security to come pick me up.

I reached my destination sooner than I thought, stopping a moment to catch my breath and to scope out the scene across the road. The jeep had pulled up alongside one of the station's two skinny gas pumps. An attendant in a peaked cap had lifted the driver's seat cushion and was pumping gas into what I guessed was the fuel tank underneath. The soldiers milled around the jeep and everyone, even the pump jockey, had lit up. As in cigarettes. Clearly those fellas hadn't heard cigarettes and gas pumps don't mix.

Fellas. Funny how that word had instantly entered my vocabulary. When in 1943, I guess.

I waited on the shoulder for a farm truck with corn stalks flapping from the back to pass. Then, my heart pounding like a jackhammer on speed, I started across the road. I kept my eye on Sullivan. He stepped away from the jeep and shook a cigarette from a white package. He lit a match and had just touched it to the cigarette when he saw me. He exhaled long and slow, squinting at me through the smoke.

Well now. The hologram Glo showed me had *not*

done him justice. He wasn't handsome like the guy I was supposed to stop, whose lean physique and sculpted features seemed genetically enhanced. Sullivan was... Let's just say he fit every physical feature that pushed my buttons. Broad shoulders and muscular build? Check. Rugged, lumberjack features? Check. Over six feet? Check, plus two inches. A real rough-and-tumble kind of fella. And was that red hair peeking out from under his hat? I loved redheads. Had Glo known that?

Sullivan checked me out too. But, while I ogled him with a *yes, please* drool, he gave no clue what he thought of me. His gaze traveled from the tips of my ugly-ass Mary Janes to the top of my chestnut curls without a blink. No hint of a yea or nay. That annoyed me right off the bat, and I admit to a petty smirk as the forgotten match he held singed his fingers. He winced and hastily shook out the flame.

I reached him and stopped a few feet away. Okay, now what? We eyed each other, me nervous as hell. Him? Who could tell? He had an excellent poker face. The other fellas noticed me then. They stopped chattering and stared. I twisted my hands around the suitcase handle.

"I was wondering," I began, so totally unnerved my voice cracked. I cleared my throat and started again. "I was dropped off here." I waved vaguely up the road. "And I'm in need of a lift into town. I was hoping, if you'd be so kind..."

I guess I shouldn't have been surprised by the snickers and wolf whistles that greeted my request. I mean, here were a bunch of soldiers headed to town for

26

weekend leave with dames and dancing on their minds, and a woman just drops into their midst, hitching a ride. I could've looked like Jabba the Hutt and their eyes would've popped out of their skulls.

Sullivan didn't say a word. He moved toward me on strong, muscular legs, and okay, sue me, but I imagined what he looked like under the uniform. His face close-up was even more intriguing—that copper-colored hair, his rugged skin, and a square jaw softened by a deep cleft in his chin. An angry scar slashed across his nose. There was a story behind that.

His eyes struck me most, dark blue, steady. Old. Not wrinkly old, but life old. Glo said he was twenty-four, like me, but his eyes were a lot older. Like he'd seen it all, more than once.

And damn it, my empathy meter kicked in.

"You say you were just...*dropped* here?" he said. He had a deep, sexy-time radio announcer voice that would have been appealing if he didn't sound so suspicious.

"Yes. My ride was supposed to take me to Ballard Springs, but..." A sign stuck to one of the gas pumps, *Gas rationing in effect for the duration,* gave me an idea. "But they couldn't spare the fuel. You know, rationing and all."

He took a long, assessing drag, cigarette pinched between his thumb and forefinger. Smoke shot from his nose like a dragon as he exhaled. "And they just left you here? On the highway?"

They called this dirt path a highway? "Hey, it's no big deal." I scrambled to soften his suspicion. "I didn't want to be a bother. They're my aunt and uncle, and their daughter, uh, my cousin, she got sick and they had to leave, and she lives far away and—"

I didn't get a chance to finish. He pulled me into his arms.

WHY, Sergeant Sullivan, I hardly know you.

That zinged through my mind between the moment he crushed me to him and when he literally swept me off my feet. I instinctively embraced him and held on for dear life as he leapt backward and we seemed to go airborne. My suitcase and his hat went flying.

Behind me, car tires ground into gravel. Shouts rang out. We fell. Sullivan toppled like a mighty oak, hitting the dirt with a thud that shook us both. I landed on top of him. The car that had veered off the road and nearly plowed into us sped off without braking.

Then, silence. I gazed at the man under me. We lay entwined in the dirt, shaking, breathing hard. His warm, tobacco-tinged breath brushed my face. For the second time today, someone had cushioned my fall. Only this time I wasn't afraid I'd killed him. He was alive and well and quite able to absorb the impact of me bouncing on his chest.

"Hey, you asked me for a lift," he said. His voice rumbled beneath my breasts. I was acutely aware of them pressing against his solid chest. I was also aware of the soldiers and the attendant, watching us with dopey grins.

"Very funny," I said, pushing against him. "Let me up."

He started to loosen his hold then seemed to think

28

better of it. His arms tightened around me. "Not 'til you say thank you," he said, mischief in his voice.

"Thank you?" I tried again to break free, not a smart thing to do. He enjoyed me wriggling on him way too much. I mean, that was definitely not a gun in his pocket, and, yeah, he was happy to see me. "Thank you for what?"

"That lead foot tried to run you down. I just saved your life."

Huh? Oh. Pretty sure that had been a clumsy attempt on Sullivan's life, but I was too freaked to argue the point. I just wanted to get up. He wouldn't let me. He seemed content to hold me like this all day, grinning like a lunatic, so I gave in. "Oh, all right, thank you."

"And say you're sorry."

"Seriously? Why should I say I'm sorry?"

He jerked his chin toward his cigarette, smoldering in the dust nearby. "That was my last Lucky Strike."

I snorted. "You should thank *me* for that one. Don't you know cigarettes are bad for you? They're dangerous."

He cocked an eyebrow. "Dangerous?"

Dang. It was twenty years before the Surgeon General would get all up in Big Tobacco's business. *Think before you speak, Beryl.* "Or, whatever," I added weakly. "Okay, I'm sorry. Can I get up now?"

He hesitated, as if there might be more to this ridiculous horizontal discussion, then released me.

I stood up as daintily as I could with an audience looking on and with, I was almost certain, Sgt. Sarcasm looking up my skirt. I straightened the seams of my stockings then leveled an accusing stare at my rescuer. I went from looking down my nose at him to looking up as he heaved his bigness off the ground. I was struck again by his powerful build. Oh, who was I kidding? I hadn't lost track of that since I'd first clapped eyes on him.

"That was a close call, Lieutenant," the gas station attendant said. "Fella musta been doin' thirty-five, forty. Coulda flattened the little lady."

Sullivan scowled at the old man and tapped the trio of stripes on his sleeve, right above a patch with a red number one on it. "It's Sergeant, bub. I'm no college boy. Though you're right, she could've been flattened, but good."

He turned back to me, touched my arm so lightly I barely felt it, yet that slight caress unnerved me more than all of our earlier intimate contact.

"Be straight with me," he said, all trace of sarcasm gone. "Do you have any enemies in this town? Anyone who'd want to harm you with such violence?"

I opened my mouth to tell the thick-headed sergeant *he* was the target but stopped mid-breath. Sullivan had no idea the big, bad, time-traveling wolf was out to get him. Should I tell him? Glo hadn't given specific instructions on that. Well, she kind of did, warning me not to blab that I'd come from the future. For my own safety, I guess. I'd read enough time travel stories and seen enough movies to know the person claiming to be from the future usually ended up locked in a padded cell.

But did that mean I couldn't warn Sullivan his life was in danger? Would it change things if he knew the truth? Cause some kind of temporal paradox? Was that what Glo meant when she talked about ripples that turn into waves that can screw with the future? And would the sergeant even believe me?

I rubbed my temples, feeling a time travel-induced headache coming on.

"Gee, Mister," I said finally, deciding to play dumb for now. "Why would anyone want to hurt little ol' me?"

He scowled. "Okay, if that's how you want it." He snatched his hat off the ground and smacked it against his leg to get the dust off. He turned to the other men. "Stretch, get the lady's bag before it gets run over. Marco, get our passenger into the vehicle. She needs to sit." He put on his hat and gazed at me. "She's had a scare and I think she's gone a little bats."

The men hopped to it. Before I knew it, my suitcase was in the jeep, and so was I. I let out a relieved breath. Maybe I had gone a little bats, as Sullivan called it. No, dazed was more like it. I watched the sergeant climb into the driver's seat. Not dazed by *him*, I told myself firmly. No way this gruff, imposing fella had anything to do with how dizzy I felt. A trip through time and nearly getting run over had taken quite a toll.

The other men piled into the jeep. The tall, skinny guy Sullivan had called Stretch folded himself like a pretzel into the small trailer hitched onto the back. He was swamped by duffel bags and held my suitcase on his lap. I felt a pang, he looked so uncomfortable.

The pump jockey came over to the driver's side and leaned an elbow on the windshield. "Two gallons, that'll be forty cents."

"That's highway robbery." Sullivan dug some change

31

out of his pocket and handed it over. "Used to be you could get a gallon of gas for fifteen cents."

The attendant shrugged. "Don't you know there's a war on?"

"That's what they tell me." Sullivan started the jeep. It coughed and sputtered then roared to life. He turned his head, looked back at the others. "Keep your eyes peeled for that Ford, fellas. He's headed toward town."

"That's a cinch, Sarge," one of the men behind me said. "There's probably not another black Ford coupe within a thousand miles."

"Just do it," Sullivan growled. The gears growled too as he shifted, and we set off.

"I appreciate you giving me a lift, Sergeant," I said after a few moments, hanging onto the seat to keep from bouncing out of the vehicle. The original jeep may have been rugged and adaptable, but comfort? Not so much. It had no cushioning under the leather upholstery, and it felt like it had absolutely no shock absorbers. Perhaps they hadn't been invented yet.

"Those mugs have to call me Sergeant, not you," Sullivan said. "Call me Sully. That quiet fella back there is Griff." He jerked his thumb toward a freckle-faced guy with a rumpled uniform. "The fella in the middle is Marco, and that's Stan. We call him Baldy."

For obvious reasons. I nodded to Stan, to Griff, then to Marco, who gazed back with dark, soulful eyes Grandma Blue would have described as bedroom eyes. They all sported corporal's stripes on their sleeves.

"And the sap in the back is Stretch. Everything okay back there, Private?" Sully called.

Stretch lifted a long, thin hand. "Copacetic, Sarge."

"Pleased to meet you." I raised my voice to be heard over the jeep's rumble. "I'm Beryl, Beryl Blue."

Dead silence. Accompanied by confused looks. Of course. These guys had probably never met anyone with the last name Blue before. Come to think of it, neither had I.

"It's Russian," I said patiently. "It was probably a hundred letters long when my great-grandpa landed at Ellis Island. Now it's a four-letter word. Blue. Beryl Blue."

"Beryl Blue," Sully repeated. "Where're you from, Beryl Blue?"

I picked the first place that popped into my head. "I'm from Portland. In Maine."

"Portland. In Maine."

Was he going to repeat everything I said? Worse, was he going to laser me with those blue eyes the whole ride? Like he could see through me, and my lies. I'd only been to Portland once, didn't have a clue about street names or landmarks. Especially landmarks that might have been torn down fifty years before I was born. If he decided to quiz me, I'd be sunk.

But no quiz. Sully simply nodded then wiggled the gear shift and stomped the clutch. The jeep shot down the road. The wind and engine noise put the kibosh on conversation.

Fine by me. I kept myself occupied by swiping my wind-whipped hair out of my face and trying to catch my breath. I mean, half an hour ago I was in the library wondering how I'd be able to manage rent, student loan, and cell phone bill all coming due on the same day without robbing a bank. What I thought were real problems until...

I side-eyed hunky GI Joe beside me. He watched the road as trees and farmhouses flashed by. He set his jaw in a firm line and sat straight and tall, holding the steering wheel with conviction.

Until I met him.

Sgt. Tom Sullivan. Sully. The fella I was supposed to save. The guy I'd been hurtled across time to save.

The man I'd been ordered to *kill* someone to save.

I shuddered. That sure put my petty little worries into perspective.

_____

4

After traveling several miles, passing farm field after farm field, repeating like the scenery in a *Scooby Doo* cartoon, we rolled into Ballard Springs. The jeep slowed as we hit city traffic. While the men behind me chattered and scoped out every black Ford coupe that passed, I took a good look at my hometown, circa 1943.

I'd been conditioned by old movies and photos to expect everything to be in black and white. Not so. The buildings were chalky granite or red brick. Green and white striped awnings hung over storefronts. Patriotic red, white, and blue bunting flapped from streetlights. Cars of all hues puttered by, leaving the smell of oil and exhaust in the air. The sidewalks teemed with men in uniform or dark suits with high-waist trousers and women in floral prints, chunky shoes, and all kinds of hats—cone-shaped with veils, wide-brimmed, narrow brimmed, feathery and flowery, and even a few straw hats with ribbons dangling from the back.

The jeep swung around a corner and I forgot all about sightseeing, forgot about Jake Tyson, hit-and-run Ford coupes and even the big man beside me. I sat up straight and held my breath as we chugged by the Higgins Memorial Library.

My library.

In my time, the four-story Victorian gothic building sagged like an old man. In 1943, it had just entered vigorous middle age. The sun warmed the brown granite to a lush honey-gold. The mansard roof was presumably leak-free, and the dormers sticking out of all four sides like pointy warts looked new. The iron banisters on the front steps were polished and clean.

That's when it finally, officially sank in. I'd actually traveled to the past.

Oh, the rest of it had seemed real enough, but felt almost like being in a theme park. I hadn't really recognized any of the buildings. Now, rumbling by my beloved library, my home away from home, looking both different and oh-so-familiar, I knew beyond a shadow of a doubt that I'd gone back in time.

My heartbeat kicked up, shifting from a nervous two-step to a full-fledged dance of terror. I wanted to leap out of the jeep and run away screaming. I might have too, if I had somewhere to run.

"Husband or fiancé?"

I jumped at Sully's question. He was watching me. Super intent. "Huh? What?" I sputtered.

"Are you here to see your husband or fiancé?" He downshifted. "There's only two reasons a girl like you would be traveling unaccompanied. Either your man has leave for the weekend, or..."

He gave me a look so full of meaning he didn't have to say it. Either I was shackled to some man, or I was a hooker.

Now, that irked me. A *lot*. Anger, a fine antidote to fear, I discovered. "Really? If you think outside the box, Sergeant, you'll find there's a third option." Okay, what was that third option? An idea sparked. A brilliant idea. "I'm on my way to join the Army. I'm enlisting."

"Enlisting? In the WACs?" he said with some surprise.

Oh. The WACs. The Women's Army Auxiliary Corps. I forgot. Women couldn't enlist in the regular army in 1943.

"Yup, I'm joining the WACs. That I am." Might as well have admitted to the hooker option the way the men snickered. Well, in for a penny, in for a pound, as Grandma Blue used to say. "And I wasn't unaccompanied. I told you, I was with relatives, but they had to leave. They'll be back to take me to the recruiting station on Monday."

One of Sully's eyebrows quirked, half suspicious, half amused, half condescending. Yeah, that's three halves, but damn, one little eyebrow packed a lot of judgmental punch. He didn't believe a word I said. And why should he? It was a flimsy story, and I was a terrible liar.

"And where are you gonna stay 'til Monday?" he asked.

Crap. I hadn't thought of that. I smoothed my skirt over my knees. "Oh, I'll find something."

"You will, huh? Don't you know every hotel, rooming

house, and inn in this city is full? They've been full every weekend since the war started. You'll have a tough time finding a bivouac."

Marco leaned forward. "She can stay with us, Sarge. I'll make some room in my cot."

Sully threw him a glare. "Mind your manners."

"What about you? Where are you fellas staying?" I asked, warming to Marco's suggestion. Not sharing the eager dude's cot but staying with them. Glo had ordered me to keep close to Sully. What better way to stay on mission than crashing with him? And I wouldn't mind sharing Sgt. Sexy's cot, if it came to that.

"We got an arrangement with a rooming house," he said. "The owner's a widow with a soft spot for the service. She converted an old carriage house into a barracks and charges us a mint for a cot, a cold-water privy, and three squares. It's no place for a dame."

"Oh."

"Yeah, oh." He glanced at me and that eyebrow quirked again. "Did you think you'd waltz into Ballard Springs and the hotel's ritziest suite would open up for you?"

"Well, no, I just thought—"

"You *didn't* think. Didn't plan on a lumpy mattress, or no mattress at all." He shook his head. "Spare me from spoiled dames who get the cockamamie idea to join the Army. You'll run home to Mama as soon as you learn you have to push a broom." He laughed, probably at my now outraged expression. "Your folks must've been batty to even let you leave the house, Miss Blue."

I hadn't been called Miss Blue like that since the last

time I faced Judge Moreno in juvenile court. It didn't sit well. "I'm no wimp, Sergeant. I'm no stranger to hard work. And how do you know it's not Mrs. Blue?"

"Oh, I know. Because if there was a Mr. Blue, he sure as hell wouldn't let a looker like you hoof like a hobo down a country road. Unless that lead foot who tried to mow you down *was* Mr. Blue? I knew there was something fishy about your story. Are you a runaway wife?"

Seriously? I was going to be eye-rolling my baby browns right out of my head with this guy. "Now you're being ridiculous."

"Maybe," he said mysteriously as he jerked the steering wheel then yanked the gear shift. The jeep rocked to a stop at the curb and he killed the engine. "This is where we're staying."

He pointed to a nearby carriage house with a peaked roof and a dirt driveway. The doors had been flung wide, and I saw two rows of cots lined up inside, some with duffel bags tossed onto them, others already occupied by lounging soldiers. Next door was a large Colonial-style house with peeling white paint and a cheerful sign reading *Ma's Rooming House* nailed over the front porch roof.

"Looks like I've got to save you again." Sully straightened his hat and hit me with a determined look. "I'll talk to Ma. I'll get you a place to stay."

I didn't argue, though I wanted to. I didn't like him treating me like a damsel in distress, but his need to play the knight in shining armor might work in my favor. It would certainly keep him close by.

The men behind me vaulted out of the jeep and fell

all over one another trying to help me from the vehicle. Sully elbowed them aside with a scowl. I ignored his outstretched hand and climbed out as daintily as I could, but I still ended up flashing my garters.

"Here you go, Miss Blue." Stretch handed me my suitcase with a shy smile. "Pay no attention to those fellas. I think you're doing a fine thing joining up. My granny says we all have to do our part, and why should us men have all the fun?"

My chest went tight. He spoke without a pinch of irony. He reminded me of my foster bother Matthias, who joined the Marines the day he was emancipated. Seventeen and no clue what he was getting himself into. I scanned the faces of the men unloading their gear from the jeep. None of them had any idea what lay ahead. Major drawback to time travel, I realized, knowing what was going to happen.

"Well, I'm off to catch the bus." Stretch hefted his duffel bag onto one shoulder and swung toward me again. "Going to the farm to see the folks and my best girl. Goodbye, Miss Blue. And good luck. So long and thanks for the lift, fellas."

"I don't get it," Marco said, watching Stretch move down the sidewalk, his long legs eating up the pavement. "That beanpole spends his leave with his folks. With all the dames crawling over this town, he goes home to milk the cows."

I thought Marco doth protest too much, by the longing expression on his face. He wanted to go home, too. They all did. That wouldn't be any time soon, I knew. Jake couldn't chase Sully to a more mundane time, could he? Jake had to come after him as the world beat itself senseless in a gruesome war. And I knew men were going to die. Maybe some of these young men, swaggering toward their makeshift barracks, laughing about the hell they were going to get up to over the next two days.

I turned to Sully. Maybe him, too. I stiffened. I hadn't thought of that. My mission was to keep him alive through the weekend. But what about after? One of the many, many details Glo had frustratingly left unexplained. Was I supposed to save his life now, just so he could fall in battle in a year's time?

Dust must have irritated my eyes, because they got wet. At least that's what I told my stoic self. No excuse for the lump in my throat, though. Sully eyed me again, so I tucked my emotions away. I had a job to do, and this was neither the time nor the place to go all gooey. Well, truthfully, there was no time or place I was comfortable letting my feelings loose, and certainly not in front of witnesses.

Sully wrestled my suitcase from me as if desperate to prove himself a gentleman with a capital *G*, then strode toward the rooming house. I raced after him, crunching through fallen leaves on the sidewalk and up creaky wooden steps to the front porch.

The screen door squeaked open and a plump figure in a blue house dress emerged. Ma, I presumed. With her lined, weather-beaten face, she looked like she'd stepped out of one of those Depression-era photos that made me grateful I lived in an age with plentiful supplies of moisturizer. She grinned, revealing several gaps where teeth used to be. And regular dental care. Totally grateful for that.

"Welcome back, Sergeant. I have your cot made up. I do hope you can encourage the other men to tone down the revelry this time. We had the dickens of a time cleaning up after you gentlemen stayed with us the last time."

Sully gave her a charming smile, and by charming, I mean knock her granny panties off enchanting. "I'll do my best, ma'am."

Ma dimpled. "See that you do. Now, who is this lovely young lady?"

"My cousin, Beryl Blue. She's come on a surprise visit. Needs a place to stay."

Ma's dimples turned to doubt as her gaze scraped over me. "I'm sorry, Sergeant. There are many cousins visiting this weekend. We're full up, I'm afraid."

I heard air quotes around the word *cousins*. He was losing her, so I stepped in, hoping to hit her patriotic sweet spot. "Sully, you forget the real reason I'm here. I'm going to do my bit, ma'am. I'm on my way to join the WACs."

"The WACs?" Ma clapped her hand over her ample bosom. "My dear, I've heard the *worst* sorts of women are joining the services. It's not the place for a respectable young lady at all. I can hardly believe your folks approve of such a thing."

Oh brother. I remember Grandma Blue saying there had been some negative talking points about women in the military during the war, but this was ridiculous.

"That's the thing, Ma," Sully said, jumping in. "Her folks are dead set against it." He slid his arm across my shoulders, making me fume and burn at the same time.

"Beryl's my favorite cousin. I told them I'd try to talk her out of enlisting. What do you say? Can you do a soldier a favor and find some space? Give me a chance to let her see the error of her ways?"

I had to hand it to him, smooth as a baby's bottom. Completely ludicrous, but smooth.

Ma's dimples came back. "Since you put it that way, I'm sure something can be arranged. Aunt Etta will just have to move out of her room and stay with me this weekend. Her room's small but comfortable, my dear. You have money to pay, don't you? It's ten dollars a night."

Funny how the motherly Ma turned all business with that last question. Hoping Glo had packed some era-appropriate cash into my suitcase, I assured her that I did, and she was all smiles as she opened the screen door and gestured me inside.

I reached down to pick up my suitcase. Sully, annoyingly, grabbed it first. I sighed. He seemed hell bent on treating me like the brainless, pampered little lady he thought I was. I decided not to cause a scene—yet—and followed Ma into a warm, spacious front hall with scuffed floorboards.

"See that your cousin gets settled in, Sergeant." Ma directed us toward a broad flight of stairs. "Her room is to the right, at the end of the hall. I'll send Aunt Etta up to collect her things. Supper's at six, and not a minute after. Don't forget your room payment, and your ration stamps, Miss Blue."

I gripped the handrail and started up the creaky steps, Sully at my side. As soon as we were out of Ma's earshot, I went on the attack. "Cousin? Really?"

"Did you want me to tell her you're my wife?"

Well now, didn't hearing that word on his lips make me tremble. With fear, no doubt. I mean, who in their right mind would want to be shackled to this opinionated, gruff, and so very tall control freak? I squeaked out a "No," and followed him to the end of a long hallway with wide floorboards and old wallpaper speckled with fading roses.

"Ten bucks for this?" Sully said when I opened the door to Etta's room. "Looks like you're paying by the inch."

"No kidding." This wasn't a room. It was a closet with a view. The twin bed took up most of the space, with a bureau tucked into one corner and a small nightstand in another.

I stepped inside, inhaling a healthy dose of lavender-scented sachet, but Sully put down my suitcase and stood in the doorway, looking at me. What, was he a vampire, waiting for an invitation to enter?

"I've got to check on the men." He gestured toward one of the two windows. I could see the carriage house through the lacy curtain and the branches of an oak tree right outside. "I'll be back for you later. Until then, you stay here. Don't leave this room."

That was unexpected. "Wait, why?"

"Because someone tried to run you down today. It might've been your husband or lover or some maniac who doesn't like brunettes with great gams. I don't know and I don't care. I don't want you wandering about giving him another chance. Understood?"

"Um, you're on leave, Sergeant. You can stand down."

"You're staying put, Beryl, and that's final. Do you understand?"

"My goodness. You sure enjoy telling people what to do."

"Comes with the territory." He tapped the sergeant stripes on his sleeve.

So charming. "All right, I'll make a deal with you. I'll stay put if you do too. I mean, what if he comes after *you*?"

Oh, what a smirk. "Don't worry your pretty head, *cousin*. I can take care of myself."

He left and I plopped onto the bed. The springs squeaked like a nest of mice being stepped on. Oh, yes, it was abundantly clear Sgt. Sullivan could take care of himself. And he could take care of me and Ma and everyone else around him.

Which begged an extremely intriguing question. Why would a man like that need a wannabe librarian like me to save him from certain death?

5

S ully had told me to stay put, but there were several schoolteachers, former foster parents and caseworkers who'd get in line to tell him I had trouble following orders. I hopped off the bed to tail him but stopped when I heard a door thud shut below.

Etta's corner room had two windows. One looked out at the street, the other to the side yard. I went to that window, and through the oak tree's branches watched Sully make a beeline down a brick pathway to the carriage house-slash-barracks. I didn't let out my breath until he stepped safely inside. I was relatively certain Jake wouldn't risk trying to off Sully with dozens of Uncle Sam's finest nearby.

I had to keep busy, so I unpacked my suitcase. I unfolded several dresses and hung them next to the evicted Aunt Etta's clothes and a flannel bathrobe in the tiny closet, surprised my hands weren't shaking. I felt like an actress pushed onto a stage without a script. Terrified, not knowing my lines, with no escape until the curtain fell. Until Jake was stopped and Sully was safe. And with no idea how to do that without resorting to murder.

"Piece of cake," I muttered.

The bureau was full of Etta's frillies, so I stuffed the rest of my clothes—stockings, silky pajamas, several pair of granny boxer panties—onto the closet shelf. I kicked off those hideous Mary Janes when I found a pair of open-toed, low-heeled blue pumps at the bottom of the suitcase, next to a leather handbag with a brass snap closure.

Glo had thoughtfully filled the handbag with makeup, hair clips, and, to my relief, a wad of bills. A *big* wad of bills. There was also a small booklet with *War Ration Book* on the cover. Inside were sheets of stamps to be used for buying rationed items. I shuddered to see the stamps marked *Coffee*. I was *not* going to like 1943.

Done, I turned to the thing I'd been avoiding. The weapon Glo had called a Cack. A harmless looking little doohickey, I picked it up and slid two fingers into a thin slot on the bottom. The metal seemed to squeeze my fingers like a mini blood pressure cuff.

"You talkin' to me?" I said, aiming at my reflection in the bureau's age-spotted mirror.

My thumb hovered over the controls, helpfully labeled arm, stun, kill. Gingerly, my heart hammering, I tapped *arm*. The Cack shuddered, like my phone powering up, followed by a high-pitched squeal that alerted every dog in the county. A bubble of light at one end winked from red to green. Good to go, I guessed. My stomach roiled.

I'd never touched a gun, not even a BB gun, and I'd

seen exactly two firearms in my whole life—Grandma Blue's rusty old shotgun that had been her dad's, and a mean-looking pistol that belonged to one of my foster fathers. He swore up and down to my caseworker there were no weapons in the home, but I distinctly recalled seeing him scratch his butt with that pistol on more than one occasion. I didn't last long in that placement.

I studied the sleek piece of metal vibrating in my hand. How did it work? It didn't seem to have any bullets. Was it like a Taser? What would happen if I fired? At a person? At Jake? Would he vaporize? Explode in a shower of ashes? That'd freak me the hell out. Probably make me puke. Ha, who was I kidding? Killing someone would make me puke. Forever.

Glo had said the Cack stayed armed for thirty seconds, one of the few questions she'd answered without me asking. As soon as the green light went off and the vibration halted, I shook the thing off my hand and shoved it into my purse. No way was I ever going to find out how it fired or what the weapon did, because I wasn't going to shoot it. I would never, ever press that kill button. Never kill anyone.

And that was final.

THE LAST WISPS of sunlight streaked through the windows, casting a tic-tac-toe shadow across the bed's flowered quilt. I gathered up a change of clothes and left the room. I had a good reason for disobeying Sully's orders at the moment. I had to find the bathroom.

Twenty minutes later, freshened up, I stood in front of the bathroom mirror, sliding a waxy stick of Jungle Red over my lips. A tap sounded on the bathroom door. Timid at first, then more insistent.

"Just a minute." I dabbed my lips with a square of stiff toilet tissue and tossed the lipstick back into my handbag. It tinged against the Cack. I gathered up the clothes I'd changed out of and turned the brass doorknob. A petite kewpie doll with soft blond curls stood in the hall, wearing a man's plaid bathrobe that seemed to swallow her whole.

"Sorry I took so long," I said, noting the way she bounced on her toes.

"Oh, no bother," she said in a breathy warble. Her eyes lit up. "Gosh, don't you look snazzy."

"You think so?" I ran my hands over the dress I'd changed into, a knee-length blue polka-dot dress that gently hugged my curves. Glo had good taste.

The bouncing woman nodded. "Oh, yes. Jeepers, those shoes, they're the living end. Where *did* you get such gorgeous pumps with rationing and all?"

Jeepers, she'd stepped straight out of a Judy Garland movie. I scrambled for a convincing lie, but didn't need it, because she rolled on.

"My name's Peggy, Peggy Smith. My husband's up at the base. Is your husband up at the base? Well, of course he is! Where else would he be? You must be thrilled to pieces to see him. Does he have a weekend pass like my Johnny? This Army's smart, giving our sweeties leave so they can blow off steam. My Johnny says if they didn't, they'd all go AWOL, all the time, and then there wouldn't be an army at all. My Johnny says there'll be no time for fun once they ship out overseas, which could be any day now he thinks. I just hope they don't send him to Italy, I hear there's flies there that'll eat you alive. And the women, barracudas, one and all. Well, honey, better stop flapping our gums. Step aside, I've got to do the necessary."

Okay then. I stepped out of the bathroom and she flew in. The door shut behind her with a *thunk*.

I went back to my room. The aroma of baking bread drifted up from below, and my stomach growled in response. It had been a long time since breakfast. The door to my room was open—I'd closed it when I left—and I wasn't surprised to find Sully sitting on the bed, his hat next to him. He'd somehow managed to get his hands on another pack of Lucky Strike cigarettes and puffed away. He'd spruced up too, with his jacket brushed, his face washed, and his damp hair like a neatly furrowed field where he'd drawn a comb through it. He looked good.

No idea if he thought the same of me. Sgt. Poker Face, as usual. Except for a quick eye-flick over me, head-to-toe, I couldn't tell if my dolled-up look made any impression. *So* annoying.

"Thought I told you not to leave the room," he said.

"Oh, did you? I wasn't listening." I walked to the bureau—a short trip—and dropped my clothes and toiletries on top. I frowned. The drawers were slightly ajar. Had Etta come to collect her things as promised, or had Sully been snooping around? Looking for what, exactly?

"Let's go." He hauled his bulk off the bed. The springs squeaked in relief. He tucked his hat under his arm and jerked his head toward the door. "Time for supper, Miss Blue."

I grit my teeth. Aside from my gut reaction to being called that, he said my name as if he thought it was an alias.

We walked side by side down the narrow hall, close enough to brush elbows. Close enough to catch his scent of tobacco and a hint of some musky cologne. Close enough to remind my libido it'd been a while since I'd brushed elbows, or anything else, with any guy.

I gave him a stealthy side eye, admiring the way his powerful legs moved, the way his shoulders filled out that uniform jacket. Admiring *him*. Sully was... Hot seemed too lame a word to describe him. I desperately needed a thesaurus. Shocking, a librarian at a loss for words. Suffice to say, Sully was a man like none I'd ever encountered.

He preceded me down the stairs as if to sweep away an attacking horde and hung back to let me enter the dining room first. Two large farm tables filled the room, with mismatched chairs on either side. Wallpaper dotted with violets lined walls covered with pictures of stern-looking men and women in Victorian clothing, probably Ma's ancestors.

Ma scurried around the tables, dropping plates in her wake, followed by a brittle-looking elderly woman, Aunt Etta, I guessed, and a teenage girl in pigtails, laying out the silver with more care. The baked-bread aroma did battle with the smell of fried chicken, inciting a riot in my beyond-empty stomach.

Sully held my chair as I sat, a quaint gesture that made me feel both ridiculous and special. Soldiers spilled through the side door and chairs scraped the floor as they sat down. Several people followed us in from the hall, including a middle-aged couple, a woman who complained about a sticky window in her room, and a beaming Peggy Smith, escorted by a slim soldier with jug handle ears. *My Johnny,* I presumed. I also presumed they'd been married the day they both turned eighteen, which must've been last week, judging by how impossibly young they both were.

"They're just kids," I murmured.

"Who? Them?" Sully glowered at Peggy, who tucked a linen napkin into her husband's collar. "I give it a month. This war's littered with hurry up marriages. Kids who think they're in love. They wake up the next day and find a stranger in their bed."

I scowled at him. Really, he might as well have a rain cloud hanging over his head. "Who was she?"

"Who was who?"

"The woman who left you with such a sunny outlook on love and marriage."

No answer. No clue either. Ol' Poker Face poured himself a glass of milk from a pitcher and ignored me. I spread my napkin across my lap. I wasn't about to beat an answer out of him.

Suddenly, Ma stood beside me. "I trust your accommodations are satisfactory, Miss Blue?"

"Oh, yes, delightful, thank you." And thank Sully, too,

I decided reluctantly, since he'd charmed Ma into letting me stay.

She cleared her throat and after a second, I got it. She wasn't looking for a five-star review. She wanted her money. I popped open my handbag and peeled two crisp and very green tens from the roll of cash inside. Sully eyed the wad with one of those suspicious eyebrows. Ma snatched the bills from my hand and tucked them into her apron pocket.

"Place your ration stamps on the table, please," she said, circling the tables. "Two red for the chicken, one blue for your greens." She bumped the swinging door with her hip and disappeared into the kitchen.

The civilians took out their ration books, tore out the required stamps, and tossed them onto the table like they were anteing in a poker game. Sully's eyebrow hitched up again as he watched me add my stamps to the pile. I slipped the book back into my handbag, careful to shield the Cack from view.

"That's a lot of dough and enough ration points for a family of ten," he said. "Too many for a spinster on her own."

My own eyebrow went up. Spinster? That was a word in real life?

Ma and her assistants sailed back into the dining room, carrying platters of golden fried chicken, mashed potatoes, and string beans, along with baskets of that heavenly smelling bread. Everyone snapped to attention, and even Sgt. Suspicious forgot his interrogation as we dug in. Conversation bubbled and plates and serving spoons clinked as the food was passed around. Things fell to a dull murmur as we ate.

"Miss Blue?" Griff said, wiping chicken grease from his chin with his napkin. "Want to see a picture of my girl?" He leaned across the table and held out a teeny black and white photo. "Her name's Beverly."

She was a plain girl with buck teeth, but he said her name like she was Miss America. "She's lovely, Griff."

He leaned back in his chair and gazed at the photo with a wistful expression. "Wish Bev could come for a visit, but her folks won't let her. She's working a lot anyways."

"Oh, is she a Rosie the riveter?" Wait, was Rosie even a thing in 1943? What year was that iconic poster created? "I mean, is she punching rivets in a factory, or whatever?"

I could feel Sully tense up beside me.

"No, ma'am," Griff said. "Her folks won't let her do man's work like that. She's a telegram gummer." My face must've gone all *WTF?* because he added, "She seals envelopes at Western Union. Bev says telegram traffic's skyrocketed with so many folks so far from home. She has to work a lot of overtime, but she don't mind. She's saving for when this is over, and we can get married."

I watched him tuck the photo into his breast pocket, next to his heart, and that pesky lump in my throat made a comeback. Would he make it home to marry Beverly? Would any of them make it? Grandma Blue's brother hadn't. I winced, ashamed I'd practically forgotten about my great uncle. Well, Grandma Blue didn't talk about him much. She was like me, pathological about keeping away from emotion. But the rare times she got broody and nostalgic, I could feel how much she missed him, how raw the loss was, even so many years later.

Some of that salty wet stuff poked my eyes, threatening to fall out. And of course, there was Sully, looking at me again, catching me in the weak-willed act.

"What?" I said. "Are you making a career out of looking at me?"

He pushed his empty plate away and lit a cigarette, blowing out the match and tossing it into an ashtray. "I've been trying to figure you out, Beryl."

Good luck with that. Several caseworkers, foster mothers, and a very determined lady shrink had tried to suss out the enigma wrapped in the mystery that was Beryl Blue. Thing is, *I* couldn't figure me out, what chance did anyone else have?

"What have you deduced, Sherlock?" I popped the last of my chicken into my mouth.

He took a slow drag, studying me. "Damned little. First, I pegged you as a dizzy dame off on a lark. Then I think maybe you're one of those independent gals, playing the field, doesn't want to be tied down. Thinks she's a man in skirts."

"How awfully sexist. You know, a woman can do just about anything a man can do. Usually quicker and better."

He shrugged that off. "I think something's on your mind. Something bad."

"You can tell that by looking at me?"

"Yup. It's your big, brown eyes. They tell me there's a story. A mysterious story."

Back at you, fella. Sully intrigued me to no end. And

not just the physical. Who was he? How'd he get that scar across his nose? Why was Tyson out to kill him? "Are you Detective Sam Spade now? Are you going to grill me until I confess?"

He scowled. "I would if it'd get me some answers. You're not the kind of dame that flaps her gums, unless it's to crack wise. Even when some jamoke tries to run you down."

A-n-n-n-d...we were back to that. "I told you, it was an accident."

"Sure it was." He ground out his cigarette in the ashtray. "Listen, I'm heading into town with the boys tonight. I want you with me."

"Why, Sergeant Sullivan, after all your talk about hurry up marriages, that's pretty bold."

"I'm not asking you to marry me, butterfly brain. I want you with me so I can keep an eye on you. Keep you safe from any more *accidents*."

What a coincidence. That was exactly my plan for him. I looked around. People began to drift away from the tables as they finished eating. I watched Peggy practically drag her Johnny from the dining room and head upstairs, the lure of a locked door and a bed with squeaky springs apparently irresistible.

A light bulb popped on in my brain. Seduce Sully. Get him up to my room and keep him there for the weekend. That would keep him out of Jake's line of fire. I wasn't in the habit of hopping into bed with a guy I barely knew, but I supposed in this case I could take one for the team. How, though? Sully was interested. I knew that from our horizontal dance at the gas station earlier, but I doubted a straight-on, *Let's go boink like bunnies* would work with this mule.

"Well, I'm not sure I want to join you, Sully," I said, trying to sound flirty. Failing, of course. Flirting was not my thing. "I was planning to stay in my room tonight and read a book."

"That's dangerous."

"What, a woman reading?" I said and he laughed, a gentle rumble that sent sparks up my spine. Oh, I could definitely take one for the team.

"No. I mean, you, here alone."

"What could possibly happen to me at Ma's?"

His gaze strafed the men lingering in the dining room, smoking, chatting. "There are a lot of wolves in wolf clothing around here. I don't want them baying at you."

"If you're so worried, why don't you stay here with me?" I punctuated this ridiculousness by batting my eyes.

His eyebrow of doom went sky high. "Nothing doing, Beryl, you're coming with me."

Score one for Sully this round. But the battle had just begun. "Frankly, I'm beginning to think *you* might be the biggest wolf of them all."

He bared his teeth. He looked like an idiot, but I think he thought he was funny.

"Sergeant, it looks like you've got yourself a date." I pushed back my chair and stood. "I'll go get my coat."

6

I straightened the hat I'd found in my suitcase, a yummy blue felt concoction with a spray of blue feathers, then dashed down the stairs. The screen door squeaked as I pushed it open and stepped outside. Everyone waiting on the porch swung to look me over. My jeep companions Marco, Griff, and Stan, several other corporals, and a smattering of PFCs gaped at me as if they'd never seen a woman before.

Every man except Sully. He greeted me with a brusque, "About time," and pressed his hand to my lower back to steer me down the steps. My skin burned from his touch, even through my coat and about eighty layers of undergarments and a girdle that threatened to cut off my circulation.

He lit a cigarette as soon as we reached the sidewalk. Most of the others did, too. I coughed and waved my hand in front of my nose. If anything killed me on this bizarre mission to the past, it would be secondhand smoke.

A beautiful night despite the smoke clouding the view, warm, with clear skies and the moon nearly full. Its brightness lit our way. Good thing, since blackout restrictions were in effect. Barely any of the streetlights were on and the few cars that passed had a slotted cap over their headlights, directing a weak beam at the street. House windows were covered with heavy, black curtains. Not a smidge of light would be allowed to escape and guide an enemy bomber to a juicy target, not if Ballard Springs could help it.

For my soldier escorts, this was a normal walk down the street in wartime. For me, a living history lesson. And distracting me from my main task—to keep an eye out for Jake.

I got back on task and scanned as we walked, but quickly realized I'd never find Jake if he'd managed to get his hands on a uniform. A literal sea of khaki trudged down the street, headed for downtown.

"Looking for someone?" Sully asked, his cigarette bobbing between his lips.

Was it my constantly swiveling head that gave it away? "Just checking out the sights. Where're we headed?"

He slowed a bit, letting the rest of the group outpace us. He offered me his elbow. I took him up on the invitation, settling my hand in the crook of his arm. That special feeling came over me again, like when he held my chair, with another, startling sensation added to the mix. Protected. I felt safe with him. Something I hadn't felt for a long time.

"We're going to the Hi-Hat Club," he said.

"Sounds dreamy." I pictured a nightclub like in those

old movies Grandma Blue loved, all art deco and polished floors, women in slinky evening gowns dancing with soldiers in crisp uniforms. "Oh, I hope I'm not underdressed. I look all right, don't I?"

He pulled the cigarette from his mouth and grinned. "You're a real piece of work, you know that Beryl Blue?"

Was that supposed to be a compliment? Because it sounded like anything but.

"Do me a favor." He shifted his gaze to the men marching ahead of us. "When we get to the club, stay where I can see you." A hot pause. "Not every soldier's like Griff, pining for the girl back home. There's some real operators in this man's Army. Even a few bad eggs. Put booze into their bellies and who knows what could happen. Especially to a woman alone."

He sounded positively dour. I got his meaning. The Greatest Generation didn't all spend their leave dipping donuts at the Red Cross. Some got up to all kinds of hell and Sully didn't want me to get caught in the crossfire.

"I'm touched, Sully, but if we'd stayed at Ma's, you wouldn't have to worry about me."

He grunted. "I'm not worried about you. I'm worried about those mugs. It'd kill me if any of them got into a brawl over a dame and got took up by the MPs. Wasting their leave in the stockade."

Well, that showed me. "You really care about them, don't you?" Another grunt, which I took as a yes. "I think maybe tough guy Sully isn't so tough after all."

He growled at my analysis of his inner cuddle-bear, but I warmed to the idea. Could that be the key to everything, the reason Jake Tyson wanted him out of the picture? Sully cared about his fellow soldiers, would give the last full measure to protect them. Maybe it was a *Terminator* thing. Jake wanted to kill Sully because he was destined to save someone the rogue time cop didn't want saved.

We continued on. I nearly spun my head off looking for Jake. I also learned those snazzy pumps Peggy Smith had drooled over were not meant for walking long distances. I had blisters on my blisters by the time we reached the Hi-Hat Club, a barracks-style building that looked as if it had been built yesterday. Smelled like it, too. Freshly cut pine tickled my nose as we climbed the wobbly plank steps and entered the club.

Inside was nothing like I'd imagined. Instead of bright and Deco, it was dim and sawdust. Noisy, beer-soaked, and a cloud of cigarette smoke hanging overhead, pushed around by ceiling fans that *thip-thipped* in lazy circles. Tables and chairs filled every inch of space, except for a bit of parquet that served as a dance floor, crowded with jitterbugging couples. A dark wood bar ran the length of one wall.

Sully swept off his hat and tucked it under his arm as we were led to a table by a man who looked to be hoarding ten gallons of motor oil in his greasy hair. Sully's hand found its way to my lower back again and he guided me across the room as if I were a rudderless ship.

We reached our destination and Sully pulled out my chair. He dropped his hat on the table then sat next to me. We pressed thighs. No choice. Tiny table, meet big man. I looked away, trying to ignore Big Red's nearness and the fire he sparked in me. With *trying* as the operative word.

"Oh, a band." I nodded at the brass quartet jamming on a small stage near the dance floor.

"That's nothing." Marco plopped into his chair. "A joint a few blocks over's got an all-girl orchestra. You should see what they wear. Or *almost* wear." He snickered.

"Every gin joint in town has a band, a cigarette girl, what have you," Sully said. "Anything to separate us from our money."

A successful strategy, judging by the crowd. But I'd never give him the satisfaction of agreeing with him, so I grinned at Griff across the table. "Does he have to be grumpy about *everything*?"

Griff let out a horsey guffaw. "Yeah, guess he does."

Then he lit a cigarette. They all did. Marco held out a pack to me, but I shook my head. Smoking wasn't my idea of a good time. I'd learned that the hard way. Two packs a day for forty years hadn't exactly helped Grandma Blue's battle against lung cancer.

A cocktail waitress pushed through the mob to our table. "Hello boys."

"Hiya, Mabel," Marco said, eating her up with his eyes.

And what a feast. She was dressed like a sexy ballerina, in a silky black tutu with a low-cut bodice, and dark silk stockings. I'd seen more skin in a shampoo commercial, but these men probably hadn't. At least not in public. Her hair fascinated me, shiny and thick and rolled into a tight halo around her head, like a brunette glazed donut. It would take an industrial strength curling iron and several days head start for me to achieve such tonsorial magnificence.

"Dance with me later, honey?" Marco rubbed his shoulder against Mabel's hip.

She adjusted her tray and looked annoyed. I would too. Sexual harassment, anyone?

"Aw, sugar plum, you know I can't," she said. "We're awful busy. What'll it be tonight, fellas?"

"Beers all around," Sully said. "With an Old Crow chaser. The lady'll have a sarsaparilla."

I choked. "Sassa-what-a?" Okay, that pampering the little lady thing could only go so far. Was I made of glass? "The hell I will. If you're drinking whatever Old Crow is, Sully, so am I."

The others laughed. "You tell him," Griff said.

Sully's eyebrow rose incrementally. "I never met a girl who drank whiskey. You think you can keep up with us?"

I sputtered. Full disclosure, I hate whiskey. I wasn't a big drinker, not even in college, but I wasn't a teetotaler either. I'd downed enough low-cal beer and dirty martinis to prove that. I could keep up.

"I do, and I will," I said.

Mabel left and the men started talking all at once, mostly about the girls in the club. I shrugged off my coat, a plaid wool that was probably chic in 1943, but for a modern girl like me screamed *Grandma's closet!*

I scanned the place, looking for Jake. A tough task. All the men were in motion, circling the tables filled with women like hungry sharks. The women, dressed like me in simple frocks and darling hats, giggled and flirted. Could've been any club, any time period, anywhere in the world. Except for the abundance of white faces and World War II-style uniforms.

Mabel returned with a tray of pilsner glasses filled with foamy beer and shot glasses containing an amber-colored liquid. Sully ground out his cigarette butt in a glass ashtray and eyed me with a shit-eating grin. He lifted the shot glass and knocked the whiskey back in one smooth gulp.

Challenge accepted. The Old Crow burned my throat and made me shudder, but I drank every drop.

Sully handed Mabel a couple of bills, and when she tried to give him his change, he waved her off. "Keep 'em coming, Mabel," he said, eyeing me. "For all of us?"

I could already feel the whiskey warming my blood. I hoped I could keep up as I'd bragged. I mean, Sully was a giant, could probably soak up an entire bottle of Old Crow before getting a buzz. I could not. But I nodded with conviction. I'd drink what he drank. Who knew I could be so competitive?

Mabel and her tray melted into the crowd and Stan raised his beer glass. "Here's to us, fellas. Across the sea in '43."

Griff grinned and held his glass higher. "Home once more in '44."

Marco and Sully chimed in. "Home alive by '45."

Lighthearted toasts, mixed with melancholy. Because of the war, the buzzard that circled over them, over everyone in this room and all the people of 1943, never out of sight, never forgotten as everyone went about their lives. I watched them drink then slam their empty glasses on the table.

"Home alive by '45," I echoed and drank too, wishing with all my might that such a hopeful toast would come true.

Marco dragged his sleeve over his mouth and jumped to his feet. "Come on, fellas. Let's find some dollies to dance with."

Stan crushed out his cigarette in the rapidly filling ashtray and stood, but Griff hesitated.

"I dunno. Not sure Beverly would want me to." He gazed at Sully, his expression agonized.

I expected a grumpy comeback, with a side of sarcasm, when Big Red surprised me.

"Go on," he said, his voice gruff. "I'm sure your girl would want you to have some fun when you're so far from home."

Griff brightened, excused himself to me, and joined the others in the GI scrum. In a moment, I saw all three men lead a partner onto the dance floor. The band launched into a song called "Taking a Chance on Love." The singer crooned as the dancers swayed.

"Aw, don't they look sweet?" I said, turning back to Sully, but he wasn't looking at them. He was looking at me. Again. Really, you'd think he'd have my face memorized by now.

"*You* don't want to dance, do you?" he asked with a twofer, a scowl and a growl.

"Clearly *you* don't want to, or your invitation would be more genuine."

"I'm not the dancing type."

I had to smile. No, he wasn't. He seemed more the throw you over his shoulder, kick down a door and toss you on the bed type. I had to fan myself at the thought. "You can relax, Sully. I don't dance, either." Certainly not the fox trot, or whatever convoluted dance they were doing out there.

Mabel stopped by with more drinks. Money changed hands, she cleared the empties, gave me a wink, and sashayed away.

Sully took a long pull on his beer then leveled a hard look at me. "I think it's time to be honest with me, Beryl." A beat, two beats, then, "Who are you? Where are you from?"

I choked on my beer. He couldn't possibly have guessed. I mean, I'd thought time travel was impossible until I got sucked into that jaw-rattling vortex. Even now a corner of my brain, the scaredy-cat corner, was in total denial that this was really happening. No way could Sully have even an inkling of where and when I'd come from.

"I told you. I'm Beryl Blue. I'm a librarian from Portland, on my way to join the WACs."

"*Librarian?*"

Now I'd done it, mentioned the one thing worse than joining the Army. "Yes, a librarian."

"You can't sell me that soap, Beryl." The skepticism practically dripped off of him. "No librarian drinks like you do. No librarian talks like you, either. And you sure don't look like a librarian. Librarian? My foot."

On behalf of librarians everywhere, in every time period, I got all huffy. "News flash pal, that's a stereotype. And it's not the first time I've heard it. We're not all old maids with our hair in a bun." My co-worker Ida Pellerin excepted. She'd been on the job nearly sixty years, so I suppose she'd earned that hair bun with the pencil sticking out of it. "We're a really diverse group."

"I think you're lying."

And I think you're annoying. "Well, I guess I am lying. A little. I'm not a librarian yet. I still have several classes to go before I get my degree. That's why George can push me around. He's all degreed and everything and I'm just the wannabe he sticks with the shelving."

"George? Who's George?" Sully dug out another cigarette and lit it.

I scowled. Really, if Jake didn't get him, that nasty habit would, especially if he kept smoking at such a heavy pace. "George is my boss. He's head librarian. And he's got this big head, like a balloon. As round as Charlie Brown's."

Northward went that eyebrow again. "I never heard of a man librarian, but maybe that's the usual where you come from."

"Where I come from? What does that mean? Portland?"

"I'm asking the questions here." He zeroed in with those suspicious eyes. "Who plays first base for the Yankees?"

The Yankees? Had I stepped from one Twilight Zone into another? "*What* are you talking about?"

"That's what you're supposed to ask when you think someone's a spy."

"A spy? That's ridiculous."

"Not as nuts as you think. There's a lot of clues to go on. You came out of nowhere. You don't know about things. You ask a lot of questions. You've got more dough than a Rockefeller, and you talk funny."

I went cold. Could that be what all the staring had been about? Since we met? All the suspicious questions? He wasn't trying to figure me out as he claimed. He'd insisted I come with him tonight not because he was concerned about my safety. Because he thought I was a *spy*?

"That's ludicrous. I am *not* a spy."

"Then why won't you answer my question? Who plays first base for the Yankees?"

"How should I know? I'm a Red Sox fan. We don't know any of the Yankees' names and don't care to learn. Hey, how do *you* know any of the Yankees? You're from Boston. That's downright traitorous."

He stilled. "How'd you know where I'm from?"

A moment of panic. I knew because I'd read the dossier on Glo's magical tablet. A list of dry facts, height, weight, birth date—September 20, 1919—all surface details that provided zero information on who the man glaring at me really was.

I didn't have to scramble long before coming up with an answer. "Your accent gives you away. It's all Boston. Now that's out of the way, Sergeant Suspicious, are we friends again?"

He snorted. "Dance around it all you like, Beryl. I know why you won't answer my question. Because you're a spy."

"Will you stop saying that?" I downed my whiskey shot in one gulp, angry at him. Furious with myself. I couldn't believe how hurt I was. The way he'd been eyeing me, I thought he might be the teeniest bit into me. "Is that how you got that?" I gestured to the scar on his nose. "From being nosy? You stuck that big Irish snout into something you shouldn't have."

"This little scratch?" He touched the jagged line. "You don't want to know that story."

"Yes, I do. I'm a librarian. We *love* stories." Especially if it would divert Sully from the topic at hand. "Tell me. How did it happen?"

"Got too close to a fight." He pulled on his Lucky, a faraway look in his eyes. "A fight between my folks."

Yikes. That was a new one on me, not having folks and all. "Oh. That's terrible. Did you call the police?"

"Why would I do that?"

"D-uh, because your father cut you? Threatened your mother with a knife?"

"Who said it was my pop with the knife?"

"Oh."

"Pop usually used his fists." He rubbed his jaw, looking wounded, though he tried to sound brash.

"But still, the police would've broken it up."

"Yeah, I guess, and they would've thrown Pop in the drunk tank. Or maybe both of my parents." I could hear a young boy's pain in his voice. "Jailing Pop would've been a waste of time, anyways. Ma would've bailed him out so he could go to work the next day. Didn't want to risk losing his job. We were lucky he had one in the Depression. He kept a few package stores in business, but at least we had a roof over our heads." He slugged back his drink and shrugged. "Told you it wasn't a happy story."

No, not at all. I'd been through my share of not happy,

too, and should be immune to a sniffle bait story like his, but damn if it didn't move me.

"I'm sorry," I said softly. I'd thought his grumpiness had come from that age-old cliché of a dame done him wrong, but the real story seemed much more complicated.

"What do you have to be sorry for?" He ground his half-smoked cigarette to bits and gazed at me through the smoke spiraling up from the ashtray. "That was a long time ago." He shifted and the steel wall slammed back into place. "Let's talk about you for a while. Who plays first base for the Yankees?"

I groaned. "Sully, you're like a dog with a bone—"

Something at the door grabbed my attention. Correction, not something, *someone*. My heart stopped. Not literally, of course, since I'd be dead, but seeing him, it sure felt like that. For a moment, I'd forgotten where I was. *When* I was, and why I'd been brought here. This wasn't some World War II reenactment. I wasn't here to play dress up, bantering with a pretend GI Joe at the stage door canteen. This was *real*. Sully was real.

And so was the man in the uniform who'd just entered the club.

Jake Tyson. The man I'd been ordered to kill.

7

J ake scanned the room and I wondered if he'd been working his way along the main drag, checking out bars and nightclubs, searching for his target. His gaze passed by us like a lighthouse beam over the ocean and I let out my breath. He hadn't spotted Sully. Jake pushed into the throng and headed for the bar.

"What is it?" Sully asked, on alert. "You look like you saw Napoleon's ghost."

"What?" Scintillating comeback, Beryl. I shifted. Better to get this over with sooner rather than later. "Will you excuse me? I have to visit the little girls' room."

He looked skeptical but rose to help me with my chair. I snatched up my glass and drew down the rest of my beer for courage, then squeezed through the tables after Jake. An impulse move. I had no plan, no idea what to do when I reached him. Certainly not kill the man as Glo had demanded. And certainly not here, in a room full of men who would be facing that kind of violence way too soon. No, there had to be an alternative to cold blooded murder. Still, I clutched my handbag, feeling the weight of the Cack inside.

My heart hammered, pumping the alcohol faster through my veins. It thumped even harder when I found Jake. He leaned an elbow on the corner of the bar, casual and cool. But I saw the way his gaze flit over the crowd, searching.

Man, that futuristic holographic tech was crap. Like Sully, the images Glo had shown me of this guy didn't do him any favors. Almost painfully pretty up close, Jake had intense, cobalt blue eyes, a sharp jaw line, and jet-black hair slicked back, not the soft waves I'd seen in the hologram. I'd noticed him as soon as he stepped through the door and now I realized why. He wore the same uniform as the other men, but he stood out. Out of place, like thunder on a winter night.

No plan came to me, so I figured I'd better sail on by to the restroom, when he stepped into my path.

"Pardon me," I managed after a moment of panic. After all, he didn't know who I was, or that Glo had recruited me to end him.

I gave him a faint smile and tried to step around him. He blocked me again.

"Excuse me." Nastier this time. I tried again to go around him. He grabbed my upper arm. Snatched me to him so close my shoulder banged his chest. His hot, minty breath rippled across my face and he stared hard into my eyes. I prepped for a knee-jab to his Little Jake, a surefire way to loosen his grip, when he spoke.

"They sent *you* to kill me?"

I froze. We were nose to nose. He squeezed my arm so tight the blood stopped flowing. My fingers went numb.

I laid my best icy librarian on him. "I do *not* know what you're talking about." I wrenched my arm but couldn't break his iron hold. My icy confidence slipped as panic skidded in. "Unhand me. *Now*."

He frowned, not a good look for him, and released my arm. My fingers tingled painfully as the blood rushed back into my hand. He took a thin silver device the size of a thumb drive out of his jacket pocket. He moved it up and down in front of me. I'd seen enough *Star Trek* to guess he used the thingy to scan me.

"No DNA code," he said, his voice barrel deep and butter smooth. He eyed me accusingly. "Who are you?"

The second time tonight I'd been asked that question, but this time I felt on solid footing. "What's it to you?" I said and he smiled, definitely a good look for him. Dimples galore. Hot. Except for the murderous time travelling assassin part, of course. "And golly, what is that strange little toy you're holding?"

"Too late. You should've acted surprised by the code scanner a lot earlier." He pushed the plastic device back into his jacket pocket. "You're an untraceable." He smirked. "Glo recruited an untraceable to find me? She must be desperate."

I shrugged, though I'd been thinking the same thing. I mean, for the millionth time, why choose me for this impossible task?

He tipped his head, like a curious parrot. "You skilled?"

Not really, but I set my expression to tough chick

mode so he wouldn't figure that out. "I don't need skills to dodge a hit and run." I'd simply needed a very determined, very strong redhead to avoid being mowed down by Jake. "Major fail on that attempt, by the way. And you might as well get used to failure, future boy. Whatever else you try, you won't succeed. I'm sticking to Sergeant Sullivan like a leech all weekend."

Jake's gaze swept me up and down. "I think I know how you're going to do that." He snickered at my outraged gasp. "That'll work for forty-eight hours but Monday he's back on base. All kinds of accidents can happen there. Then he'll be moving out, on to the next training base. After that, overseas. I can blend in every step of the way. No one will notice me. You'd better stop me before then, or you won't be able to stop me at all."

He taunted me like a villain from a grade-Z movie, Evil with a capital *E*, but I took him seriously. "Why are you doing this, Jake? Money? A boatload of cash?"

He grinned. Had I hit the nail on the head?

"Does it matter?" he said. "Why are you trying to stop me?"

Yeah, *that* billion-dollar question. The easy answer—because I was stuck here. Stuck, with Glo's threat always at the back of my mind. A threat that kept that pilot light of panic in my belly lit. But my real motivation? I looked into the big mirror over the bar, spotted Sully's reflection through the undulating crowd. He sat alone at our table, fully engrossed in his beer.

He needed my help. He needed *me*. And no one had needed me for a long time.

"I guess I'm starting to like the big lug," I said, turning

back to Jake. "And because I'm not so fond of bullies. Particularly money-grubbing bullies who don't think about consequences."

He went grim. "Everything has consequences as far as Time Scope's concerned. You know how powerful they are. What they can do."

I nodded, though actually, I didn't. I wasn't naïve enough to think the company did what they did out of a love of history. I was sure they made a major profit zipping people through time. Maybe their shoot-to-kill order had a lot less to do with their so-called rules than with their bottom line. Jake going rogue could be a major threat to their corporate reputation. And their stock value.

"Wait." He got in close again, searching my face. "You *don't* know, do you? That explains no DNA sig. I was right, Glo *is* desperate. Reaching back into time for an untraceable. When are you from? The way you talk, I make it the 1990s. Or early twenty-first century."

He hit that pretty easily. "Never you mind," I snapped. "Look, let's make a deal. You go on your merry way, forget all about Sullivan, and we'll all live happily ever after."

"What kind of deal is that? What's in it for me?"

He was a Han Solo rip off, apparently. He loved only money. I thought about promising him every dime I had in my bank account but didn't think seven hundred dollars would be enough to stop him.

"What's in it for you is I don't kill you." I opened my handbag and tilted it toward him, so he could see the weapon inside.

He laughed. "Do you even know how to use that? I don't believe you could hurt a fly."

My goodness he excelled at goading. An effective strategy. I narrowed my eyes, fuming. "Wanna bet?"

Another laugh, another display of dimples. "So, that's how it'll be? As they say in your time, the game is afoot." He stepped back, did a ridiculous bow, like a courtier of old. "I'm looking forward to our dance."

Then he melted into the crowd.

I STUMBLED back to the table.

My head spun as if caught in a tornado wind, and not just from the alcohol rushing through me. No one in my time except a total Sherlock Holmes geek would ever say *the game is afoot.* I guess he'd meant *game on* or some other lame challenge. Whatever. He clearly wasn't about to back down. I had to stop him in the next forty-eight hours, or he'd kill Sully. Jake knew the only way to do that would be to kill him first.

I welcomed the sight of Mabel dropping fresh drinks on our table. I needed something to douse the blaze in my stomach. Thinking about killing someone was all fine and good in the abstract, but in reality? Terrifying and nauseating. There *had* to be some other way.

Sully held my seat. I plopped down with zero elegance.

First things first, keeping Big Red safe. Jake had leeringly hit on my original scheme, the most logical plan. Seduce Sully. Spend the next two days with him in my cozy little room at Ma's. I'd lost the first round in the battle. Time for a second sortie into the seduction zone. I waited until Sully had sat down again and shot him a dazzling smile, punctuated by a toss of my hair.

He was not impressed. He frowned at me like a stern father. "What'd that fella want?"

"What fella?"

"Don't play dumb Dora with me." He took a fast drag and exhaled in a huff. "Guy by the bar. You two seemed awful chummy. You talked for a long time."

Sully sounded kind of jealous, but that was good, right? The seduction thing would be easier if he helped.

"He propositioned me," I said. "I told him I wasn't interested. There's a more interesting guy here tonight." I threw some eyelash batting on top of that cheesy line.

He still wasn't buying it. "You said you were going to the powder room. It's that way, Beryl." Cigarette ash flicked everywhere as he hitched his thumb over his shoulder. "You *went* to meet him. Who is he?"

"He's nobody. Less than nobody." I gulped down my whiskey, scrambling to shut down this line of questioning. "You know what, I think I'd like to dance after all. What d'ya say, Sully, want to cut a rug?"

That suspicious eyebrow went up. After a long pause, he got up and held out his hand. "Okay, sister, it's your funeral."

I blamed anxiety and alcohol for my legs being so wobbly as he led me to the dance floor. Then he took me into his arms, slid a hand around my waist and pressed his palm to the curve of my back, pulling me to him, and my nervousness faded. He closed his warm, strong fingers over my trembling hand and everything and everyone vanished. The fear, Glo and her threats, Jake and his deadly game being afoot, all whisked away. Every single thing.

There was only him.

Sully began to move, and I followed his lead. I couldn't help thinking how perfectly we fit. Physically, better than any man I'd ever been with. Emotionally, we fit. Two damaged people from different times, radically different worlds, but with the same hard luck. How was it that we fit so well together? So strange. Okay, with Glo pulling the strings, maybe not so strange.

He gazed down at me and his eyes crinkled with a smile I could only define as disarming. *Totally* disarming. Maybe Sully felt that electricity too. Or maybe he was laughing at the way my handbag, which dangled by the strap from my wrist, kept bopping him in the shoulder. Or how I kept trouncing on his toes.

I smiled back. "I never claimed to be Ginger Rogers." Not even Mr. Rogers in the ballroom dancing arena. My experience was limited to one awkward spin around the dance floor with an elderly foster-uncle at a wedding and watching the occasional episode of *Dancing with the Stars*.

I did my best not to trip as he swung me around. "You're not uncoordinated," he said. "Maybe you just don't know the steps. Don't they foxtrot where you're from?"

Actually, no, but I got his meaning. The spy business again. Annoying, but at least he'd taken a break from badgering me about Jake. "Where I'm from? You mean Berlin or Tokyo, right?"

"Maybe Moscow. You said your name is Russian."

I narrowed one eye. Was he calling me a Communist? He pulled me closer. The barbed retort on my tongue cut off as he pressed his cheek to mine. His oh-so-male scent wrapped around me. I felt dizzy. Or maybe that was from the whiskey flooding my veins.

"You're hiding something, Beryl Blue," he murmured. His warm breath tickled my ear, sending sparks shooting down my spine. "I promise you I'll find out the truth."

We swayed together as the band segued into a smooth version of one of Grandma Blue's favorites, "You'll Never Know How Much I Love You." The vocalist nailed the song's heartache and longing.

After a bit, Sully pulled away a fraction. "Thought you told that palooka to beat it."

I opened my eyes and came back to the present, or the past, as it were, to see Jake watching us from the sidelines. "Apparently he didn't get the message."

"Tell me straight, Beryl, is that the fella you're running away from?"

"I'm not running away from him or anyone else."

Sully's face went deadly serious. "Then why do you look so scared when you eyeball him?"

Because he wants to kill you, dummy. But I couldn't say that. Not without at least a week's worth of explanation. I settled for a lame, "I am *not* afraid of him."

Sully glanced to the right. "Let's put it to the test. He's coming over. The dope's gonna cut in, I guess."

I wrenched out of Sully's embrace and gasped. Jake was making his move? Here? He steamrolled through the dancing couples, eyes on us. I couldn't see his hands. What if he had a Cack? Would he dare fire it in this

79

crowd? Or what if he went low-tech and had a knife? My frantic gaze ping-ponged between Jake and Big Red. He could shiv Sully here on the dance floor, quick and dirty, and when he'd finished, get lost in the mob of khaki.

"Sully, get out of here," I said, struggling to open the clasp on my handbag and get at the weapon inside. I could hear the panic in my voice. "He's going to kill you—"

"Beryl," he said. A soft growl that did the trick. I stilled. As calm as the Dead Sea. He gazed into my eyes. "I'll protect you, if you'll let me."

Now, I've been all about taking care of myself for a long time. Had to. Needed to. But I didn't see any other way. A clipped nod from me and Sully crushed me to him, twirled me around and slammed us into Marco. That knocked Marco off his dance partner's pillowy bosom, where he'd been blissfully resting his head.

"What the hell, Sarge?" Marco squinted in confusion. "What gives?"

Sully got right to it. "Need a diversion. Fella's trying to steal my date." He nodded toward Jake. "That one, the guy who looks like Tyrone Power."

"Right." Marco grabbed Stan by the lapels and shoved him into another soldier. Poor Stan squawked in surprise, but his sacrifice had the desired effect. Soldiers cursed, women shrieked, fists flew. In five seconds flat, a full-scale brawl had broken out. Jake was swallowed up by the mob.

"Sully, you're brilliant," I said, ducking to avoid a hairy-knuckled fist.

Sully torqued like a dancer in a Fosse musical,

punched the hairy knuckles guy in the jaw, then grabbed my hand. "Thank me later. Let's go."

He tugged me behind him, and we bobbed and weaved our way through the melee. We emerged out of the scrum seconds later, unscathed. Well, relatively so. My cute little hat had been tipped all askew. I straightened it as we zipped by our table. Sully snatched up his own hat and I grabbed my coat. I didn't look back until we reached the door.

As Sully yanked me out into the night, I grinned in satisfaction to see someone's flying fist say hello to Jake's pretty face.

8

The sounds of the GI rumble faded as we hustled down the stairs to the sidewalk. I took a huge breath of relief. A mistake. The night had cooled. Crisp fall air poured into my lungs, making my head spin like a dreidel.

"Whoa." I teetered, grateful Sully held my arm. Otherwise, I would have fallen flat on my butt.

"I knew you couldn't keep up. You're drunk." He sounded kind of pleased.

"I am not." I sighed. Then hiccupped. "Yes, I think I am drunk. And possibly blind. Why is it so damned dark?"

Sully snatched my coat from me because I tried to put it on upside down. "It's the blackout. You want me to turn on a few lights? Send a signal to your comrades for a bombing run?"

He held my coat while I shifted my purse from one hand to the other and slipped my arms into the sleeves. "Come on, Sully. You know I'm not a spy."

He grunted, an annoyingly neutral sound. Then he

gave me a little push and we began to walk in the direction of Ma's.

"One good thing about the darkness, " I said, tipping my head up to gaze at the clear night sky. "No light pollution."

"No what?"

"I mean, it's so dark you can see all the stars."

He chuckled. "Of course you can, brainless."

"You don't have to be insulting about it." Truth? I wasn't insulted, I was giddy. From the adrenaline of the fight and from the whiskey, but mostly from the hint of affection in his voice.

A jeep sped by, filled with burly men in uniforms with armbands that read MP—Military Police. The vehicle screeched to a stop outside the Hi-Hat and the MPs poured into the building.

"I hope the fellas don't get into too much trouble on my account," I said, and by that I meant Marco and the other good guys. As for Jake, I hoped the MPs would arrest him and lock him up for the duration of the war. That would put an end to his stupid game, with the win in my column. I glanced at Sully. *Our* column. His quick thinking had saved the day. Again.

"Don't worry about those knuckleheads," he said. "They can take care of themselves." The big faker. I heard the concern in his voice. "You gonna tell me why I had to start a brawl in the first place? Why is that man haunting you?"

I sighed. I wanted to tell him. I really did. That sure would make things easier. But I doubted he'd believe me. I still had trouble believing that I was breathing 1943's air, never mind that people could zap themselves back and forth through time at the tap of a button. Sully would sooner believe I was a spy. Oh, right, he pretty much did.

"I told you, Sully. The guy hit on me, I shot him down. I guess he's a persistent fella. And you saved me." I remembered I was supposed to be seducing him, so I shot him an adoring look and fluttered my eyelashes to beat the band. All that got me was more head spinning and another suspicious eyebrow.

"Are you flirting with me, Beryl Blue?"

"You bet I am." More eyelash action. "What girl wouldn't?"

He scowled. "You're not just *any* girl. What do you want with a guy like me?"

Oh, I could think of a few things. "Don't be doing that, Sully. You're a total babe." That earned me a confused look. "I mean, you're a handsome fella. A good guy. No, a *grand* guy."

His lips twitched before he managed to re-scowl them. "You *are* drunk. Look at me sober and you'll see a mug who's never amounted to spit, and never will."

I gazed at him, at that determined chin leading the way home. Under the sarcasm I heard the pain, a pain I knew too well. Self-loathing, my shrink would call it. Sully's perfect childhood dodging knives and fists could be the reason why. I hugged his arm with both of mine and squeezed. Not in a sexy way. Well, okay, with a generous amount of side boob getting friendly with his bicep, so kind of sexy, but mostly I meant it in a supportive way.

"Never amount to anything?" Just save the future,

that's all. "So *not* true, Sully. You're..." I searched for the perfect word but came up empty. I really needed that thesaurus. "You're special."

He looked down at me, poker face sliding into place, but for once he didn't give me a dismissive snort. And he didn't pull away, so it was all good, and we walked that way, close and comfortable, until we reached Ma's. Could've been an ordinary couple, walking home from an ordinary date, except for the 1943 thing. And me tossing nervous glances behind us, fearful Jake had given the MPs the slip, and now slithered after us like Gollum after his precious. Plus the guy next to me, so unlike any man I'd ever dated.

We reached the boarding house and climbed the porch steps. He turned to me at the front door.

"This is my stop, Beryl." He detached my tentacles from his arm. "I'll stay here until I know you're safe inside."

Oh. Then where would he be? Unsafe, outside. Earlier, I'd thought he'd be fine in the carriage house barracks. But if evil Jake would make his move on a crowded dance floor, what would stop him from trying to take Sully out while he slept peacefully and unaware on his cot? Even with all of B Company snoring nearby.

"You can't leave, Sully. I mean, will you come up to my room? You know, to make sure I'm safe in there, too?"

His square jaw got even squarer. If that was possible. "*This* is as far as I go."

Why did he have to make saving his life so difficult? "What is it?" I said softly, looking up at him. "Are you afraid to be alone with me?"

He smiled. A nice change from his usual scowl. "That's not it at all. You're beautiful, Beryl. You got more ginger than a woman has a right to, but—" A hard pause. "I care about your reputation, even if you don't. Besides, you're drunk and there are rules about that."

Ethics. Respect. Sully could teach some frat boys and high school jocks a lesson about that. "Sully, I can hardly believe you're real. Maybe you're not, and this is all a dream. Or a bad reality show I can't get out of."

"This is why girls should never drink. You start talking gibberish. Off to bed now, Beryl. *Alone*. Good night."

He started to go, so I had to resort to drastic measures. I fell against him, lifted my arms, and looped my hands behind his neck. Not much finesse, but it did the trick. Stopped the man in his tracks.

"How about a good night kiss?" I purred.

Eyebrow sky high now. Both of them. "You're awful fast."

Fast. A Grandma Blue word. A ridiculous word from a more prudish time, when a woman wasn't supposed to make the first move. "It's only a kiss, Sully, not a marriage proposal."

I wriggled against him. Shameless, I know. But it was for the greater good, for the mission, right? Had nothing to do with the fact that I wanted him to kiss me, wanted him to spend the night with me. And not just as the guy I was supposed to save, but as the guy I kind of sort of liked. Was growing to like more and more with each passing second.

Nope, it had nothing to do with that at all.

He bent his head and looked into my eyes. I could feel

his heartbeat, hammering hard. He wasn't as immune to my charms as he pretended to be. Were the walls of Jericho crumbling?

He touched my face, almost without thinking, it seemed. His gaze held mine. I saw heat, longing, and something deeper in his eyes. My heart flipped. He stroked my cheek with his thumb.

"Beryl." His warm breath brushed my face, my name like a caress in that husky rumble.

Who was flirting now? It certainly worked. I tingled all over and my knees went weak, and not just from the whiskey. His lips were inches from mine. Close enough to feel his warmth. I'd been around the block enough times to know when a guy wanted to kiss me. I tipped my head back, parted my lips, inviting him...

"Who plays first base for the Yankees?" he murmured.

I jerked back, hands falling away from his neck. Burned, and sorely tempted to pop him in that luscious, teasing mouth. "Nice. See if I try to save your life now."

"What's going on here?" The inside door creaked open, and we both turned to see Ma, wearing a flowered housecoat, a frilly nightcap, and a supremely suspicious expression.

Great. Pulled over by Ma the Morality Police, and Sully so eager to avoid a ticket. Now I'd never get him upstairs. But no way could I let him out of my sight all night. I scrambled for an idea, thought as fast as my whiskey-addled brain would let me.

"O-h-h-h... I'm going to faint..." I threw my forearm across my forehead like a diva in an old movie and swayed dramatically. "I'm going to..."

87

I let my legs buckle. Slowly, and only when I was sure Sully would catch me. He scooped me up. The feel of his steely arms around me, my head cradled against his broad shoulder, his delicious scent wrapping around me, it took every ounce of will power not to swoon for real.

"My cousin is unwell," he muttered.

He said that like I was mentally unwell, but Ma interpreted it differently. I opened my eyes a slit and saw her glower at Sully.

"You mean she's imbibed too much, Sergeant. Shame on you for letting her get into such a state."

Sully grunted, taking her abuse like a man.

"I suppose you'll need to assist her to her room?" Ma sighed. "Very well, bring her in."

The screen door squawked. I gave myself a mental thumbs up for my successful scheme as he carried me inside. When he got to the stairs, I decided I better come to. Sully might be as strong as a bull, but I doubted he could carry me up those steps without straining something.

I opened my eyes and, with a theatrical groan, slipped out of his grip. But I didn't let go. I hung onto him for dear life as we climbed to the second floor.

"You come *right* down once the young lady is settled, Sergeant," Ma called after us, her voice reeking disapproval. "You know I don't allow monkey business in my place. I have a reputation to uphold."

MA'S scolding voice followed us up the stairs and down the hallway. I let Sully practically drag me toward my room while I searched for my next ploy. Some way to keep him up here. All night. Hitting on him again would be weak. He'd already shut me down, and, jeez Louise, I wasn't about to beg. I liked him and all, but a girl had to have some pride.

He opened the door to my room and clicked the light switch. When he tried to set me upright, I played full-on wasted and went as limp as an overcooked noodle. He caught me before I hit the patterned carpet.

"Son of a gun," he grumbled, helping me to the bed. "Next time I say you're getting sarsaparilla, you're *getting* sarsaparilla."

He sat me down, unwound my fingers from my hand-bag's strap and dropped it on the bureau with a decided clunk.

"What's in there, rocks?" he asked, with a suspicious quirk of his eyebrow.

"Maybe." I stifled a yawn.

He knelt and eased off my shoes then began to undo my coat buttons. I didn't help, and it didn't matter. He did the job with the skill of a man who had put a drunk to bed many times before. That made me sad. Grandma Blue could be a pain in the butt, but she'd been a sober pain in the butt.

After Sully peeled off my coat and tossed it over the bed's foot rail, I took his hand. "Stay with me."

Our eyes locked for a hot moment before he stood and glanced at the door he'd left open. He turned back to me. "I can't, Beryl. I like you, a hell of a lot, but I'm not gonna take advantage of you."

I flopped back against the pillows and stretched out my legs, inciting a squeaky bedsprings chorus and getting an instant case of bed spins. "Why not? Because I'm a *spy*? Because I'm drunk? Because I'm a drunk spy?"

He frowned. "Don't be sore at me."

I gazed up at him. He nearly filled the room with his height and broad shoulders. "I'm not mad at you," I murmured. "I'm sore at..."

Glo, and by extension, Jake. I was sore at *them*. Furious, really. I'd been perfectly happy living my life...okay, a little bored...okay, a *lot* bored. But I was happy, well, not exactly happy, but okay with my boring, dull, going nowhere, unhappy life until Glo dragged my ass so many years into the past. Introduced me to Sgt. Sexy, told me to save his life, *or else*, and left me high and dry. And now I had no clue what I was doing, except kind of falling for this big ol' redhead who wanted nothing to do with me.

I sighed the mother of all self-pitying sighs, and threw up my hands, totally surrendering. "Whatever. This whole thing's fucked up."

Now, in my time, people rarely blinked to hear someone drop an F-bomb. But this wasn't my time. Sully went all horrified, like I'd just declared Adolph Hitler dreamy, once again reminding me of that fact. He quickly closed the door, as if to contain my profanity before it could tsunami down the hall.

"For a librarian, you sure know some colorful words," he said, coming back to the bed.

"Note to self, don't use the F-word. You Greatest

Generation boys don't like it when a lady swears." I hitched up my skirt a tiny bit, reached underneath, and unhooked my garters with a relieved sigh. Those garters had been jabbing into my thighs all night. How did women ever survive in these prehistoric times?

I peeled off my silk stockings and dropped them on the floor. I began to wriggle out of my girdle, which squeezed me like a python strangling its victim. Sully went pale and retreated to the window overlooking the garden.

"Can't have Civil Defense giving Ma grief about lights in the windows," he said, pulling down the shade.

He moved to the other window, which overlooked the street. He reached for the shade, then paused and peered out into the night. Searching for Jake, maybe, and uh, get a clue Big Red. If Sully could see Jake outside, that futuristic underwear model most certainly could see Sully inside. He was a large target, especially framed by the window with backlighting and everything.

"Sully, will you get away from that window?"

"Are you finished undressing?" he muttered, his back to me.

"Yes," I sighed, finally freeing myself from my girdle prison. "Now, please, come away from the window."

He lowered the shade and turned to me. "It's that fella. You're really afraid of him, aren't you?"

"I guess. I'm afraid he'll hurt you."

He snorted, like that was impossible. "Pop taught me how to throw a punch." He came back to the bed and gazed down at me. "My mom taught me how to duck."

I gave a grim smile. Dark humor, my specialty. I was

beginning to suspect Glo had used one of those online dating sites that used eighty-five points of compatibility to match me up with Sully.

I tilted my head, studying him. "You know, I wish someone had warned me about you. I thought you actually needed my help. Instead, I meet a solid tree-trunk who can take care of himself just fine. You're a giant, walking, talking tree, like an Ent. A big, hot, fucking red-headed Ent. Oops, F-word again. Drop a dime in the swear jar."

"You know, you're talkative when you're soused," he said with a rumbling laugh.

Oh, how I was coming to love that laugh. It tickled my spine.

"Soused," I said. "What a word, soused. Everyone should get soused once in a while. Even my grandma Blue got hammered sometimes. Four times a year, Thanksgiving, Christmas, and—" I went from giddy to maudlin drunk in a nanosecond. I swear time travel must trigger PMS, because my emotions had been all over the place since I'd landed in 1943. "And two other times," I said, trailing off.

Sully shrugged off his jacket and tossed it over the foot rail next to my coat. The bed squeaked as he sat. "Easter and the Fourth of July?" he said softly, loosening his tie.

"No," I murmured. "The anniversary of the day my parents died, in April. And every year on the eighteenth of December."

"You're not going to cry now, are you, Beryl?"

"No. I never cry."

"Good to know." He brushed away the tear that rolled down my cheek with his thumb. "Your parents?"

I liked that, the simple way he asked that. "Car fire," I said, just as simply. "It was only me and Grandma Blue after that."

"And December eighteenth?"

"That was the day my grandma's brother was killed. In the Battle of the Bulge—" I snapped my mouth shut. That gruesome battle was more than a year away. "He was killed in the war," I finished. "She didn't talk about him much, but I knew she missed him."

"They called that the war to end all wars," he said, and I realized he thought I meant World War I. "And here we are again, at war."

We stared at each other a moment, my questions unspoken, his worries clouding his face. How many of Sully's men would face the same fate as my great-uncle? Was Sully's number up too? Was he fated to sacrifice himself to save another soldier, or a bunch of soldiers? A heroic act Jake wanted to derail by taking Sully out now?

I reached up and touched his face, trailed my fingers down his cheek, across reddish stubble that had sprouted along his jaw. Another tear threatened to fall. Even if I saved him now, he might die.

"Sully, are you afraid?"

"Of what? The enemy? I'd be stupid to say no. How about you? What're you afraid of?"

"At the moment, just about everything." But mostly him. The thought of getting attached to him terrified me. Everyone I ever loved had been taken from me. Sully would be taken from me too, either way. If Jake succeeded, he would die. If I succeeded in this insane mission, I'd go home, and Sully would be taken from me by time.

He took my hand, laced his fingers through mine, his touch warm and reassuring. "I'd better go."

"Am I that unappealing?" I meant to tease, but it came out kind of hurt. *Oh, Beryl, what happened to you? You never used to let a man get under your skin like this.*

Sully gave me a look so intense my breath caught. "Christ, Beryl, that's the opposite of what you are. Why are you so anxious to destroy your reputation?"

"I don't care about that. I *want* you to stay. Please. Stay so I can protect you." Our hands were still entwined. I gave a gentle tug. He didn't resist. The bedsprings squeaked in surrender as he stretched his long body next to mine, facing me, our joined hands between us.

"What about Ma?" he asked.

"She can find her own redhead."

He smiled into my eyes. "Beryl Blue, you're a real piece of work."

I felt a grin spread over my face as my eyes closed.

9

I woke up with a headache the size of Montana. And a roiling stomach. I opened my eyes. Slowly. Dust motes floated in the sunbeams that slit through the edges of the window shades. Even that little bit of light made me wince.

"Sully?" A wad of cotton seemed to fill my mouth. "What time is it?"

No answer. No surprise. He was gone.

"Shit." I threw off the covers, scrambled out of bed, stabbed my feet into my shoes and flew out the door in one quick movement. The beating drum of my hangover caught up to me halfway down the hall and I had to stop to catch my breath. I had to stop at the bathroom, too, no matter how desperate my need to find Sully. Other needs were just too powerful.

Afterward, I paused long enough to wash my hands then resumed my frantic flight. All kinds of gruesome scenarios ran through my head, each and every one of them ending with Sully dead in a ditch, with Jake cackling maniacally over his body.

I'd reached full panic mode by the time I got downstairs. Then, I froze. Men's voices murmured from the dining room, including Sully's distinctive rumble. I peeked inside and there he sat at one of the tables, wolfing down his breakfast.

My relief morphed to anger pretty fast, and I bombed into the room, ready to engage.

"You look like hell," Sully said, eyeing me head to toe.

He sure didn't. He wore the same uniform as yesterday, but he'd shaved and washed up and changed into a fresh shirt. He looked tasty. My anger melted away.

"Good morning to you, too," I said, surprised by the warmth in my voice. And the heat that flamed my cheeks. "I blame the whiskey for my current condition."

"I tried to warn you." He tapped Griff on the shoulder and ordered him to vacate his seat, which Griff did with bleary-eyed good humor. Sully helped me to sit, then resumed his chair and pushed a bowl of stick oats swimming in milk toward me. "Do you want something to eat?"

"Not on your life." I held my stomach and reached for one of the silver coffeepots in the center of the table. Steam poured out of a spout as long and curved as a swan's neck. "Just coffee. Black coffee."

"I wish," Marco said from the other side of the table. He hunched over his bowl, his oatmeal untouched. Looked like the whiskey had caught up to him, too. And someone's fist. A purplish shiner darkened one eye. I felt duly guilty. He and the others had thrown themselves into the breach for me, no questions asked.

"That's tea, Beryl." Sully watched me pour the steaming amber liquid into a cup. "Coffee is rationed. Been rationed for a while. Not sure you know that."

"Of *course* I know that." I lifted my cup and sipped. I preferred my tea sweet enough to give me a toothache, but since I knew sugar had also been rationed, I wasn't about to hunt for the sugar bowl and give Sully more ammo for his *Beryl-is-a-spy* arsenal.

"They say we'll have coffee at the front," Stan said, shoveling in oatmeal with one hand, holding a cigarette in the other. "So at least we have that to look forward to."

"What? Coffee, or the front?" Marco said. "I could do without both. Just give me a real bed, with a real pillow and I won't gripe again for the duration of this lousy war."

I leaned toward Sully. Not too close, since I hadn't changed or cleaned up yet and no doubt smelled like I'd rolled out of an old west saloon. "Why did you leave me?" I asked in a low voice. My cheeks flamed again. Had I gone menopausal all of a sudden, turning on the hot flash machine whenever Sully came near?

"You know why I left, Beryl. No one saw me leave, no one can call you fast, and no one has to feel my fists." He shot me that disarming grin. "Besides, you talk in your sleep."

That was news. "I do?" I'd rarely spent the night with a guy I was seeing. I liked to sleep alone. At least that was my excuse. My shrink would suggest I feared getting too close. Whatever, I never knew such an interesting factoid about myself. "Did I say anything...unusual?" Like, blurt out my PIN or the result of the last forty years of presidential elections?

"Give a girl a drink and she'll say all kinds of things."
He snagged two biscuits off a platter, dropped them onto
a plate, then nudged my shoulder. "In German."

Oh, he was teasing. I grabbed a biscuit too and
scanned the table for butter, finding none. Biscuits
without butter were an abomination in my book, but I
supposed that was also rationed. I ate it anyway. It had a
strong flavor of potatoes.

Sully bit into a biscuit and eyed me again. "Tell me
about that fella at the Hi-Hat last night. The one who
blackened Marco's eye."

"The guy packs a helluva punch," Marco said, proving
he'd been eavesdropping. "The MPs almost got him, but
he slipped away, the clever bastard, er, excuse my French."

Was Jake really that clever? I mean, making a move
on Sully on the dance floor seemed more desperate than
smart. Too bad the MPs didn't catch him. They would've
relieved him of any futuristic weapons and transporter
doodads he carried, leaving him stranded in 1943 forever.
And solving all my problems without me breaking a
sweat. Now, we had circled back to square one.

"Beryl? You gonna answer, or stare at your cup all day?
Why are you so afraid of him?"

I looked at Sully, then around the room, sure all ears
were tuned in. Including the elf-like lobes of the evicted
Etta, puttering around at a sideboard by the windows,
stacking spoons and bowls.

"Look, Sully, it's a long story, and I'd prefer to tell you
when we don't have an audience. Let's go somewhere we
can talk privately." And by that I meant my room, with the

door locked, safe and sound, and possibly up close and intimate as we chatted.

Sully scarfed the rest of his biscuit and pushed away from the table. I thought he'd seen it my way until he pulled me across the hall into the parlor, a cozy room with a fireplace, a braided rug, claw-footed furniture and the distinct smell of peppermints and old people. And books, to my delight, shelves and shelves of books, lining one wall.

I steered to the bookshelves to have a look while Sully roused the room's lone occupant—a young private in a rumpled uniform, snoozing on the leather-bound sofa. Sully gave him a shake and the guy snorted awake.

"Jeezum crow!" the kid cried, startled and bleary-eyed.

"Beat it, bub." Sully jerked a thumb toward the door. "We want to be alone."

The man both leered and grumbled at that command then did as ordered. Sully closed the door after him and stepped to a cherry table the *Antiques Roadshow* would kill for. A cathedral-style radio sat on the tabletop. He turned the knob. The speaker whined and crackled as something classical with lots of violins came on.

"This ought to keep any big-ears from listening in, if that's what worries you," he said. "Now you're free to spill the beans."

He gestured to the sofa. I reluctantly put down a dusty copy of *A Tale of Two Cities* I'd been checking out, went over, and plopped down. The cushions still held the sleeping man's warmth. Sully sank down beside me. That simple act turned up my inner furnace again. I wished I had internal air conditioning, because I'd switch it to *hi-cool* and leave it there forever.

"Wait, Sully, before we begin, *please* don't do that." He'd taken a pack of Lucky Strikes out of his breast pocket and was about to light up. Where did he keep getting those gross things?

The first suspicious eyebrow of the day made an appearance. "Don't do what? Smoke?"

"Yes, smoke. It's just, I really don't like cigarette smoke." I waved a hand in front of my face. "Could you just...not?"

"I never met a dame who complains more than you," he grumped, but stuck the cigarette back in the pack and the whole thing disappeared into his pocket. He sat back and eyed me like a spoiled kid denied a toy. "Happy?"

"Immensely."

"Good. Now, can we get back to that nincompoop who's chasing you?"

"Would you believe me if I said he's chasing you?"

He rejected that with a wave of his hand. "He's after you, has been since we met, and who knows how long before that. You know him from somewhere. Did you two have a love affair?"

"What? That's ridiculous..."

Wait, maybe not so ridiculous, if that's what Sully would believe. He certainly wouldn't believe the truth. A story churned in my head. Not a well-plotted story. My brain was too whiskey-mottled and hung over to craft the great American novel. Pulp fiction would have to do.

"His name's Jake and yes, he's after me. He's...he's my ex, uh, my former boyfriend." Sully sat up straight and I knew I had his full attention. "We mixed it up for a while but then I told him we were done. I told him I wanted to do something valuable for my country and I was going to join the WACs. He didn't like that idea. Far from it. Now he's following me, trying to stop me any way he can."

"I knew it." He balled his fists on his thighs. "He tried to run you down, the bastard."

I felt terrible getting him all riled on my behalf, but his ferociousness had a surprising effect on me. I went all gooey inside. I wasn't used to having a protector.

"Did that fink go AWOL to chase after you? Or is he based at Camp Davis? I'll have a word with his C.O. The fella will be on KP for the duration. If I don't break his neck first."

His jaw worked, as if grinding rocks with his teeth. Sully's poker face had a tell, and that was it. The fella was *furious*. If I told him Jake's uniform was merely a costume, that he only pretended to be a soldier, he'd probably explode.

"Whoa, Sully. What difference does it make *where* Jake's from? The thing is we have to hide, stay out of his way until I can leave or...whatever."

He burst up off the sofa. "Come on, let's get out of here."

"Upstairs?" I asked hopefully.

Those wise blue eyes lasered in on me. "Beryl, we've only known each other a short while, but I think you know by now I'm not the kind that hides from trouble."

"No. I mean yes. Yes, I know that." *Damn it.*

"Good. I'm not afraid of facing the bull when he's angry, and that cheap pair of pants is one angry bull. We need to get outside, stick our necks out, draw him out and see if he tries to chop." His eyes glittered. "Then I'll pummel him."

My mind went to a dark place. If Sully had that stick-your-neck-out strategy at the front, he'd be toast. I gazed at him soberly, willing those awful thoughts away. "But why go on the hunt for Jake, when he's hunting y— Uh, me? *I* say we run and hide. Until hurricane Jake blows away."

He shot me a fierce look. "Beryl, you can't run away, *can't* hide. The thing you're scared of won't go away unless you face it. Whether it's Hitler and Hirohito, or some two-bit Valentino that likes to bully girls."

Gotta say, I admired him. His plan bordered on nuts and possibly suicidal if he knew the truth, but I admired his gumption. I was the queen of running away, both literally and figuratively. Even when I'd been placed in a warm and cozy foster home where I felt like I might actually fit in, I ran. *Especially* when that happened. I'd run from anyone who tried to treat me like a human being. Even the books I loved so much were a form of running away, but in a good way.

"You ready to go find this weasel?" he asked.

"I suppose resistance is futile?" I peered up at him. He was so tall. Menacing, almost. Jake wouldn't stand a chance hand-to-hand. With a weapon, from a distance, like a sniper? I shuddered to think what could happen to Sully. "We're doing this no matter what I say?"

"Damn right we are."

I sighed. No way would this end well. But I couldn't stop the tides or a tornado once it formed, and I'd begun to realize I could no more stop Sully than I could tap my heels together and wish myself home.

"One question," I said. "Why? Why are you risking yourself for me?"

"Because—" His blue eyes snapped fire. His voice got rough. "Because I don't like men who hurt women and I want to tell him so to his face. Before I kill him."

10

————

Sully offered me his arm as we left Ma's. I slipped my hand through the crook of his elbow, and we headed for downtown, putting operation Make Sully a Target into full force. Sending Jake a challenge. Find me, kill me. The finding job would be easy. Sully positively swaggered down the sidewalk. Plus, he'd left his hat behind, and his glorious copper hair shone like a beacon in the midday sun. He provided a big, broad target that would make the killing part super easy.

"I *really* don't think this is a good idea," I said for the millionth time.

"You worry too much," he said.

And you take too many chances. I anticipated getting a bad case of whiplash today from swiveling my head, keeping an eye out for Jake. But I had no choice. If Sully was determined to see this insane plan through to the hopefully not bloody end, then I guessed I had to be too. I might have serious doubts about my ability to complete the kill-the-assassin part of my mission, but I sure could do everything possible to keep Sully safe.

Fears and whiplash worries aside, I felt a bit more human after I had cleaned up and changed back into the Mary Janes and the skirt and sweater-set I'd been wearing yesterday. I'd opted out of the girdle, though. To hell with authenticity. That thing was beyond uncomfortable.

"Sully, what'd you do before the war?" I asked after we had walked a bit in silence.

"This 'n that."

"Which means?"

Second suspicious eyebrow of the day. I was keeping count. "This. 'N. That."

And here I thought I'd put that whole spy thing to rest. "You really are annoying. You think I'm going to tell the enemy you had a job pumping gas or played ball in high school?"

"A fella can't be too careful." He relented with a chuckle. "I didn't do much to speak of before the war, anyway. Weren't a lot of jobs to be had. Me and Pat scrabbled around, picked up some dough carrying crates, pushing a broom, even washed dishes at the Parker House for a while. A swank joint, lots of swells and debs, movie stars, too, so we did all right."

I nodded, getting most of his old-timey slang. "Pat?"

"My brother. He's in the Navy, and before you ask, I don't know where he is. If I did, I wouldn't tell you, Mata Hari. Loose lips sink ships."

"Sully, don't you *ever* give up?"

"Nope."

His eyes teased me. I'd say that set me on fire once

again, except the fire hadn't tamped down one bit since we'd left the boarding house. Okay, since last night. Well, since we'd met, to be honest.

"How'd you end up in the Army? Didn't you want to join the Navy, like your brother?"

"Not on your life. I'm partial to dry land." He patted his coat pocket, started to pull out his cigarettes, then gave me a sheepish look and pushed them back in. "Pat wanted to get as far away from the old man as he could, joined the Navy back in '40, the day he turned eighteen. He was at Pearl when it got hit. Ma had a hellish couple of weeks waiting to get word if he was all right."

Must've been hellish for him as well, I decided, from his voice and gloomy expression.

He shot me a quick glance. "I would've enlisted, too. But Pop got sick and lost his job. I was the only one pulling in dough, so I had to stay and take care of both of them. That kept me from getting drafted."

His voice had taken on a defensive note, like I'd think he'd been shirking, or that he was a coward or something. "I understand. You stepped up to help your family, Sully. You did what you had to do."

"I s'pose." He shrugged. "Time's change. Now no man's exempt, no matter what the reason. I got my draft notice and here I am. In the Army, soon to be in the fight. Like Pat."

"Do you have any idea where you're headed?"

"I don't know. I honestly don't." Blunt and frank and not even trying to tease me about prying for inside info. "I'm playing infantry roulette. Uncle Sam spins the chamber, and I go where it lands. Mud trench or mountain or desert. In some country, somewhere, over there."

I tensed. *Over there.* Italy, North Africa, the Philippines, Normandy, Alaska, so many other points of conflict. Wherever he went, there'd be battle. This war truly was a world war. I squeezed his arm. Because, what else could I do?

We turned onto Main Street. Sully lasered in on every soldier we passed looking for Jake. A nearly impossible task, like trying to find a needle in an olive-drab haystack. The mobs of men on weekend leave joined the hundreds of locals out and about, thronging the sidewalks and darting in and out of the shops. In my time Main Street was almost a ghost town. Now? We passed a tobacconist, a hat shop, and a tailor, each place stuffed with customers. At a shoe store, women whipped out their ration books like credit cards to buy one of the two pair of new shoes they were allotted each year. The revolving door at Woolworth's spun like crazy.

My head spun just as madly, keeping an eye out for future boy. I focused so much on looking in a hundred and one directions, I almost missed the library as we walked past. *My* library. I stopped and stared up at that majestic old building. Only yesterday I'd rolled into work here five minutes late, as usual. Only yesterday I'd gone upstairs to shelve those returned books and fallen from that ladder. Only yesterday my world had been flipped upside down.

"Want to go in?" Sully asked.

"What about the plan? Shouldn't we stay outside?"

"We should. But this place seems...important to you."

Picked up on that, had he? Was it my near blubbering and wistful expression that had given me away? "Well, I guess it kind of is. I'm a librarian, after all. Do *you* want to go in?"

"Sure. I like libraries."

"Really? I don't picture you as the bookworm type."

"If you can be a librarian, Beryl, then I can be a bookworm." He shrugged. "I've been going to the library since I was a kid. It's quiet. It's free. A place to get away from the old man. There was a branch around the corner from our place. Sometimes me and Pat would go down to the big one at Copley Square, where all the mucky mucks go. When we could get away."

The affection in his voice as he spoke of his brother made me jealous. I'd always wanted a sibling. Sure, I'd had tons of foster brothers and sisters. Some of them were caught in the system like me, others the biological spawn of the good people who'd taken me in, but it wasn't the same. It wasn't permanent, and there was no shared memory. Of good things, like Christmas when we were four. Or bad stuff, like the accident that had killed my parents.

Or even... I gazed up at the library again and my chest tightened. Or even to share one of my most precious memories, the first time I'd walked through those dark wooden doors. The first time I'd entered the wonderful world of books.

Sully watched me, of course. He seemed to have a GPS in his brain that told him to turn and stare at me whenever I started to get weepy and sentimental.

"Are we going in or not?" His words were rough. His voice was not. Soft, almost tender.

I couldn't speak, so I simply nodded. Side by side, we climbed the smooth granite steps. My heart hammered and the memories pulsed. Me, wearing a short dress and lacy white gloves like a girl in an old movie, holding the iron rail with one small hand, the other hand safely cocooned in my mother's comforting grip. As excited then as I felt now.

Sully opened the door and held back for me to enter first. I stepped inside and my breath caught.

The place looked almost exactly as it would more than seventy years from now. Almost. No audiobooks and a massive newspapers and periodicals section compared to my time, but the rest was achingly familiar. The spacious first floor, the dark paneled walls, rows and rows of shelves, sagging under the weight of so many books. The high ceiling with suspended globe lights and the second-floor mezzanine in the back. Sunlight streamed through the arched windows.

Plus, the smells. Mahogany, steam heat, newsprint. And that special scent of *books*—binding glue, mustiness, and a hint of vanilla.

I'd come home. Sort of.

I turned to Sully and grinned, feeling positively giddy. He caught my mood and returned a knockout smile of his own.

"Come on." I tugged his coat sleeve and he followed me across the main floor to the back. The ancient elevator's bell dinged, the brass-plated door clunked open, and half a dozen people spilled out. Several more crowded on.

Too cramped, and too slow, so we climbed the stairs that curled like a snake around the elevator shaft, our shoes clacking on the tile.

We came out on the mezzanine level. I leaned on the brass railing to watch the people bustling about on the first floor. They pored through the stacks, sat at reading tables, or lounged on comfy chairs. Men, women, school kids, seniors. People wearing feathery hats, shiny shoes, suits and dresses, as if they were the star attraction at their own funeral. A far cry from the yoga pants and tee-shirt couture of my library days. At the front desk, a librarian with a gray hair bun stamped a woman's books with martial efficiency and turned to her next victim without cracking a smile.

"Look at this place, Sully," I said, grinning again. "The Hi-Hat may be *the* place at night, but Saturday is *all* about the library."

Sully leaned his elbows on the railing next to me. "I guess this place *is* important to you." He turned his head and searched my face. "I thought you'd never been to Ballard Springs before."

His voice trembled with laughter, softening his suspicion. A little, anyway. "Oh, give it a rest. Please?"

I tugged his sleeve again and we headed down the wide bridge connecting the mezzanine to the reading room. We took a turn around the stuffy, high-ceilinged room filled with stuffy old almanacs and atlases lining stuffy old shelves, then started back across the bridge.

Sully slowed then stopped as we neared a large table with a map of the world spread across the top. Pins and tacks of varying colors were stuck in many places.

"What's this?" I asked.

"It's for tracking battles. A lot of libraries have one. Isn't there a battle map in your library?"

More teasing, or maybe real suspicion this time. With no eyebrow of doom to clue me in, I couldn't be sure.

"*S-h-h-h!*" a small, squeaky voice said. "You're not supposed to talk in here."

I looked down, and down some more, to where the voice had come from. A girl of five or six, with frizzy brown hair and a frilly blue dress sat cross-legged on the floor under the map table. She had a picture book spread across her lap. She looked up at us with scolding brown eyes and put a finger to her lips, shushing us again.

"Don't be bossy, Ida," came from a woman reading *The Song of Bernadette* in a nearby armchair.

Ida? *No.* Could this little thing possibly be my elderly coworker from seventy plus years in the future? Ida Pellerin, walking librarian stereotype, glasses, hair bun and all.

"But Mama, you *know* they're not supposed to talk in the library," she said in an annoyed whisper. "They *have* to follow the *rules.*"

Oh, definitely Ida. Apparently, she'd been a regular at the library since day one, training for her future career.

"Mm-hmm," Ida's mama murmured, turning a page in her book.

"I'm sorry, little girl," I whispered, trying not to sound freaked out. I mean, talk about a reality check. How many times did I have to remind myself this wasn't a cosplay game? Or that I wasn't sprawled unconscious upstairs on the top floor of this very building, trapped in a head trauma-induced dream? This was reality. Total, mind-bending reality.

Baby Ida *hmphed* at me, placed her book on the floor and stood up. She balanced on tiptoe, straining to see over the tabletop. Sully, who'd been studying the battle map with the intensity of a general planning a major offensive, looked down at her with a gentle grin.

"Want a boost?" he asked, then glanced toward Ida's mother for permission. She granted it with a distracted nod. Sully groaned and pretended to strain as if Ida weighed a thousand pounds and not a mere forty as he lifted her up. That made Ida beam. And me melt.

He held the girl in his arms and pointed out the different continents, telling her which army was where. When he got to Asia, he said, "That's the Orient. My brother is there."

Ida's face scrunched in thought. "The Orient. That's where Japan is." She pronounced it *Jah-pan*. "That's where my daddy is. He's sleeping there so he can't come home, Mama says."

Sully visibly stiffened. As did I. That buzzard came back, circling again, reminding us of war, and its heavy cost. Poor Ida. I had no idea she'd lost her father at such a young age. I promised right there and then I'd be extra wicked nice to her when I got back to the future.

"I'm sure he's dreaming about you, sweetheart," Sully said, his rumble in tender mode. "I bet he's dreaming about his pretty little girl every night."

My heart caught in my throat and something stirred in me. Something raw and breathtaking and unfamiliar. Something I could barely begin to understand.

Sully put Ida down, rumpled her curls, and she skipped away. He turned to me, his eyes a little shiny. Or maybe that was the light.

"Let's get the hell out of here," he said, his voice tight.

I nodded, stunned. Who was this man? Yesterday, he'd been gruff and suspicious and magnetic, all at once. A while ago back at Ma's, he'd been so fierce, threatening to split Jake in two to protect me. And now, so gentle with a child he didn't know.

My emotions whirled as we moved toward the stairs. *Don't judge a book by its cover,* Grandma Blue always said. The Book of Sully had turned out to be a much, much more complex read than I could have ever imagined.

Suddenly, Sully froze. He'd stopped so abruptly, I nearly crashed into him. I followed his thunderous gaze to the floor below and every hair on the back of my neck stood at attention. Jake stood just inside the door. He stared up at us with a shit-eating grin, his hat pushed back at a rakish angle. He lifted both hands and wiggled his fingers in a taunting, *come get me* gesture.

Sully's entire body tensed up and a furious sound like a bear caught in a trap rolled up his throat. My heartbeat picked up to a speed faster than light. I feared he'd vault over the mezzanine railing to get to Jake and kill himself in the fall. Finishing what Jake had started out to do without that bastard even breaking a sweat.

Not on my watch.

I grabbed Big Red by the arm and gave him a shove. A fruitless effort against such a solid object, like trying to topple the Washington Monument. But my sneak attack startled him enough to snap his focus from Jake to me. For a moment.

"Come on," he growled and plowed down the stairs, taking the steps two at a time.

I rushed to keep up. By the time I reached the ground floor, Jake had fled. Sully crashed open the front door and disappeared outside, chasing after him. I followed, apologizing for the disturbance on my way out, earning laughter from some of the patrons and a pinch-faced glare from the librarian at the desk.

I caught up to Sully pretty fast. He stood on the sidewalk, scowling at passersby. My racing heartbeat slowed in relief.

"He got away," he spat. "Dammit."

"Good," I said, getting one of Sully's patented frowns in return. "He found us like you wanted. But what could you do to him in the library? Beat him senseless? With women and children around?"

The anger drained from his face, replaced with something akin to shame. "You're right," he said after several moments. "How about a bite to eat? You hungry?"

A bite to eat? My hangover had cleared up enough to give me an appetite, plus it was nearly three o'clock and I hadn't eaten anything since that biscuit at breakfast. So yeah, I was hungry, but also suspicious.

"Sully, what are you up to?"

"Let's pick up some grub," he said, with a devious grin. "There's a park near here. We'll have a picnic."

"A picnic?" The day was relatively warm for October, with a smattering of wispy clouds drifting across the sky, but not exactly picnic weather. "We'll be the only nonfeathered loons in the park. An easy target for—" I stiffened. Exactly Sully's strategy. "You're out of your mind."

He accepted my diagnosis with a shrug. "Why not? You said yourself, he found us. He can find us again. Only this time it'll be just the three of us and not half the city in the way."

"No, Sully. That's suicide. I forbid it."

Eyebrow up for the third time today. Or was that the fourth? "You're awful pushy for a librarian."

"And you're as stubborn as an old mule. How you manage to obey any order from your superiors is beyond me."

He puffed up, positively pleased with himself.

"Don't give me that grin, Sergeant. You're going to get us *both* killed."

That got a reaction. His poker face twitched a little. "You're right. We should go back to Ma's."

I brightened. "That's the first sensible thing you've said all weekend."

He held up a hand. "Let me finish. We'll go back and I'll lock you in your room then go look for that guy on my own." He pinned me with a heated look. "You're too much of a distraction, anyway."

Right back at you, fella. "Well, we know *that's* not going to happen. I'm sticking with you, no matter what."

"Now who's being stubborn?" He snorted. "Looks like we're having a picnic."

I indulged myself in a long-suffering sigh. Why did he always have to win?

11

——————

I looped my arm through Sully's and he steered us toward Linden's, a sandwich shop about a block down, next to a Rexall Drug store. Linden's was still around in my time, but Rexall had become a dollar store. The smell of perfume, pickles, and the ever-present wall of cigarette smoke hit me as we stepped inside.

A burly guy in a white apron past his knees pushed up to the counter. "What'll it be folks? We got chicken salad and pastrami today." He leaned in and lowered his voice to a furtive whisper, as if revealing state secrets. "We got *eggs*. No one in town's got eggs. They been scarce for weeks. Uncle Sam's taking them all. Hard boiled or egg salad, your choice."

Sully ordered four egg salad sandwiches, pickles, and a Coke for each of us before I could get in a word. I frowned. Would he ever stop treating me like a helpless girl? I didn't object to the order, though I didn't like egg salad. I mean, who does? But if it came with bread sliced from those pillowy loaves stacked on a shelf behind the counter, then yes please. Some people have a sweet tooth, I have a bread tooth.

A few minutes later, Sully forked over a dollar bill and the man behind the counter handed him a paper bag containing our lunch. The glass Coke bottles inside clinked as we moved to the door and back outside, on our way to the park.

We stopped at an intersection to wait as a rickety farm wagon, pulled by a pair of knobby-kneed horses, lumbered around the corner. Several children chased after it. So did a couple of floppy-eared beagles. A bed sheet with a hand-lettered sign, *Scrap Drive Today,* fluttered on the wagon's side. Clearly the drive had been successful. Rusty garden gates, old push mowers, bedsprings and all kinds of metal junk filled the wagon's bed to overflowing.

"Looks like everything but the kitchen sink is in there," I said. "Oh, wait, there *is* a kitchen sink."

Sully laughed, loud and long, like he'd just heard that expression for the first time. I cringed. Had I introduced an idiom before its time? No clue. I was a librarian, not an etymologist.

"Sarge. Hey, Sarge!" someone shouted. "Miss Blue, over here."

Sully shifted to alert mode and so did I, until I spotted the man calling out to us—Stretch, the long-legged private who'd given up his seat in the jeep for me. He waved to us from behind a velvet rope, where he stood in a long line of soldiers, teens, and a smattering of gray hairs waiting to get into the Bijou movie theater. The overhead marquee advertised today's matinee, the pulse pounding, red-blooded serial *Batman*. Could this film have been the first of the million and one movies featuring the Caped Crusader?

"Hiya, Miss Blue," Stretch said when Sully and I ambled over. He took my hands and squeezed them both. I'd seen people do this in old movies, a greeting less formal than a handshake but not as intimate as a hug.

I squeezed back. "Good to see you, Stretch. Are you enjoying being home on the farm with your family?"

"Gee, yeah, I'm having a ball." He swept off his hat to reveal seriously blond hair. Towhead, I think Grandma Blue would have called it.

A gaggle of young women surrounded him and I wondered which of these bobbysoxers could be the girl he'd mentioned going home to see. The one wearing braces that looked like ancient tooth torture devices? Or the one with her coat draped over her shoulders, showing off an hourglass figure? Hopefully not her, for Stretch's sake. She checked out Sully with a *gimme* expression that made me want to hang onto him with both hands.

"My folks are happy to have me home," Stretch said. "Might be the last time I get to see them before..." His grin faded and he swallowed, a faraway look in his earnest blue eyes. "Before we ship out."

I practically saw that war buzzard's shadow swoop over the kid's face. I didn't know what tortured me more —what I knew he might face once he got into battle, or his uncertainty. No, the real agony was that I couldn't tell him. Or Sully. Couldn't warn any of them about what was to come. That could mess with the timeline, according to Glo. Cause ripples that would turn into waves that impacted every moment of time forever and ever.

Stretch brightened. "I've got an idea. Why don't you come for Sunday dinner tomorrow? I've been telling the folks about you, Sarge. Telling them about Miss Blue, too. I bet they'd love to meet you both."

Sully, who'd been searching the crowd, snapped toward Stretch, and suddenly went all deer-in-the-headlights. Another interesting chapter in the Book of Sully. Jake and the enemy trying to murder him didn't faze him, but sitting down for a meal with Mom, apple pie and a gingham tablecloth seemed to scare him spit-less. Guess I couldn't blame him. That Norman Rockwell painting thing scared me too.

But I couldn't turn the kid down. He seemed so earnest and eager about the whole thing. "That's sweet. I'd *love* to meet your folks, and I'm sure Sergeant Sullivan would enjoy that as well." I elbowed Sully in the side. "Right?"

"Oh, yeah. That'll be fine, Stretch." He cleared his throat. "Thanks."

Stretch flashed an excited grin. "Swell! How about you and all the fellas come? My mum makes the best lamb stew in the county. No ration stamps required."

"Sounds like a plan," I said.

He gave us the address, we agreed on a time, and left him to his movie palace matinee.

We resumed our walk and soon passed between two stone lions into Ballard Park. There were more trees than in my day, and the World War I monument was shiny and new, instead of tarnished and splotched. The park was much larger than in my time, too. City buildings and a new fire station had eaten into its acreage, but the park's greenery still ringed the crystal-clear springs that had given the town its name.

"How does a soldier on leave find his way to a park?" I asked.

"I told you there's no room at the inn, or anywhere else in this town." Sully nodded toward a bench, where a man in a rumpled uniform curled up, catching forty winks. "Fella has to make do the best he can."

We strolled along the winding path toward the park's center then down a gently sloping hill. The scent of grass and shag bark hickory nuts carried on the air. Sully aimed us at a spot close to the water and completely out in the open. He put the bag holding our lunch on the ground then shrugged off his jacket and spread it over the ground, gesturing for me to sit. I did, stretching out my legs. I'd ditched my stockings along with the girdle today and the grass tickled my bare ankles.

"Excellent military strategy, Sergeant," I said as he hunkered down next to me. "There's no one else here. Our backs are to the path, the water is in front of us. Those oaks flanking us have really thick trunks. *Perfect* for Jake to hide behind and..."

I stopped before I could say, *and shoot you dead*, because I hadn't said anything to Sully about a weapon. He thought he'd deal with Jake face to face. I tossed a worried look at the trees, roughly forty feet away on each side. Colorful leaves fluttered down, making a pile on the ground. I'd forgotten what Glo had said about the Cack's range, but Jake could probably lean against the tree trunk like a lazy thing and fire at will.

"Don't you have any faith in me, Beryl?" He pulled a bottle opener from his pocket and popped the top off the Cokes. He handed me one—the glass bottles were *so* tiny —then tucked both caps and opener into his pocket.

"I have total faith in you, Sully." I lifted my Coke to him in a toast, while with my free hand, I dragged my handbag close to my thigh and opened it so the Cack would be easy to get at. "It's *Jake* I'm afraid of. He's persistent. He'll find us."

"I'm counting on it." He did a quick scan of the clearing then stretched out on his side, propping himself on one elbow. The bag crinkled as he dug inside. He pushed a sandwich wrapped in waxed paper at me. "Go on, eat."

I unwrapped the sandwich. The waxed paper, slippery and sticky at the same time, reminded me of Grandma Blue. I took a tentative bite. The bread was heavy on carbs, the egg salad heavy on mayo, but dang, if it didn't spark my appetite like nobody's business. I snarfed the whole thing down.

"Sully, tell me some more about your childhood." I sipped my Coke and grimaced. I hadn't drunk any soda without artificial sweetener in forever. Tasted like super sweet cough syrup. "You said you liked to read. Were you a good student?"

"I said I liked the library, didn't say I liked to read." He laughed, probably at my horrified expression. "Guess that's something you shouldn't say to a librarian. Yeah, I was a fair enough student. Enough that Miss Wilkinson in tenth grade told me I should think about college. A pipe dream. No dough."

"I hear that song. I'll be paying college loans until I'm fifty." He shot me a funny look. *Oopsie.* College loans were probably an alien concept in this day and age. I'd slipped up again. "So, what about your parents? Are they still together? Married, I mean."

"Sure they are. What kind of question is that?"

I lifted a shoulder. "If they fight like cats and dogs, maybe they're better off apart."

He pushed the last of sandwich number two into his mouth. "Nope. It's 'til death do they part, Beryl. Fighting all the way." He shifted position and sat up, looking around again before settling his gaze back on me. He nudged my shoulder with his own. "What about you? Any brothers and sisters?"

I shook my head. "Just me, Mom and Dad. And then Grandma Blue. She took care of me after...the accident."

"It still cuts you. How old were you?"

"I was six. Correction, six and a half. That half thing is so important when you're that age, isn't it? Still, I don't remember much. Just little details, like being in the back seat of the car."

I broke off my gaze and squinted up at a couple of military planes tracking across the cloudless sky. The distant putter of their engines cut through the stillness around us. My memory drifted back to my younger self in the car that day, seated in the back, my black patent leather shoes with the delicate gold buckles barely reaching the front of the wide seat.

"It was raining. We were going someplace. I don't

know where. We must've been late because we were flying. There was a flash and then the car just— I can't remember. A freak accident, Grandma Blue said whenever I asked about it. A hit and run that sparked some kind of electrical fire. I remember choking on the smoke that filled the car. Crying, trying to get to my parents, to my mother in the front seat. But there was too much smoke." I let out a bitter sigh. "And that's it. I barely remember what they look like."

I bit back a sob. Sully touched my arm then took my hand, lacing his fingers in mine. He didn't say *I'm sorry*, like people do and I was glad. He didn't say anything.

"Anyway..." I dragged a thumb under my leaky eyes. "Some guy driving by stopped to help. He got me out of the car, held me in the rain until the cops came and then all I remember is crying. And a nurse. She wore a dress so white it made me blink. And one of those..." I touched my head. "One of those old-fashioned nurse hats. Stiff and starched." Which had always struck me as odd, and possibly even a false memory, given how stressed out I'd been at the time. "She hugged me and told me everything would be okay. Only, it wasn't okay. My parents were gone."

We sat a moment with Sully holding my hand, his thumb stroking my knuckles, his gaze on me strong and steady. After a bit, I smiled.

"Grandma Blue was a tough old bird. She taught me to be tough too. I had to be after she left me. Being alone is no picnic." I stiffened. "You know, I never told anybody any of this. Why am I telling you?"

"Because I'm here?"

I shook my head. That didn't explain it. My therapist had been there too, every Thursday at four p.m. She'd tried to get me to talk but I never did. I never told anyone about the pain, the grief that shrouded my heart to this day. I'd kept it locked away. I'd run away from it. Beryl Blue's modus operandi.

I studied Sully's face and looked into those wise, lived-it eyes. "It's more than that. I think you *get* me. All of me. You understand."

He touched my cheek, his fingers warm on my skin, and gazed deeply into my eyes. The air between us seemed to shift. That same breathless something I'd felt in the library shivered through me. My heart, always so carefully guarded, opened like a daffodil on a spring day, welcoming an unanticipated and unfamiliar surge of joy.

Acting on impulse or instinct, I leaned toward him. He met me halfway and we kissed.

Our kiss began soft and tentative, as if questioning, unsure. We tasted each other with slow, tender movements. Exploring, giving, not demanding in any way. Genuine. A kiss we'd never have been able to share last night, with the whiskey and Jake and my own desperation between us.

Then Sully took charge. He parted his lips and kissed me fully, no longer holding back. I didn't hold back either and we melded together for a long time, lost in the moment. Lost in us. He slipped his fingers through my hair, stroked my cheek, caressed my neck. He moved lower to cup my breast under my open coat. Even through my dress and all that underwear, heat flamed as if he'd touched my bare skin. A deep moan rolled at the back of his throat. I echoed the sound.

A harsh wind suddenly whipped up, blowing my hair, and peppering my face with dust. My eyes popped open and I wrenched out of Sully's embrace with a gasp.

Jake loomed over us—the Cack pointed directly at Sully's head.

SUNLIGHT GLINTED off the weapon's sleek metal. A challenge blazed in Jake's hyper-blue eyes. I cursed myself for letting my guard down. For giving into my heart and getting distracted by a simple kiss. Jake had no doubt lurked nearby, waiting for his moment to attack, and I'd stupidly given him that chance.

Beryl Blue, the only person in all of time able to stop this lunatic from murdering Sully, had failed her mission. Completely.

Sully reacted instantly. He bit off a strangled, "Son of a bitch," and flew to his feet. He flung up his dukes like a bare-knuckled fighter in an old-time boxing match. Silly and sexy and kind of scary all at once. But mostly silly. Jake nimbly dodged Sully's fists.

I caught the dog-whistle whine as Jake armed the Cack. I broke out of my self-blame stupor, snatched my own weapon from my handbag, and leapt up. Terror shot through me. My hands shook. I couldn't hold the Cack steady. Or press the arming button. Or see any buttons at all.

I flailed like a fool as the two men fought. Sully got in

a lucky punch, smacking Jake in the jaw with a fast uppercut. Jake *oinked* in pain and staggered back, but the Cack stuck to his hand like a bloodthirsty leech. He quickly righted himself and took aim—straight at Sully's heart. Out of time, I dropped my weapon and activated karate action Beryl. My skirt rode up and my panties flashed as I aimed a killer slap-kick at Jake's shooting arm.

Too late. Jake fired.

No, not fired. The weapon *cacked*, literally. What came out I didn't know. Not a bullet, but some kind of scorching laser pulse. A knee-weakening rotting eggs odor lashed my nose as sizzling hot electricity exploded from the weapon's tip. My kick disrupted Jake's aim just enough. The blast shot by Sully dangerously close and pinged the ground, kicking up dirt and grass and a frightening amount of smoke.

I didn't give Jake a second chance. I attacked again. Full frontal offense. Jake fought back, but barely. He must've been the worst student in defense class. His punches and kicks never connected, not once. How had he gotten so far up the Time Cop food chain with pathetic skills like that?

Sully had frozen, stupefied, at the weapon's blast, but when my opponent finally connected—a stinging bash to my cheek with the Cack—he snapped out of it. With a curse that would make a sailor tremble, he hurled himself at Jake. Bad timing. Jake grabbed my ankle to stop a kick to his groin just as Sully plowed into him. Momentum and Sully's sheer size did the rest.

The three of us rocketed forward and cannon-balled into the water.

The springs of Ballard Springs are cold at any time of the year, but in October? Like ice. Frigid water shot up my nose and flooded my mouth. I surfaced, sputtering. I swished wet hair out of my eyes to see Sully and Jake thrashing about, arms locked around each other like Sumo wrestlers battling to the death. Jake shoved Sully underwater. Sully burst up, roaring like an angry kraken, and pushed Jake under. Jake came up, coughing, and thrust Sully into the drink again. They rolled and twisted, submerged and emerged, each man cursing and choking as he came up for air.

The tide turned. Jake spent more time underwater than on the surface. He weakened, but Sully did not. The gentle giant who'd tousled Ida's curls at the library had disappeared. So had the tender man who'd comforted me a few moments ago, and even the angry papa bear who swore to get Jake at all costs. A soldier had taken his place. A man bent on stopping the enemy the only way he knew how.

By killing him.

"Beryl," Jake choked when he managed to surface. "Help me—"

He cut off as Sully plunged him underwater again. I had to do something. "Sully, stop!" I grabbed his arm. It was as unyielding as iron. "You'll kill him."

He shook me off. "So? Save the krauts a bullet."

I seized his arm with both hands and yanked. "Please stop! You're a better man than this."

Suddenly, like an elastic band snapping, he let Jake

go. Sully sagged and the frenzied fire in his eyes went out. Jake splashed to the surface, coughing and gasping for air. He rushed by Sully up to the grass and bolted.

"Coward," Sully spit at Jake's back.

He swung toward me. His big chest heaved, water dripped from his hair and down his face like rushing rivers. Blood ran from a cut on his chin. He didn't seem affected by the cold and wet, but I shivered, goose bumps on my goose bumps. Or maybe I trembled, not from the cold but from the way he looked at me. Like I was a lab experiment, or a strange animal in the zoo.

"Sully, what's wrong?"

His eyebrows drew down like thunderclouds. "Everything's wrong," he said, as frigid as the water soaking my clothes. "Beryl, *who* in the hell are you?"

I cringed at the sharp edge in his voice, the stony set of his jaw. The hurt and betrayal in his eyes. "What do you mean?"

"Don't be coy. You've been lying to me from the beginning. No ordinary girl can fight like that. Especially against a man."

"S-s-sexist much?"

"Quit it, Beryl." He scraped his hand through his wet hair. "I once saw some fellas in Chinatown fight like you did. It was hard and fierce. Guys were laying money down on the winner. How does a librarian know how to do that? Who are you? Who's that bastard? And what in hell was that...metal thing he had?"

The Cack. He'd seen it fire. "It's a flashlight," I lied. Unconvincingly.

Sully growled. Literally growled. "Jesus Carnegie

Christ. *More* booshwa. You must think I'm the world's biggest dope." He swiped water off his face and spiked me with an angry gaze. "No more lies, Beryl. I want the truth."

I sputtered. How ridiculous could we be? Standing here, arguing. We were still in the water. My skirt floated around my thighs like a lily pad. "All right I admit it. I'm a spy. I'm a badass spy and I'm chasing down Pretty Boy Floyd because he didn't pay his taxes. That's the truth. Happy now?"

"Ah, shit. Look at me, a sap, falling for a pretend librarian who can't stop lying."

That stung. Bad. As in, knife meet gut bad. Because it came from him. The first man, the first person, I'd let get close to me in like, forever.

"And what are you?" I snapped. "I thought you were just a hapless Joe, targeted by a lunatic. But what you are is a killing machine. Uncle Sam's going to get his money's worth out of you. You're a brute and a bully and I don't know why I ever l-let you k-kiss me."

I slapped my hand over my mouth but too late. Damage done. Sully winced. Shrunk into himself as if I'd punched *and* slapped him. Then kneed him in the jewels for good measure. Anger and the cold flushed his face, but the expression in his eyes completely wrecked me. Hurt and burning with shame, like earlier, outside the library. A shame so deep and agonizing it tormented him.

As if he deserved every accusing word.

Way to go, Beryl. And, true to form, I couldn't set it right with an apology. Oh no, I've never faced up to my mistakes, never thought of anyone's feelings, least of all my own. I'd say anything, do anything not to have any feelings at all.

"Look, I'm freezing to death." I sloshed toward to the bank and up onto the grass. My soggy Mary Janes oozed muck. They were *kaput*. So was all hope of anything that kiss had promised with Sully. "I'm going back to Ma's. I need to change."

I punctuated this with an involuntary shiver that shook my whole body.

He followed me to the remains of our picnic and showered me with spring water as he shook himself like a dog. "Yeah, you go back." He snatched up his coat and stabbed his arms into the sleeves. Tried to, anyway. His shirt was too wet. "I'm sure you know the way."

"Wait. Where are *you* going?"

He eyed me in a decidedly unfriendly way. "I'm going to get drunk, Beryl. *If* that is your real name." He gave up on the jacket and flipped it over his shoulder with a grunt. "I'm going to get good and drunk. And try to forget that I ever met you."

12

I went back to Ma's.

What else could I do? Chase after Sully? Hang on him and beg his forgiveness? Totally not my style. Besides, I was too cold. Besides, addendum, Sully would probably brush me off like an annoying fly. Because that's all I was to him. An annoying, lying, deceitful bug who'd been nothing but trouble since he'd met me.

"Big redheaded dope," I muttered as I snatched up that stupid, useless Cack and shoved it into my handbag.

I gathered up the remains of our picnic trash then struggled up the hill to the sidewalk. My shoes squished and my wet coat felt like it weighed a thousand pounds. I told myself to be glad Sully had ditched me. For all his charm and gruffness and lips that could melt a girl inside and out, he was what Grandma Blue would call bad news. I mean, he'd nearly killed Jake. Would have, if I hadn't stopped him.

I moved quickly. Questions and doubts pounded my

mind. Who was Tom Sullivan? What did I know about him beyond what Glo had told me? Was any of it true? I already suspected Glo had lied to me about some things. Maybe everything she'd told me had been a lie. For all I knew, she was a time traveling criminal mastermind and Sully was her muscle, chasing after Jake, a hit man on a rival mob's payroll. Hit man out to get another hit man, with Glo pulling my strings, trying to trick me into eliminating the competition for her and...

Okay, Beryl, you've dipped into potboiler territory. Put the brakes on.

Ma's place wasn't far, maybe half a mile, but still, I'd turned into a walking popsicle by the time I climbed the porch steps. I left puddles all the way to my little room. I tossed my handbag on the bed, gathered up dry clothes and dragged off to the bathroom for a hot bath, a long mope, and maybe even a good cry.

Minutes later, I climbed into a porcelain tub with claw feet and sunk into steaming hot water. My day with Sully ran over and over in my head. The comfort between us, the way he'd helped me open up, and that sweet kiss. The fight with Jake, and then *the* fight. Why had I let myself say those mean things? How had I left myself so open? Sully was the first person I'd ever really spoken to about the accident, and he hated me.

I scrubbed slime and gunk off my skin with a cloth I'd found in the bathroom cupboard. Why should I care what Sully thought about me, anyway? Why did I let him bother me so much?

I hadn't felt this emotional and unguarded, or this vulnerable in a long time, not since Grandma Blue had left me. I'd shut off all emotion, put up the walls, and locked everyone out. Hadn't let anyone in since. I'd run away if I felt a smidgen of affection for a foster mother. I'd dumped any guy, hard and fast, if I thought there was the least chance I could get into him. I didn't want to feel, wouldn't let myself feel *anything* after losing so much.

Then along came Sully.

"Who cares," I muttered and dunked under the water. I needed to wash the man out of my hair. Not to mention the leaves and twigs and whatever else had been snagged in my tangles during my impromptu swim.

Feeling slightly better, I got out and pulled the stopper chain. The bathwater gurgled like an empty stomach as it swirled into the drain. I quickly dried and dressed, then fluffed my damp curls and listlessly brushed my teeth, staring at the red blotch on my left cheek where Jake had hit me during our fight.

I so wished Glo would pop in here and take me home. I wanted to go home. Couldn't *wait* to go home. Back to the future, where I could brush with real toothpaste, not this powdery stuff that tasted like baking soda laced with iodine. Home to a proper shower and shampoo with twenty-one essential ingredients for clarifying and conditioning tricky hair like mine, not just soap in a bottle. Home to my mostly sweet but occasionally evil cat, Jenjen.

Home, away from this temporal nightmare and far, far away from that big redhead who had no right to wiggle under my skin and into my heart the way he had.

A sudden gale whipped up in the bathroom. The lacy curtains over the window twisted and danced. A flare of bright blue light bounced off the mirror, nearly blinding me. I spun around, my heart thudding. Could that be Glo? Had she somehow read my whining thoughts and had come to take me home?

The undulating form took shape. I gasped, swallowing a mouthful of that awful toothpowder in the process.

Not Glo—it was Jake.

HE LOOKED as if he'd stopped at a salon for a makeover before popping in here. His uniform was dry, clean, and pressed. His hair washed and combed. His face, shaved. Except for the Kicker he held in his left hand and the Cack holstered on his hip, he looked like Hollywood's version of GI Joe. Handsome, hot, heroic. Minus the heroic part.

I couldn't speak, could barely move. Jake stood between me and the door, and I had no weapon. I'd left my handbag on the bed where I'd tossed it when I came in, the Cack tucked securely inside. Beryl Blue, anti-Boy Scout, never prepared.

Jake stepped closer. I brandished my toothbrush like a knife but relaxed—a smidge—when he perched on the edge of the tub.

"Nice shiner," I said, indicating his bruised left eye. "You get that from fighting me or Sully?"

He touched his face and winced. "You. You've got a nasty right hook."

"Thank you. What do you want?" I tried to sound chill when I so was not.

"Thought we should have a chat. You saved my life today."

I tucked the toothbrush into my toiletries bag with shaking hands. "I saved you, so what?"

"Glo's gonna be furious. You stopped Sullivan from killing me. You blew your mission."

"Well, your pathetic begging had something to do with it. Besides, he wasn't *really* going to kill you," I said, trying to assure him. Or myself? I'd seen that dangerous look in Big Red's eyes. "You kind of deserved it, popping in on us in the park like that. That was ballsy *and* risky."

"Risky? You think?" he said with a boatload of sarcasm. A ghost of a smile curved his lips. "Was Sullivan angry I hit you, or that I interrupted your, what's it called? Make out session?"

I flushed. Didn't want to, didn't want future boy to know how much that kiss had meant to me, and what he'd ruined by busting in on us.

I took a calming breath. "Never mind about that. You focus on yourself."

"*You'd* better focus on *me*, Beryl. I haven't given up. You had your chance to stop me today, and you let it slip away. Not that I'm not grateful." He bobbed his head in a little bow, like a pretentious dork. "But it was foolish and rash, and awful stupid. Thinking with your heart, not your head. Not a smart strategy in the time-perp retrieval game. You'd better learn that now."

"Why should I?" I jammed my hairbrush into my bag

and gathered up my things. "I'm no time cop. As soon as I finish this stupid assignment I'm going home."

He frowned and I actually thought I saw something like pity flash in his eyes. "Why Glo chose someone as useless as you for this mission is baffling."

Useless. I'd heard that adjective before. It ranked right up there with unwanted and unwelcome in my dictionary of pain. Along with orphan. "Watch it, pretty boy. You want another beat down like I gave you in the park?" I spoke as coolly as I could manage under the circumstances. The circumstances being that he'd pissed me off.

He smirked.

"Wait." I glared at him. "You threw that fight? Why?"

He laughed. God, it was a mean sound. "I liked it when you thought you were winning."

For real? This guy was the king of goading. And it worked. "You're a jerk."

He replied with another infuriating smirk.

"You know, it just occurred to me that you used that time travel device..." I gestured to the Kicker in his hand. "To pop in here. Glo told me she can track your DNA through that thing. She probably already GPSed you and is coming for your ass right now." I tried on a smirk of my own. "You better fly out of here before she catches you."

His gaze flicked to the window, as if he thought Glo might bust through feet first, SWAT-style, and slap on the cuffs. "Sounds like Glo's been sharing Time Scope's classified intel with you. I bet she's not telling you everything."

As if I didn't know that. I trusted Glo a splash more than I trusted him. Which meant, not at all. I declined to let him in on that little secret. I should've told him to tornado the hell out of here and leave me alone, except, got to admit, he'd caught me on his hook quite nicely.

I lifted my chin. "She's not telling me everything? What's that supposed to mean?"

"You think Time Scope will let you go home? With all you know about the future?"

I couldn't hide my surprise, or my alarm.

"Are you really that naïve?" He snorted. "Time Scope's a corporation, dedicated to making money, that's all. They'll do anything, *anything* to keep that status quo."

"And you want to change that status?" Color me confused. "Is that why you're after Sully? Does he have something to do with Time Scope?"

I didn't see how he could, what with time travel not being invented until a long time from now. Unless Sully figures out... Nah. No offense to that redheaded ox, but he didn't strike me as Professor Inventor.

"That's for you to figure out," Jake said dismissively. "The rest is obvious or would be if you weren't so dim. The *only* way they'll send you home is if you do what you were sent here to do. Kill me, then maybe, *maybe* they'll be grateful enough to drop you back into your useless, dull little life."

I ignored his barbs and focused on the harsh reality of what he'd said. Glo's words screamed in my mind. Do the job, or I wouldn't live to see tomorrow. I'd been so focused on Sully I hadn't thought about that threat. Did that mean Time Scope would take me out if I failed? My alert level dialed up to eleven. So did my fear. This trip through time had turned into a horrifying nightmare I couldn't claw out of no matter how desperately I tried.

Jake's long, lean body unfolded as he rose from the edge of the tub. Almost as tall as Sully, he seemed infinitely more intimidating.

I cringed against the sink. "Why should I believe it's just Sully you're after?" I asked, my voice no more than a scared whisper. "You already tried to run me down. What's to stop you from killing me, too?"

He instantly backed off. Then, kind of...closed up. Smirk-less, quiet, still. Except for those snapping blue eyes that held my own.

"Beryl." His voice deepened and he spoke slowly, as if he considered me both thick *and* dense. "I'm not going to kill you. That's one thing you can trust me on. I would *never* hurt you."

I blinked. What the hell? What happened to the cocky jerk who'd been...? *Oh.* Holy crap. Ho-lee crap. "You are *not* serious. You...you *like* me?"

I wouldn't have believed it if I hadn't seen it with my own eyes. His sculpted cheeks blushed a startling shade of scarlet.

This one-on-one convo had taken a turn for the weird. Beyond weird. Time to go. I darted to the door, started to yank it open. He flew up next to me in a flash and slapped his palm to the door, smacking it shut. Trapping me inside. We were almost nose-to-nose. He smelled of soap and time travel.

"Get out of my way." I prepped for a knuckle pop to the throat. He had a prominent Adam's apple. It would hurt wicked bad. "I should've let Sully drown you."

He eyed me, tons of emotions I couldn't identify galloping across his face. "But you didn't. You stopped him." Every syllable snapped out angrily, as if my failure to let him be murdered amounted to a cardinal sin. "You know why? Because you're a pushover. Weak, soft-hearted. You talk all tough, but you don't have what it takes to keep Sullivan safe. You should go home. Just give up and go home. I can send you. Right here, right now."

He thrust the Kicker in my face. I eyed the device with longing. The screen flashed with words and numbers, and I could just make out a two-word command: *Enter Date*. As simple as that. Enter the date, press send, this thin piece of amazing tech would power up, and my pixels would tornado home.

I looked at Jake. He could be bullshitting me. Or trying to eliminate me altogether. How did I know he wouldn't send me to the plague-ridden Middle Ages? Or further back to Jurassic Park? A raptor's brunch wasn't exactly how I pictured my demise.

"If you send me home, Glo's going to be furious." Not that Glo's feelings concerned me at this point.

"She'll never know. You leave, I find Sullivan and finish the job before the night is out. History is changed, everything changes, and Glo's none the wiser."

Jake's finger hovered over the Kicker's screen. I tensed, plotting how I could snatch the damned thing from his hot little hands.

"I won't make this offer again, Beryl. Say the word, and you're on your way home."

A word jumped to the tip of my tongue, but not the H-word, home. The S-word. *Sully*. The only thing anchoring me here. If I went home, if he died, the future would be toast. Scary, but abstract, like thinking there's a zombie in a dark room. You don't know until you turn on the light whether or not you should pee your pants. Sgt. Sexy was anything but abstract. I'd seen him, touched him. Kissed him. If I went home, that beautiful, grouchy man would die.

And that mattered. A lot.

I squared my shoulders. "Thank you for the offer, but —" It hit me like Dorothy's house landing on the Wicked Witch, hard and fast. "Wait. How do you know my name?"

He stiffened. "What?"

A soft tap-tap sounded on the door, like a timid woodpecker.

I lowered my voice. "When Sully was trying to drown you, you called me Beryl. And just now you said it. I never told you my name."

A slight pause before that smirk made an encore, though not as cocky as before. "Guess I heard Sullivan say it. During the fight."

"Really?" I said, heavy on the skepticism.

Another knock on the door, more urgent, followed by, "Beryl?"

Peggy? Again? That girl had a bladder the size of a peanut.

"Just a sec," I sing-songed at the door, then, to Jake, "I don't remember Sully using my name. You're lying." At least I thought he lied. I couldn't remember anything clearly beyond Sully and Jake and their soggy fight.

Peggy's knocking picked up the pace, becoming a steady beat. You could almost dance to it.

"You may know my name, Jake, but you don't know me. I'm not going home, and I'm *not* going to back down. You don't scare me. Time Scope doesn't scare me. I'm going to save Sully. You got the drop on me once, but not again. Next time I see you, I'll be armed. I'll wipe that smirk off your face."

I tried again to open the door, but he pressed against it with all his weight.

"Why?" he asked. Uber-serious now, his eyes glittering.

I swallowed my fear and anger, and the dregs of that tooth powder, too. I looked him right in the eye.

"Because it's the right thing to do. And I'm tired of running away. Now, get out."

13

Peggy must've had to release Niagara Falls, but she didn't rush in when I finally opened the door. Instead, she peeped into the bathroom as if she expected to see a monster in the tub. She looked behind the door, then back at me, her kewpie doll face scrunched up.

"I thought I heard a man's voice in here," she said, scandalized.

Not anymore. *Let's see who gets to Sullivan first*, Jake had taunted. Then he'd typed in a code on the Kicker and tornadoed away.

"No one in there but me and my shadow," I said, tossing Peggy a wan smile and hoofing it back to my room.

I hung up my wet clothes then, gazing into the mirror, I pinned back my hair with bow-shaped clips I'd found in my suitcase. Glo had selected another winner for my outfit, a sleeveless jersey dress the color of violets, matched with an embroidered three-quarter sleeve jacket that hugged my waist. A smart ensemble, Grandma Blue would've called it. I might've called it that too if I wasn't so preoccupied.

My fears and worries had increased a million percent. If Jake had found me, he could easily find Sully. And seriously, *how* had Jake found me? Glo had sworn up and down my DNA couldn't be tracked by their future tech, so how had Jake not only known to find me at Ma's but had tracked my location inside the building so precisely? How had he gotten so clean and dry minutes after his underwater brawl with Sully?

I tossed those questions onto the steaming stack of questions and mysteries piling up on my temporal jaunt and shrugged into my coat, still damp and smelling of wet wool. I scooped up my handbag from the bed. The Cack inside weighed it down. I vowed not to let the weapon leave my sight for the duration of my time here. Next time I saw Jake, I'd be ready.

Then I went to find Sully.

Dusk had fallen and the streets were already clogged with khaki. Wolf whistles and the occasional rude remark flew at me, a woman alone. I shook it off. Sully said I could take care of myself, and I could. The only thing I couldn't protect myself from was him. He'd crawled under my skin so deep I'd eagerly taken the plunge from half-assed protector to all-in defender of his big self. From reactive to proactive, as my therapist would say.

I went straight to the Hi-Hat Club. GIs swarmed every inch of the place, but I didn't see the soldier I wanted. I caught Mabel's elbow as she wended through the crowd.

Not a smart move. She nearly dropped her tray, weighed down with bottles and glasses.

I ignored her glare and got to the point. "I'm looking for Marco and the fellas," I said. Shouted, actually. A crowd ten times larger and rowdier than last night filled the club. I wondered if some of these guys had been here since yesterday, catching cat naps between drinks.

Mabel's gaze swept over me. "Look, sister, if Marco shook you off, maybe he don't want to be found."

Meow. "Look, sister, I'm not playing that game. I'm looking for the big guy, Sergeant Sullivan. I *really* need to talk to him."

"You mean Red?" Her gaze passed over me, lasering in on my belly. "I don't figure him as the type to get a girl in trouble and ditch her." She put some glasses down on a table, ignored a few leering compliments, then turned back to me. "It's suppertime. You should be dogging the joints that offer the goods."

"The goods?"

"Cow grub. Black market steaks. I was you, I'd start at Louie's over on Dublin."

I called up a mental map of the city, couldn't locate Dublin Street.

She grunted in exasperation. "Two blocks to the right of city hall."

"Oh." John F. Kennedy Boulevard. "Thanks," I threw over my shoulder and headed back outside into the sea of uniformed testosterone.

I passed the library and the theater where we'd seen Stretch in the afternoon. My heart ached remembering the way Sully and I had bantered, the comforting feel of his solid arm under my hand as I held onto him, the giddy sense of adventure. The park, and the kiss. Now, I felt empty without him. And scared. I had to find him. Jake wasn't messing around.

No sign of him at Louie's. Or at The Lantern, the El Morocco, and several other eateries. I grew more frantic by the moment. I pushed through the crowds. My feet ached. My ears rang from all the wolf whistles. I was leered at and had my butt pinched. I had to hip check a wild-eyed drunk before he could cop a serious feel.

And still no Sully.

Damn it, Big Red, where are you?

I approached a long brick building housing Jonesy's Bar & Grille, the next stop on my tour of the nightclubs and hotspots of Ballard Springs. I groaned at the long line waiting to get in, soldiers and a gaggle of dolled up ladies who could very well be of the night variety. I didn't want to wait, so I marched up to the bouncer. Or, rather, the doorman I figured by his uniform of white gloves, a smart cap, and a knee-length coat with fringed epaulets, like something out of a movie.

"I'm meeting someone here," I said, as brassy as the buttons on his blue coat. "Can I scoot in and see if he's inside?"

"I don't know, can ya?" he smirked.

I rolled my eyes. Lord save me from the grammar Nazis, in any time period. I pulled a twenty out of my bag, pasted it to his palm, and locked onto his bloodshot brown eyes. "I think I can."

His face went all giddy. Maybe a twenty was like a

hundred or even a thousand in my time, with inflation and all. He fell back and the door swung inward.

A grumble from the people in line followed me as I stepped into a curved foyer with polished marble floors, dotted with tall ferns in huge pots. Very art deco, far classier than most of the other places I'd been to tonight. To the right I saw a hallway to the restrooms and what I guessed was the back exit. To the left, an archway that opened into a packed dining room—easy to tell from the clink of plates, the music, and the buzz of conversation and laughter.

I scanned the crowd for a distinctive pair of broad shoulders and that lighthouse beacon of red hair, as I'd done at a dozen other places. This time... I let out my breath. My neck muscles un-kinked, and so did the rest of me. Final-fricking-ly. Sully, safe and sound, gathered with his men around a button-sized table near the center of the room. He was in shirt sleeves, his jacket draped over the back of his chair.

"Check your coat, hon?"

I swiveled to see a curvy brunette standing inside a tiny room stuffed with coats and even a few furs. She cracked her gum and eyed me with curiosity.

"Good idea." I shrugged out of my coat as I crossed the foyer. It was warm outside, but nowhere near as hot as in here. As steamy as a lobster in a pot, as Grandma Blue might say.

The brunette reached out and took my coat. "You here all by your lonesome? No date?" She sounded appalled.

"Oh, he's inside. I'm meeting him." I hoisted my handbag onto the counter to put away the ticket she handed me and the Cack inside *thunked* on the countertop.

Her super-plucked eyebrows shot up. "You hoarding scrap iron in there?"

I laughed—not too far off the mark—and headed for the dining room.

A cloud of body odor, clashing perfumes, the aroma of grilled beef, and the ever-present cigarette smoke nearly smothered me as I stepped down two shallow steps into the big room. I wound through the tables, eyes on Sully. Couples crowded a small dance floor, swaying to a tune by an all-girl orchestra. And yes, they were barely dressed, just as Marco had claimed. Well, barely dressed for 1943. I'd seen Catholic school uniforms more risqué than the short skirt the sax player was rocking.

I stopped a few paces from Sully. Affection swelled, though I should've been screaming mad at him. For abandoning me, for putting himself in danger, and for making me wear out precious shoe leather looking for him. Making me frantic that Jake would catch up to him before I could.

But I couldn't. Couldn't summon an enzyme of anger. Looking at that beat-up mug, his rumpled tie and equally rumpled hair, and even when he lit a cigarette, I couldn't be mad at him for a nanosecond.

"Sully?" I said softly.

He glanced over. Our gazes snagged. We looked at each other a long time, his expression, as usual, impossible to read. I didn't know what I expected. Anger? Dismissal? A flippant, "Hey, fellas, look, it's Mata Hari." I chewed my lip, prepared for anything.

He dropped his cigarette into the ashtray. Kicked back his chair and stood. He closed the distance between us in two quick strides. Oh, I was prepared for anything, anything except what happened next.

He drew me into his arms.

HE HELD ME, different from how he'd held me when we'd danced last night. *Way* different from when Jake tried to run us down and Sully had jumped us out of the way. He wrapped me in his embrace, cocooned me, enveloped me, as if he'd thought he'd never see me again.

My head spun at the feel of his arms around me, his body against mine. He bent and pressed his stubble-rough cheek to mine. I inhaled his scent. An intoxicating mix of whiskey and soap and maleness.

"Beryl." His warm breath tickled my ear. The way he said my name tickled too. A capitulation, a confession, so much meaning in that one word.

I pulled back and gazed into his beautiful eyes. The smoke, the music, the noise, the voices all faded. My fears, my worries about Jake, Glo, and everything else faded too. Cliché alert—it felt as if we were the only two people in the room. In the world.

"I'm sorry, sweetheart," he rumbled. "For today, for what I did in the park. Cripes, when that fella hit you, I couldn't even..." He pressed his forehead to mine and sighed. My knees went weak. "I'm a grade-A heel. Can you ever forgive me?"

"I'm the one who should be sorry," I murmured. "Can you forgive *me*?"

"There's nothing to forgive." His eyes smiled into mine. "But you do have a lot to explain."

That brought me back to planet Earth. So did the waiter who approached the table. He carried dinner plates lined up his arm like dots of paint on a palette. Semi-charred slabs of T-bone filled each plate. Sully released me abruptly. I grinned. Apparently, a big, juicy piece of steak was the only sight more welcome than me in this world of rationing and shortages.

"We'll talk later," he said. "Will you join us for dinner?"

Before I could answer, he grabbed a chair from the next table—much to the occupants' surprise—and scooted it between his own and Marco's.

He patted the chair's seat. "Drop that pretty rump here, sister."

Now, how could I turn down an invitation like that?

I settled next to him. "I see you've made good on your promise to get drunk." The dinner plates the waiter put on the table were outnumbered by the many empty—or on their way to being empty—shot glasses and beer bottles.

Sully's eyebrow shot up. What number was that? "Don't nag, sweetheart. I'm not as pie-eyed as they are." He gestured to his companions. "Not by a damn sight."

Pie-eyed? Near drooling, I'd say. Marco slurred a hello to me. Stan could barely lift his hand in a limp hello. Griff giggled like a schoolgirl. It was only seven thirty, for heaven's sake.

"I've been too busy looking for you to get drunk," Sully said. "Been beating the bushes, trying to find you."

My turn to raise an eyebrow. That was breaking news.

"I know I stomped off like a fool." He pulled his plate toward him and picked up his knife and fork. "Took a long while to come to my senses. All I could think was, what if that bastard goes back to her? To finish what he started? I went back, *ran* back to get you. You were gone. I searched the park then went to Ma's. No dice there either. Ma said you left. I put on dry clothes then started hunting everywhere. The library, restaurants, every gin joint in town. Got more frantic at every stop. Every place you weren't." He pointed at Marco with his knife. "That's when I met up with the fellas here."

"I see." I watched with gushy fondness as Sully sliced into his steak and shoveled a piece into his mouth. He chewed with an audible sigh. "You came here, where you thought you might find me hiding under a T-bone?"

He looked a bit sheepish. "Lay off. A man's gotta eat." He stabbed a piece of beef with his fork and brought it to my lips. "A woman, too, I'm thinking."

Now, I'm not normally into steak. Way too expensive on a wannabe librarian's pitiful salary, for one reason. But it had been an awful long time since those egg salad sandwiches. I was hungry. I grabbed that sucker like a dog snarfs kibble.

"The whole time I was running around, I couldn't stop thinking." Sully fed me another piece. "About you. About *him*. About what happened." He gazed pointedly at my face, no doubt at the purpling bruise I couldn't quite cover with makeup. "That damned... That...coward *hit* you." He popped another chunk of beef into his mouth and chewed as if tearing into Jake's neck.

"He didn't hurt me, Sully." And now I knew why. He hadn't been trying. Unlike me. I'd been trying my head off to hurt Jake, a fact Sully seemed to have conveniently forgotten.

"Doesn't matter. No real man hits a girl."

I had news for him. Some men do it because they think that *makes* them real men. "I'm all right, Sully," I said gently. "No harm done. Takes a lot to break me. Beryl Blue, made of steel."

He gazed at me, his expression dark, almost primal. My heartbeat kicked up. Made of steel, except one important part of me, I was discovering.

He broke away, snatched his cigarette from the ashtray and took a hard drag. "Yeah, well, he *could've* hurt you," he muttered.

"How about a memento of your night out, fellas?" A young woman in a slinky black evening gown sashayed up to our table. She held up a camera, which must've been a workout because the thing had to weigh nearly thirty pounds. "May I take your picture?"

"Only if I can take yours, beautiful," Marco said, leering comically.

The camera girl giggled and batted her long eyelashes at him as if that were the first time she'd heard that line tonight. Smiles, a few more leers, some price-haggling, and she got everyone to agree to buy a copy. As soon as the cash changed hands, she got down to business.

"All right, everyone scooch in."

Chairs scraped as the men moved to one side of the small table. I slid my chair closer to Sully. The camera girl lifted the contraption and looked down into what I presumed was the viewfinder. Weirdest. Camera. *Ever.*

"Miss, you gotta scootch in," she said. "I can't get you in the picture at all if you don't scootch in."

I scootched furiously, then found myself airborne as Sully lifted me from my chair onto his lap. He grinned, his cigarette dangling rakishly from his lips. He maneuvered my arm around his shoulders then slipped his own arm around my waist, pulling me close. His right hand found its way to my knee.

My lips twitched. He was drunker than I thought. Why else would Sgt. What-About-Your-Reputation indulge in such copious PDA? Not that I minded. His touch, his nearness, and his wonderful Sully-ness sent my blood thundering through my veins.

The camera girl winked. "Now, that's nice and cozy. Everyone smile."

I smiled then blinked, blinded by the flare of the gazillion-watt flashbulb. The photographer handed each of us a ticket and wound a small dial on her camera.

"Your copies will be ready at the coat check in an hour," she said.

"Can I give you a hand in the darkroom, doll?" Marco's bushy eyebrows waggled up and down like two caterpillars having a seizure. "We can see what develops."

"Fine by me, Joe," she said. "But I gotta warn you, we'll probably bump into my husband in there. He prints the pictures. When he's not beating up mashers like you."

She waved and toddled off. Marco groaned and the

others guffawed. They moved their chairs back into place and conversation and consumption of food and beverages resumed, but Sully didn't let me leave his lap. A cozy and comfortable position to be in, much to my surprise.

"Beryl..." he said, gazing at me, sounding uncertain and a tad shy. He crushed out his cigarette in an ashtray then tightened his arm around my waist. "I thought I'd lost you, after what happened today. When I said those things. Can you ever forgive me?"

I flushed with guilt. "We both said things we didn't mean."

"No, you were right. I'm a monster, a cold-hearted killer—"

"I was angry. I didn't mean it. You know it's not true."

"It *is* true. I'm just like my pop." He seemed sober as a judge now, all wisps of tipsiness gone, replaced with a seriousness that made me tremble. "Pop served in the Great War. Saw things no man should ever have to see. It changed him, turned him mean. An angry drunk reliving the battle of the Argonne is not a pretty sight." A heavy pause. "He beat my mother. He beat us, too, but he hurt her worse. I couldn't take it. I snapped. Used my fists to solve the problem. To solve all my problems. Today, at the park..."

He faltered and I stroked my fingers along his strong jaw. "It's okay," I murmured. "You don't have to talk about it."

"Yes, I do." An angry fire darkened his features. "When I saw that guy hit you...saw him *hurt* you, I went berserk. Couldn't stop myself. I couldn't think about anything, except my rage and my need to stop him from hurting you again. Even if that meant killing him."

Everything clicked into place. Sully's fury, and his brutal attack when Jake hit me with the Cack. He'd been protecting me the only way he knew how. The way he'd learned to defend his mother.

"Oh, Sully."

"You see?" A grim smile tugged at his lips. "I am my father's son."

My heart broke for him. "You're nothing like your father. You're protective. You care for people and want to keep them safe. That's what makes you a good soldier. That's what makes you a good man."

He let out a relieved breath and squeezed my waist in a hug. "And you're a good woman, Beryl." He reached up to tuck a lock of hair behind my ear. "Now that I've found you, I'm not letting you out of my sight again."

"Well, I found you, but let's not quibble about it."

He chuckled then nuzzled my neck, making my breath both stop and quicken, if that was even possible. "You know something, Beryl Blue?" he said softly. "You're a real piece of work."

The band rolled out a slow tune and a woman with tightly coiled dark hair began to sing. She had pipes that could shame a finalist on *The Voice*. The song, "I'll Be Seeing You," I'd always thought maudlin and sappy.

But tonight? With Sully holding me so close, as I stared into his wounded eyes, seeing the frightened, angry boy behind his tough guy façade, I felt the aching, yearning melancholy of the song's every note. I knew what the couples clinging to one another on the dance floor longed for and desperately hoped for. The chance to see one another again. In that old café or at the wishing well or anywhere at all.

And what about us? Would I ever see him again? If I could complete my mission and stop Jake, what then? Hopefully Time Scope would send me home, Sully would go on with his life and that would be that. Just as Glo intended, right? I mean, there wasn't any reason for us to see each other again. Not like I'd gotten stuck on the guy and felt myself falling in—

"Aw, ain't you two sweet?" Marco said. He, Griff, and Stan eyed us with indulgent smiles, as if they were a trio of matchmakers pleased with their rousing success.

That popped the bubble. I cringed, and Sully, that stone solid hunk of granite, blushed. *Blushed.* Why? Had he figured out the disturbing direction of my thoughts? His story about his father had touched me deeply. Had he seen that on my face? Seen the way my heart had opened to him? Could the others tell? Did everyone in the place know about that powerful emotion knocking on my heart?

That four-letter word, sometimes a noun, more often a verb. A word that scared me more than anything. A word I wouldn't even allow myself to think, let alone say out loud.

I bounced off Sully's lap, grasping for my chair like a blind woman, trying desperately to calm the storm inside me. It couldn't be possible. I'd just met him yesterday. It didn't happen that fast, except in books and movies or in Vegas. There had to be a logical explanation for the dizziness and racing pulse and general gushiness that gripped me when I got within ten feet of Sgt. Sexy. A crush. Some kind of time travel induced emotional vertigo. Or a serious case of carnal flu. Maybe a combo of all three.

I mean, yeah, we'd kissed, if you could call it that. It had been almost chaste, barely any tongue. So what if I couldn't stop thinking about how his lips felt on mine? So what if I couldn't stop thinking about Sully himself and the way his very presence set me on fire? It meant nothing. It certainly didn't mean I was falling in...that irrational condition...with him.

Nope, not possible, because let's face it. I simply didn't know how.

14

I ordered a drink and something to eat, trying to put up an emotional wall between me and Sully. Though I'd been ravenous when I walked in here, my appetite had vanished, but I figured I better get some more protein and a dose of carbs into me so I wouldn't pass out. Especially if Jake put in an appearance.

"Why if it isn't Beryl Blue," a voice trilled, as I pushed my empty plate away and dabbed a napkin to my lips. I looked up to see Peggy, dolled up in a floofy orange evening gown, with her Johnny by her side. "It's me, Peggy Smith, from the boarding house."

I wanted to say I didn't recognize her since she wasn't banging on the bathroom door, but she gave me such a delighted-to-see-you grin I told my snark monster to give it a rest.

"Hi Peggy," I said. "And, Johnny, is it? Looks like you two decided to come up for air."

A sound like a lamb's bleat came out of Peggy's mouth. "You say the most amusing things. Johnny, say hello to Beryl and her beau. Johnny thinks it's too crowded in here, and hot as blazes to boot, but I'm having the most marvelous time. It's simply too wonderful, with the most delectable food and do you know I've had two of the most delicious drink, a gin fizz, the waiter calls it. I feel positively woozy, and golly doesn't that girl singer have the most wonderful voice? My Johnny doesn't like girl singers, or girl orchestras for that matter, but I do, and I want to stay all night and listen to them no matter what my Johnny thinks."

She finished this lava stream of verbiage with a loud and probably much-needed intake of breath. Johnny didn't say a word. To be fair, nobody could say a word, but he looked the most miserable about it. He stood there like a lump with a pained look in his dark eyes. What happened to the lovebirds feeding one another at the table last night? Trouble in paradise?

"Do you mind if we join you?" Peggy snatched another chair from our unfortunate neighbors and crowded into our table. Johnny did the same.

Drinks were ordered—another gin fizz for Peggy—followed by chit chat about where Peggy and her Johnny were from. Hilarity ensued as beyond-wasted Stan tried to pronounce Poughkeepsie and Sully lit into them about New York's baseball teams. He had a real thing for baseball, apparently, and I thanked the ghost of Ted Williams Sully hadn't decided to grill me about the Dodgers. I mean, they were from Brooklyn, not Los Angeles? Who knew?

After a bit, Peggy tapped me on the shoulder. "I need to visit the powder room," she whispered.

I was all, *have a nice trip* before I realized she wanted me to go with. My eyebrows shot up. Apparently that thing about women going to the bathroom in groups had historical precedent. I couldn't shut her down. She looked as if she had something important on her mind.

"Sully, Peggy and I are taking a walk," I said as I pushed my chair back and stood. "Please watch out for yourself while I'm gone."

He bolted to his feet and looked me square in the eye, the first time we'd connected since I'd vaulted off his lap. His gaze turned fierce, his posture doubly so and my inner furnace went from hot to boiling to sizzling. Whatever magic he possessed that could do that to me with just a look, the fella ought to bottle it.

"I'm going where you're going," he growled.

I didn't argue, and he led the way. He pushed through the crowd like a snowplow, spearing every GI we passed with a suspicious look. He stopped outside the bathroom door and I breathed a sigh of relief. I did not want to explain to Peggy why he'd followed us in or why he scoured each stall as if he thought he'd find the enemy hiding in the toilet bowl.

I put my hand on his arm. "I can take it from here. You watch your back."

"My goodness, your sergeant is protective," Peggy said after the door closed on Sully's scowling face. "Of course, I don't blame him, not one bit. Those soldiers can get so terribly rowdy on leave and sometimes they behave in a way that's less than proper. My Johnny says he doesn't want me to set foot on the street without an escort and..."

She nattered away as we passed through a fancy

sitting room with armchairs and ashtrays that looked like umbrella stands and into the bathroom proper. She ducked into one of the narrow stalls, still talking, her voice muffled through the marble dividing wall.

I tuned her out, preferring to focus on the old-fashioned toilet and the chain suspended from a tank above that I had to pull to flush. I couldn't resist flushing it again, and once more for good measure. A flagrant waste of water, but I found it quite fascinating.

Afterward, I stood in front of an ornately scrolled gold mirror that ran the length of the wall and washed my hands in a marble sink. Peggy and another woman were beside me, powdering their noses. Literally. And I'd always thought that phrase a euphemism. I was learning a lot tonight.

"So, I guess your Johnny's the strong silent type, huh?" I said to Peggy's reflection. I angled my handbag so the Cack would be out of view and extracted my lipstick. Her Johnny hadn't said a word since they'd joined us. Not that Peggy made it easy, but she had to breathe at some point. He could've piped up during the lull.

Her big blue eyes flicked to the other woman, who snapped her compact shut, smoothed her skirt, and gave us a polite nod as she left. As soon as the door whispered shut, Peggy burst into tears.

"Good grief, Peggy, what's wrong?"

"E-e-everything. Johnny and I had a terrific fight. He's *so* stubborn. I can't convince him to budge an inch. Not one inch."

She paused to sniffle then launched into a soliloquy that made my jaw drop.

"I want to get married. I thought my Johnny wanted to get married, too, until we went to City Hall yesterday morning to get the license. He acted jumpy and nervous when we signed the papers then refused to go to the Justice of the Peace to officially tie the knot. Well, you can imagine that got me steamed, and I had to *drag* the reason out of him. He told me he changed his mind. He says it wouldn't be fair to me with him marching off to who knows where, facing who knows what, and what if he gets hurt, wounded or even k-killed? He says where would I be then, a widow at eighteen and left all on my own? I tell him I don't care but he's as stubborn as an old mule and insists we wait until he comes back, if he c-comes b-back at all."

She lost it completely then, wailing and bawling. But finally, not talking.

I handed her a linen hand towel from the vanity table and jumped into the breach. "I thought you two were already married."

She dabbed her eyes and dried her cheeks. "Did I say that? I meant that we're all but married. In every sense, if you get my meaning."

"Yeah, I get you." Johnny didn't want to buy the cow if he could get the milk for free, as Grandma Blue would say, along with things like, the best way to keep the fox out of the barn is to keep the door closed. She'd started with those cryptic warnings when I was about twelve and puberty had roared in.

Peggy blew her nose and listlessly tossed the cloth in the direction of a wicker clothes hamper. "Well, I suppose I made my bed, now I have to lie in it."

She heaved the kind of sigh probably first heaved by Eve right after she took some bad advice from a snake. Full of regret and self-blame. It annoyed me. No, not annoyed. Made me angry. Why did women so often get the blame, and frequently took the blame, for the dirt men did to them?

I uncapped my lipstick. "Peggy, settle down. It's not your fault."

"But, you see, it is. Getting married was my idea. So was coming here all alone. Johnny wrote to me, telling me to stay at home with my folks, that he would see me when he got leave before shipping out and we would discuss our future then. But I wanted so badly to see him *now*. To be with him. I love Johnny with all my heart, and I want to be his forever. You know how that feels. I've seen the way you look at Sergeant Sullivan. You're in love with him."

I stilled, my lipstick an inch from my lips.

She giggled, sounding like a clogged drain through her tears. "Oh, you don't think anyone's noticed, but I have. Maybe none of those fellas you're with. They're men, after all, they wouldn't notice if your hair was on fire. Men don't notice anything, except for a good piece of pie and a nice pair of legs. But a woman can tell these things. You're over the moon for him. And truth be told, I think he's in love with you. Any man who can't be parted from his girl for more than a minute while she powders her nose is a man in love."

Impossible.

Or...maybe not? Was Sully's attention merely concern for my safety, or something more? Did he know where my busy brain had been going earlier? That pesky L-word? Did he feel the same way? I mean, he barely knew me. Would probably freak the hell out if he knew the truth about me. No, it couldn't be possible. But my heart hoped, way down deep.

"You're in the same boat as me," Peggy said. "The man you love is about to go away, maybe forever. I want to grab every moment I can with Johnny. I want a part of him to keep with me always, and that means marriage, no matter what the risk. I think you understand why I travelled here, Beryl. Why I risked my reputation and everything to be with my Johnny. Us girls would go anywhere, do just about *anything* for the fellas we love."

I stiffened. Even kill for them?

She turned back to the mirror to repair her makeup. I studied her teary-eyed reflection. She was as delicate-looking as one of those old-fashioned china dolls. But if her champion debate team ability to hold the floor was any indication, she wouldn't be ignored. Or denied. Maybe her Johnny was being sincere in his concern for her future, but she'd filibustered his objections to end up where she stood now. Facing the end with no denouement.

Peggy was far braver than me. I bet she blurted those three little words a hundred times a day, when I couldn't even think them. Glo should've picked her for this mission. If anything, she could talk Jake to death.

I blotted my lips with a piece of toilet tissue and slipped my lipstick back into my bag. I turned to her. She deserved her Johnny.

"Don't lose hope, Peggy. Something might be done.

No, something *can* be done." I spoke with more authority than I felt. "Sully will help." Really going out on a limb now. "I'll have him talk to Johnny. He can pull rank or something. You just chill and let me see what I can do."

"Oh, Beryl." She beamed, nearly blinding me with her smile. "I'd be the happiest girl in the world if your sergeant could get my Johnny to— Oh, murder!"

She gaped at her fingers, now greasy and stained red. She shot a loathing look at her lipstick tube.

"My lipstick is leaking. These darned paper tubes are such a bother." She scrubbed her fingers vigorously. "All this awful rationing and shortages. I know the army needs the metal for bullets and such, but is it too much to ask for a bit of scrap to be set aside for proper lipstick tubes? So we can fix our faces without making a mess? Doesn't Uncle Sam want us girls to look good for our boys, to keep up morale?"

We finished soon after that. Sully pushed off the wall he'd been leaning against and eyed me, his expression a cross between a scowl and amusement.

"I thought you'd be in the john all night. How long does it take to fix your face?"

That phrase again, *fix your face*. What an absurd figure of speech. "Sounds like you missed me," I said with a grin.

He grunted and I took his arm. Peggy bounced ahead of us into the dining room like Tigger, as if on springs of happiness. In her mind, the problem was solved. My sergeant would make everything right.

I side-eyed Sully, worried I'd made a rash promise. I remembered how he got all grumpy when he spoke about "hurry-up" war marriages. Would he view a shotgun wedding with any less disdain? Or weddings and marriage in general, after what I'd learned about his parents? I doubted he'd be thrilled I'd dragged his name into this scheme. Glo wouldn't be happy either, I suspected. Anything that deviated from the mission would probably be a no-go in her book.

Seriously though, at this point, I didn't care. Even if Sully *like* liked me, as Peggy had claimed, it didn't matter. It wouldn't work between us. Could never work. We had no future. But Peggy and her Johnny did. That was doable. Something could be done. I'd find a way for those two crazy kids to be together, lock, stock, and wedding ring.

At least someone would get a happy ending. I'd make sure of it.

15

Back at our table, I sipped my beer and mulled over Peggy's predicament while the others shot the breeze.

The soldiers got into what any generation of workplace pals get into when they go out for a drink—bitching about their coworkers. Some guy named Curly cheated at craps. Another dude screwed up so much he was always on KP duty, peeling potatoes until his hands were raw. And Lieutenant So-and-So was a royal pain in the rear but what could you expect from a Ninety-Day Wonder?

Sully seemed uninterested in jumping on the bashing bandwagon. He finished his drink, caught my eye, and jerked his head toward the exit. Time to go, I guess. I wasn't exactly thrilled to venture outside and make him a target again but didn't object. We stopped in the lobby to pick up my coat and our copies of the photograph then stepped out into the night.

The crowd had ballooned since I'd entered Jonesy's a

while earlier. The street teemed with people and laughter and cigarette smoke drifted on the air, a scene as chaotic and as testosterone filled as a Super Bowl victory celebration. Sully led me through the mob and steered us onto a less crowded side street.

"Where are we headed?" I asked, after we'd walked along side by side for a short time.

"Back to Ma's place. Where we can be alone." He gave me a sidelong glance, making my pulse race, until he dropped the hammer on that declaration. "It's time for us to talk."

Uh-oh. A conversation that began with those words, spoken in just that way, never ended well. "Sully, no. We can't go back to Ma's."

"Why not?"

Because of the obvious. Something I should have thought of earlier. "Jake knows I'm staying there."

Sully aimed another glance my way, suspicious this time. "How does he know that?"

"I-I'm not sure. Believe me, I wish I knew. But I suspect that's where he is, waiting for you...er...me." That's what I would do. Why bother to traipse all over Ballard Springs, when he could wait in the shadows at the boarding house for his quarry to come to him?

Sully abruptly stopped walking and seized me by the shoulders, turning me to him, his eyes blazing into mine.

"Beryl—" He cut off, looking furious and tortured at the same time. "I want you to clear the air once and for all. And for the love of Jesus and all that's holy, you're gonna tell me the *truth*. Is that fella Jake your lover?"

A smile tugged at my lips, though this was no

laughing matter. He'd finally referred to Jake by his name, not some snarky nickname. It still sounded like an insult.

"No, Sully. Absolutely no," I said. The one thing I could be completely honest about. "That's the last thing Jake is to me."

"You sure? The way he's chasing you, the way I saw him look at you at the library makes me think otherwise."

Sully was clearly more observant than me. I hadn't noticed. Except that moment in the bathroom, the look on Jake's face then, the heat in his voice. But I'd hand-waved it. I'd been mistaken, the light was weird, Jake had indigestion, anything but the creepy reality that he might have a thing for me. Because, seriously? He was a criminal. Plus, I was supposed to kill him. A great conflict for a romantic suspense story, but in reality? *Ick.*

"There's nothing between us," I said decisively. "*Nothing.*"

He released me with a nod, and I thought I saw relief in his eyes. Had Sully been jealous of my pretend ex-boyfriend-slash-stalker?

"Tell me, then," he said as we resumed walking. "If that fool's not a spurned lover, why did you tell me he was? Why is he after you? Why does he want to hurt you? You know him somehow. You both know how to fight in that odd way. How'd you learn how to do that? And what in hell was that hunk of metal he had?"

I let out a gusty sigh, scrambling for something plausible that didn't involve time travel. Not because Sully wouldn't believe me, though I was reasonably certain he wouldn't, but because I didn't want him to think I'd been messing with him. Playing him for a sap, as he would say. I didn't want him to think badly of me.

There it was, in all its pathetic glory. I wanted...no, I *craved* his approval.

I took a breath. "Okay, Sully, here's the deal. The truth. You were right all along. I *am* a spy." I let that sink in. "I'm sorry I lied about Jake. About telling you he's my ex-boyfriend. I had to fib to keep you from asking questions. As you said, loose lips sink ships, and all that. I really work for the..."

FBI? No, wrong one. CIA. Only, not the CIA, it got that name during the Cold War. Started out as something else. Damn it, brain, fine time to stop working.

"I'll just say I work for a secret organization I can't tell you anything about." Okay, sort of true. "Jake's an agent for us and he's gone rogue." Mostly true. "I've been assigned to stop him any way I can. Kill him if I have to." Completely true, except for the *if I have to* part.

Sully's brow scrunched. "I don't get it. You're tough and smart, but how does a girl get to be a spy?"

"You know, Sergeant Sullivan, you're almost completely perfect, except for the sexism. You can't wrap your head around a woman doing typically male stuff, can you? Just wait a few years. Then you'll see that us girls can do a *lot* of things. A lot of amazing things."

He made a *whatever* face that irked me to no end. "You're avoiding my questions."

Yes. Yes, I was. "It's like this. You're not the only one who can do their patriotic duty. Everyone has to do their bit in this war, even women. I've lived an unconventional life. I've acquired a particular and unusual set of skills.

There's a critical need for what I can do, and Uncle Sam drafted me to do it. Just like you were drafted." Almost completely true. I resisted the urge to pat myself on the back.

He grunted. Point in my favor, I guess. "What about that metal dingus? Don't give me that ish kabibble about a flashlight. I saw that thing work. It kicked out a heat ray like something from a Buck Rogers picture."

And now my truthiness had come to an end. "Uh, that's classified, sorry to say. It's a weapon, something new. A prototype." I patted my handbag. "I've got one too. It's so dangerous I don't even want to use it. But Jake's a ruthless piece of shit. He'd use it in a heartbeat. He's vowed not to be taken alive and doesn't care who he takes down with him. That's why I keep telling you to be careful."

He nodded, seeming to swallow that load of BS whole. "Why you, Beryl? Why do you, of all the spies have to do such a dirty job?"

The question I'd been asking myself nonstop since this crazy time travel ride had begun. "I was the only one available," I said with a shrug. "The other agents, the men, are busy with more important spy stuff. I'm on my own." And that was the truest thing I'd ever said to him. The sad truth.

"You're not alone, Beryl. You've got me." He slipped his arm across my shoulders and hugged me close. "Now, let's go back to Ma's and face that traitorous weasel."

Convinced he'd go without me if I said no, I didn't put up a fight. Didn't even utter a mild objection as we headed back. His touch and his heated words had robbed me of speech, anyway. *You've got me.* A solid promise from a determined, Rock of Gibraltar man. I'd always been about going it alone, so to find someone I could rely on and trust implicitly was a major deal.

Well, technically, Glo had found Sully for me. Had she known he'd turn out to be so heroic?

I put all my questions aside as we reached the boarding house. We approached from the opposite side of the street. When we got close enough to do a proper reconnaissance of the property, Sully adopted a defensive pose, moving with his elbows bent, as if he held a rifle. He'd been on watch for Jake the whole way back, but now we'd reached a place where the enemy most likely would be, the soldier had clicked into place.

We crouched behind a Dodge coupe up on wooden blocks, its tires removed. Sully scanned the scene across the street. "All's quiet on the western front," he muttered.

I got his meaning. It seemed *too* quiet over there. No signs of movement at Ma's, or in front of the house, or near the carriage house barracks next door. No shadows lurked at corners or hid in the few parked cars. Not even a breeze rustled the scrubby forsythia bushes flanking the boarding house's front steps.

"Maybe he gave up," I said doubtfully, my heart hammering.

"Maybe," Sully replied, with an equal dose of doubt. His gaze shifted to the Cack I'd removed from my handbag and held clutched in my hand. "How does that thing work?"

"It's simple. Well, I *think* it's simple. I've never actually fired it." I lifted the weapon so he could see it clearly in the moonlight. "There's two settings, kill and stun." I hovered my thumb over the circular black tabs embedded in the sleek gray metal, then motioned toward the arming tab above the other buttons. "You have to press this button first to activate it, then it'll fire."

The distinctive whine of a Cack powering up suddenly cut through the night air. Sully frowned. My heart lurched, and not in a good way. *I* hadn't pressed arm.

A moment later, a silhouetted figure burst out of the darkness behind us.

"Sully, *run!*" I shouted as Jake fired and a blinding flash lit up the night. A sizzling beam blasted into the sidewalk a nanosecond after Sully and I bolted from the spot. Smoking bits of pavement spurted in all directions. Asphalt projectiles pinged the car we'd hidden behind like bullets. Jake fired again and scorching heat missed us by a fraction as we tore across the street toward Ma's.

Sully grabbed my hand and we flew up the steps and into the house, barely taking a breath. He slammed the door and turned the lock.

"Damn it all," he spat, leaning against the door and breathing heavily. "That bastard caught us with our pants down. Again." He eyed the Cack still in my hand with a mixture of awe and loathing. "That weapon's a son of a bitch. Beats my M-1 all to hell."

I shoved the thing into my handbag and peered through one of the narrow windows beside the door. Jake stood on the sidewalk next to the Dodge, his face visible in the moonlight. He stared at Ma's, looking satisfied, almost pleased we'd escaped. A second later he ambled away as if out for a Saturday evening stroll.

"He's gone." I turned from the window and threw my arms around Sully's neck, hugging him tight. My nerve endings sizzled with fire, my whole body alive and pulsing with the adrenaline of fear and excitement and relief that Sully hadn't been harmed.

I pulled back and our eyes locked. My breath caught. So did his. Electricity shot between us. Impulsively, I hiked up onto my toes to kiss him, but he stopped me, held me at arm's length. Hurt flushed through me and he must've seen it on my face because his gaze on me turned fierce.

"Beryl, wait," he said in a desperate tone. "I want to be clear about something before we...before anything else happens. With us."

He sounded gloomy, but his words sparked hope deep in my belly. "Go on."

He cleared his throat nervously. "I've only known you a half a minute, but you've come to mean something to me. I've never met anyone like you. You put up with me. You've seen me at my worst—"

"And I've seen you at your best," I said, thinking of him in the library with Ida. And how gentle he'd been with me at the park before Jake had crashed the party. His kindness with Stretch and his other men, and his openness about his father. "You've got a big heart, Sully."

He accepted that with a self-deprecating scowl. "Maybe. But it's a heart I've kept under lock and key for far too long. Until I met you. A girl so full of life you make me dizzy. A girl who isn't afraid of anything. Not me, or that palooka you're after, no one and nothing." His voice dipped to a husky murmur. "Beryl, I know we just met, but I want you like I've wanted no other woman. You mean something to me. We..." He touched my face, a gentle caress. "*We* mean something and whatever happens between us is important to me. Not a passing thing, Beryl. What I'm saying is, I think I'm falling in—"

I pressed a finger to his lips. "Don't say that word. It's a jinx. I've lost everyone who's ever said that to me. You mean something to me, too, Sully, but we don't have to put a name to it. We just have to *be*. I learned that from something Peggy said tonight."

"Only one thing?"

I smiled. "Okay, in the middle of a lot of things, Peggy said something very wise. Her Johnny will ship out soon. She said she wanted to make this short time they had together count. To grab every moment and memory with him before he goes. I want to do that too. With you."

I placed my hands on his chest, feeling his steady heartbeat under my palms. I didn't know what this was between us or where it could go. I didn't want to think about it, or what could happen tomorrow. All that mattered was this moment and this man. All that mattered was us, together. Here and now.

"Sully, I want to be with you. Last night I was drunk and stupid and said a lot of things that probably scared you half to death. But tonight, I'm as sober as can be. I know this is bold, but I want to be with you, reputation be damned. We may only have this night. Let's make it count."

He eyed me a long time, that poker face betraying

nothing. He covered my hands on his chest with both of his. My heart sank. He was going to push me away. Pat me on the head and send me to bed like a misguided child.

Then he smiled into my eyes. "Beryl Blue, you're a real piece of work."

He took me in his arms and kissed me.

THIS KISS WAS nothing like the one in the park. That had been an introduction, our lips blending sweetly, tentatively. This kiss was...not. Rough, demanding, take no prisoners. He wanted me and I needed him. Right now, this moment. This kiss sealed the deal. The war, my mission, and Jake faded from my mind. So did the past and the future. Sully and I, together, were the only thing that mattered.

We stood there in the dim light of Ma's front hall and kissed and tasted and caressed, pressed together, touching each other with the joy of discovery. His lips lingered against my throat, sending fire rushing through me to every part of my being. I slid my hands under his jacket and felt the contours of his muscled back, wanting more, wanting all of him.

We parted a moment and gazed at each other, solemn and joyful at the same time. Then Sully seized my lips again. His mouth closed over mine like an explorer who'd been searching for his treasure for a long time, finally staking a claim. A full bore, flag in the soil declaration. I was his.

And I was. Completely. Me, Beryl Blue, the scaredy

cat who ran from intimacy and commitment as if a horde of ghosts and bill collectors chased after me. I'd gone all in. For Sully. For us. With a breathtaking, liberating conviction, I was his.

"Who's there?" a sleepy voice called from the back of the house, yanking us apart. "Is something wrong?"

Footsteps creaked along the floorboards, heading toward us. My heart thundered and my blood rushed. Sully wanted me, I wanted him, and all was right with the world. No way would I let Ma the Morality Police break us up again.

I took Sully's hand and laced my fingers with his. "Come on," I whispered and tugged him toward the stairs —and my room. "Let's go before she catches us."

He squeezed my hand and without another moment's hesitation, we went upstairs.

16

I awoke to the gentle peal of church bells in the distance and a warm body next to me. I lifted my head from Sully's sturdy shoulder and watched him sleep. His hair was tousled, and his thick eyelashes brushed his rugged cheeks. His dog tags nestled in the copper-colored hair on his chest and they rose and fell as he breathed.

My heart fluttered. And so did just about every other part of me, thinking about last night. The two of us together, our bodies joining as one. Giving ourselves to each other completely. Embracing the moment. Even his laughter at my confusion when he'd called the condom he taken from his wallet a *French letter* made me tingle. His joy at knowing something know-it-all Beryl didn't had been adorable. His power and skill when we'd made love had been unforgettable.

As if he felt my gaze on him, he shifted. His eyes slowly opened. "Good morning," he murmured.

I sighed and snuggled next to him. I didn't want to leave his side, this bed, this room, this time. I didn't want to leave him, ever. Then my heart ached, literally ached, because I knew that could never be. He'd have to leave, and soon. He'd have to go back to camp, pack his duffel, and head out. Parts unknown. Future unknown.

If I kept Jake from getting to him.

The bedsprings squawked as Sully reached for his uniform jacket, crumpled on the floor. He pulled out a pack of Lucky Strikes and his copy of the photograph we'd had taken last night. I'd tucked mine safely into my handbag. He lay back against the pillow, cigarette pack on his chest, and tipped the picture to catch the sunlight slipping around the window shade. The photo had come out pretty good. I could still smell the perfume and smoke that had drifted through the nightclub, could still hear the music, and the feel of Sully's arm around my waist.

"What's that beauty doing with a mug like me?" he said.

I gazed at him and my heart swelled. He always put himself down. He had no idea how magnetic he was. Not conventionally handsome nor picture perfect, like Jake. He had so much more. Character, strength, goodness in his heart. Not bad in the sack, either. I hadn't kissed that many frogs in my dating career, but I'd kissed enough to know a prince when I found him.

"Sully, stop it with the negativity. You've completely rocked my world. Too bad..." I trailed off. Too bad it would soon end, one way or another.

I put our inevitable separation from my mind and focused on the moment. I didn't nag as he slipped the photo back into his pocket and exchanged it for a cigarette, but I did sigh in disapproval. He got the message. Flashing me a sheepish look, he put the nasty thing away.

I rested my head on his shoulder again and he stroked my hair. "Tell me about your orders, Beryl. Did you say you have to kill that bastard if you catch him?"

I snuggled closer. Hard to do. The bed was so narrow, we were already practically conjoined. "Let's not talk about him. Not now."

"I have to. I have to understand why my country would ask a woman to kill a man in cold blood. Even if you are a spy, even if it's necessary, killing a guy is a damned dirty business." His voice rumbled beneath me, filled with disbelief and confusion. "And I can't believe you could..."

"That I could kill a man?" I finished for him. The major question of all the questions plaguing me. Could I pull the trigger on Jake? I kissed Sully's shoulder and traced my initials in the soft hair on his chest. For Sully? To save him? I was beginning to think I could.

I flinched at a sudden pounding on the door.

"Beryl? Beryl! It's me, Peggy Smith."

Groan. The real world intrudeth. "The bathroom's down the hall, Peggy," I called.

"Please, Beryl, I need to talk to you. It's about my Johnny."

"Oh, crap, I forgot." I sat up. The thin blankets fell

away and Sully's lazy gaze trailed over my body, centering on my naked breasts.

"The honeymoon's over?" he said distractedly.

"They never had a honeymoon. She told me yesterday they're not married, and he has no intention of marrying her."

That got his attention. He tore his gaze from me and eyed the door with a thunderous expression. "*What?*"

I shushed him. "Some kind of nobility thing, not wanting to leave her a widow with no man to protect her."

"We'll see about that." He shoved off the covers and the springs squealed wildly as he hopped out of bed. I watched him put on his government issue boxers. His body was beautiful, a word I wouldn't share with him, but the shoe fit. He had strong, hard thighs, a tight butt, and back muscles that rippled as he grabbed his trousers and stabbed his legs into them. The complete, romance novel cover boy package.

Peggy pounded the door as I hunted for something to wear. Sully had put on his shirt and tie by the time I scrambled into a frilly bathrobe the evicted Etta had left in her closet. I eased the door open a crack and swallowed a shriek at the ghoul that stared at me from the other side. Peggy had twisted her golden hair into a thousand pin curls and white cream plastered her face. She looked like a zombie mime.

"Beryl, Johnny's going back to the base after breakfast," she wailed. My fingers twitched like I had a remote and could lower her volume. "I've talked and talked, but he won't listen to me at all. You have to do something."

Ma popped out from the stairwell down the hall. She

started toward us. "What's all this ruckus so early on the Lord's day?" she called.

A big hand flashed in my peripheral, and the door slammed. "Cripes, Beryl," Sully said in a teeth-gritted whisper. "You want the whole house to know I spent the night here with you?"

News flash, they probably already did, thanks to Mr. Squeaky Bed. "What about Peggy? And Johnny? And getting them hitched? What'll I tell her?"

"Tell her I'll take care of it." He finished tucking in his shirt and held up a hand. "Not right *now*. Go put on your face. I'll meet both of you downstairs."

"Wait, meet you downstairs?"

He snatched his jacket off the floor and shrugged into it as he strode to the window. He winced at the pitiful moan of wood scraping wood as he slid the window upward.

"Sully, you're seriously not—" He swung a leg over the sill. Yes, he seriously was. I ran over. "You'll break your neck."

His blue eyes twinkled. "Would you cry if I did?"

"You know I would."

He seared me with a look that made me flush. He lifted his hand and touched my cheek, his voice going barrel deep. "Marry me."

I went still. Two words packed with almost as much power as that dreaded four-letter word. And from him, the man who scowled at the mere mention of matrimony. Was it terrible that I wanted to say yes? Say to hell with what it would do to the timeline, or messing with history, or any of the things Glo had gloomily warned about?

I wanted to stay with Sully. Forever and ever.

Because I was in love with him.

I blinked, stunned at the plain, terrifying, undeniable truth. I didn't know how it had happened, and it didn't seem possible to have happened so fast, but I'd fallen in love with Sully. L-O-V-E. Not just passive love, but active, pulse-pounding, dizzy-making, irrational-thinking, happily ever after in love.

And the kicker? I wanted him to love me back. I'd been all about running. Running away from anyone offering me love. Closing my heart and denying I even knew the definition of the word. Now I looked right at it. How he felt for me blazed in his eyes. How I felt for him soared in my heart.

But our love was hopeless. We could never be together. Never.

"Go," I said. My heart shattered to see the hope in his eyes fade. "And keep an eye out for Jake."

"You're a nag, you know that?"

He kissed me quick, stealing my breath. I watched anxiously as he reached out and grabbed a tree branch, shaking loose a bunch of leaves. The branch sagged ominously. How could it not with that big gorilla swinging from it? But it didn't break. The branch dipped low, an easy jump. Sully hit the ground with a thud, straightened his jacket, and gave me a jaunty salute.

Then he was gone.

"WE'RE OFF TO CHURCH NOW," Ma said as I came downstairs twenty minutes later. I'd had the chance to freshen up and now wore a navy-blue linen dress with white cuffs and belt, my hair tied back with a ribbon the same color as my dress.

Ma worked her hands into a pair of lace-edged gloves while Etta pinned a straw hat onto her gray bun. Dear Etta. She'd given up her room for me. I doubted her good morning smile would've been so friendly if she knew what a workout her bed had gotten last night.

Ma eyed me as if she knew, in every squishy detail. "We're off to church," she repeated, her gaze boring into me. "Would anyone care to accompany us?"

I looked around the front hall as if there were a ton of other people here eager to volunteer, instead of just little old me. What would be the point of me tagging along? I'd already traveled a fair piece down the road to perdition, what with all my various and sundry sins. And if I went all the way and carried out my mission, I'd be guilty of breaking commandment *numero uno*. After that, no amount of churching could ever put the brakes on my trip to the hot place.

Ma sighed, seeing her chance to get me into the fold slip away. "Very well. There's oatmeal on the warming dish on the sideboard, and fresh milk in the icebox."

I thanked her and she and Etta left, sweeping up Griff and a few other washed-and-combed GIs waiting on the porch. She led them down the street as if she were General Patton marching off to battle.

I went into the dining room. No Sully. I told myself to remain calm. He knew to watch out for Jake. He would join me soon. A smattering of soldiers populated the room, including Marco. He slumped over the table, staring into a heaping bowl of oatmeal as if he expected it to speak to him.

"Rough night, Marco? Didn't you sleep well?"

"What makes you think I been to bed?" he said in a raspy voice.

Fair enough. I went to the sideboard near the windows and lifted the lid off the oatmeal crock pot, getting an impromptu facial from the steam. The smell of cinnamon and oats woke my stomach up. I took a bowl from a tall stack. Its floral pattern had faded from years of spoons scraping and elbow grease washing. I picked up the ladle to scoop a heaping portion of oatmeal, suddenly startled by a *tap-tap* on one of the windows. I looked up, expecting to see Sully grinning at me from outside.

Not even close. Glo stood in the sun-dappled yard. She shaded her eyes and signaled for me to come out.

Well, well. Of all the people I'd been wanting to see since I'd landed here, she topped the list. She'd left me on Rand Road with a zillion unanswered questions. Dumped an impossible mission on my unwilling shoulders. Left me to flail around as best as I could. I'd flailed, failed, and fell in love. Not exactly the outcome she'd been hoping for.

Queuing up a long string of angry complaints, I abandoned breakfast and headed outside. The kitchen door creaked as I opened it, and I walked into another perfect day. Almost too perfect. Did Time Scope have some kind of control over the weather? That wouldn't surprise me.

Glo had moved away from the window and now leaned against the gnarled trunk of the tree that had abetted Sully's escape a little while ago. I stalked over, passing a soldier sleeping on a wooden bench, his coat spread across his chest like a blanket. Cigarette butts were strewn everywhere, mashed into the dirt and browning grass.

I got right to it. "*Where* have you been?"

"I thought you'd be glad to see me," she said, raising an eyebrow. Not in an endearing Sully way. In an annoying Mr. Spock-like way, as if she were an alien totally unable to understand why anger shot from my eyes and smoke poured out of my ears.

"I am glad to see you," I said. "Because we need to have words. Lots and lots of words. You disappeared, dumping me here alone, a stranger in a strange land."

She held up a hand. "Not true. I've been keeping an eye on you. From a distance. And so far, you've been doing a dismal job. Mission *un*accomplished."

The mission. The fricking mission. "Oh, I'm sorry, I didn't know you were on a schedule. You should've rush ordered Jake's assassination."

"Keep it down, sister," the soldier on the bench grumbled then turned onto his side.

I lowered my voice, but my temperature didn't cool down a bit. "Come on, Glo. It's not like you asked me to pick up your dry cleaning. You're asking the impossible. I just can't..." My voice dropped to a whisper. "I can't *kill* anyone."

She studied me, her expression still hard, but I saw a flicker of something in her eyes. Compassion, maybe. Or empathy. "To be honest, if people saw things my way, you wouldn't have to. You wouldn't be here at all."

I blinked at this unexpected honesty. "Does that mean I *don't* have to do the job? Then why don't you send me home and get someone more bloodthirsty for this mission?"

Any sympathy I thought I saw in her eyes vanished. Hard as nails Glo roared back, full force. "Sorry, Beryl, it doesn't work that way. Time Scope's not going to say pardon us for bothering you and send you home."

"That's what Jake said."

She stiffened. "Jake? You *spoke* to him?"

"Yeah, yesterday, and the day before. He knows I'm working for you. He's not threatened by me at all. Pretty much called me a wimp to my face." Her eyes glittered with anger, surprising me. "What, you think I should've taken him out then? I guess I could've, but I didn't have my weapon with me at the time. And, come on, face it. I can't kill Jake. Or *anyone*."

She took a deep breath and seemed to get hold of herself. "Beryl, I'll tell you one last time. You've *got* to complete the mission."

"Or what? You'll kill me instead? I want to make sure I'm clear on that. You dropped that on me like a bomb then took off. I won't live to see tomorrow if I don't do what you want, right? That's what you said." I heard the rising panic in my voice. "Are you going to kill me if I don't kill him?"

Long pause. Oh, I knew that kind of pause. I was queen of that kind of pause. She scrambled to come up with a lie.

"I didn't mean it that way," she said finally. Lamely. "I was trying to impress on you how important the mission is. What I meant to say is, if you fail, and Jake doesn't, if he kills Sergeant Sullivan, then the whole future is changed. *Your* future is changed. Irrevocably."

"My God, what is it that Sully does to make—"

I broke off as the devil I spoke of came down the path from the carriage house. I watched him walk, moving with assurance, his back military straight. Our gazes snagged and every hot moment of our night together flashed into my mind. And flushed through my body. I boiled like a furnace, aching to be in his arms again.

Glo's gaze bopped between me and Sully. I thought I saw a satisfied little smirk on her face before her expression went dark again.

Sully started to come over, but I held up both hands. "No worries, Sully," I called, getting another grumble from the soldier trying to sleep. "I'll just be a sec. You go in."

He studied Glo, and after a tense moment, he gave a reluctant nod and did as I suggested.

"He seems awful sweet," Glo said as the door closed behind him. With her terminal scowl, that didn't seem like a compliment. "What are you going to tell him about me? About this meeting?"

"Another lie, what else? I already told him I was a spy."

"You? A spy?"

"Thanks for the vote of support. It's better than telling him Jake and I are lovers, which was the first story I went with— Hey, you okay?"

She choked, the same strangled noise my cat Jenjen made when hucking up a hairball. Not attractive in the least.

"I'm fine," she said finally, catching her breath. "Now, about the mission?"

"Can you at least give me props for getting the job half done? I've kept Sully safe. Believe me, that's not easy. He's a damned big target."

That got me another Mr. Spock eyebrow. "You like him."

What gave it away? The affection in my voice? Or the fact that when Sully came within five feet of me, I blazed hot enough to heat every room at Ma's for the winter?

"I don't like Sully," I lied. "We just...get along. And I'm worried about him." I felt suddenly hollow. "Glo... Does he make it? Through the war, I mean. You must know. Does he survive?"

She looked me straight in the eye. "What does it matter, if you don't stop Jake now?"

There it was, Glo's money shot. No matter what I said, or how much I protested, I was still on the hook. I still had to murder someone.

"What does Sully do? Does he invent something or make something? I mean, what's so important that Jake would go so far to stop him?" My voice echoed the fear in my heart.

She sighed. "He helps someone during the war. And Beryl, I swear that's all I can tell you. Now, if you want me to get you home, set the timeline right. Stop Jake."

"I didn't ask for this job, you know," I muttered.

"I know." Her voice softened. Well, as soft as I'd ever

heard from her, anyway. "But no one gets to choose their path. Bumpy or smooth, you have to take that path and make the best of it. Your path happens to be extra bumpy."

"What else is new?" I said and went back into the house.

17

"You compromised Miss Smith," I heard Sully growl at Peggy's beau when I stepped into the dining room. "You risked her reputation and her good name, and for what? For your own selfish needs."

I went to scoop myself some oatmeal, feeling sorry for Johnny. I half expected Big Red to grab the poor kid by the collar and start shaking him. That would be like a Great Dane taking on a Shih Tzu. Not a fair fight.

"Well?" Sully demanded. "Is that behavior befitting a soldier in the United States Army?

"No, Sergeant." Johnny hung his head. "I only meant—"

"I know damn well what you meant. Now, I mean every word when I say you're going to do what's right by that young lady." He jabbed a thumb at Peggy, who sat at the table near the now sleeping Marco. Her pin curls and the white face goo were gone. She wore her Sunday best frock and straw hat, her hands folded primly in her lap.

"But Sarge," Johnny sputtered. "I'm only thinking of Peg and her future."

"I don't want to hear any excuses," Sully growled. "You're going to marry her and marry her today."

"Then what?" Johnny cried. "I dunno what's gonna happen. I don't want to leave her all alone with no one to take care of her, if I should... If something should happen to me." He shut his mouth with an audible click.

Sully rested his hand on the young man's shoulder. "I understand, son. I truly do." I caught a whisper of emotion in his voice. "But you have to do what's right. No ifs, ands, or buts. Think of her, and her folks."

Stan staggered in. His bald pate glinted under the dining room light. "What's going on?" he asked, heading toward me.

I handed him my oatmeal-filled bowl. "Much drama. Sully's taking care of it."

He grinned. "Sarge is good at that."

I took two more bowls from the stack and filled them. Oh my, yes, Sully was good at a *lot* of things. Especially making me melt into a puddle just being in the same room with him. I tamed my raging hormones as best I could and brought the bowls to the table. Peggy beamed at me. It looked as if she would get her dearest wish and she didn't have to say a word.

"Go get ready, Private," Sully said. "In one hour, we're gonna find a Justice of the Peace and get this settled once and for all. Have I made myself clear?"

"Yes, Sergeant," Johnny said meekly.

Sully nodded. "Good. Now get out of here and let me have my breakfast."

Johnny fled. Peggy followed, stopping to hike up on tiptoe to kiss Sully's cheek before leaving the room. He looked most uncomfortable.

"Very nicely done, Sergeant Sullivan," I said when he sat down next to me at the table.

"I feel like a heel," he muttered, shooting me a guilt-stricken look.

"You shouldn't. Our situation is different." I pushed a bowl toward him. "Here, eat," I coaxed before my tradi-tional, old-fashioned sergeant could beg to differ.

He picked up a spoon. "Who were you talking to outside?"

Yup, Sully was capable of a lot of things, chief among them being suspicious. Only a beat before my next lie poured out. "Relax, she's one of us. She's been tracking Jake for me but hasn't found him."

He dug into his breakfast, still doubtful. I could tell by the way he muttered into his oatmeal.

I ate, too. The milk was creamy good and full of fat. The oatmeal didn't have enough sugar for me, a member of the high fructose corn syrup generation. But someone else had done the cooking, so all was right in my world. Almost. Still no coffee.

"Don't forget we're supposed to go to Stretch's this afternoon for Sunday dinner," I said, less than thrilled. I didn't want Sully out of the house and out in the open again. I wanted him close and in close quarters and, maybe, just maybe, a repeat performance of last night's exquisite dance. But we'd promised Stretch, and I didn't want to disappoint the kid.

"I *did* forget," Sully said with a groan. He glared at the

doorway Johnny had bolted through, with Peggy on his heels. "We have to take care of the lovebirds first. Where do you suppose Ma keeps her telephone directory? Ought to be a few JPs listed in the book."

There were. The phone book had been printed in 1939 —paper rationing and scarce printing supplies meant no current directories were available—but Sully announced with reasonable certainty that the marrying men listed were most likely still in business.

In precisely the hour Big Red had ordered, Peggy and her Johnny piled into the back seat of the jeep and we sped toward the residence of Henry Holmes, Justice of the Peace. The vehicle puttered to a stop outside a house almost identical to the one in the movie *Psycho*. I stared up at the top floor windows as we trooped up the front walk, expecting to see Norman Bates' skeletal mother staring out at me.

"More of you? I thought Henry married the whole county yesterday," Mrs. JP said when she opened the inside door and saw us on her porch. She turned out to be more Kathy Bates than *Psycho's* Mrs. Bates—plump, salt-and-pepper pin curls, shrewd brown eyes. She swung open the screen door with a smile. "Come on in. You're in luck, we're just back from church. Wipe your feet, gentlemen. I'll have no muck in my parlor."

We crowded into a tidy front room full of knickknacks and braided rugs, smelling of gardenia toilet water and pipe smoke. Henry Holmes sat in a wingback chair that nearly swallowed up his skinny self. He rose and folded his newspaper.

"The fee's two dollars, gentlemen," he said, with an

old-school New England accent I hadn't heard since Grandma Blue had left me. He peered at Sully and Johnny in turn, his gaze as shrewd as Mrs. JP's. "Two dollars *each*. No discounts for a double wedding. This *is* a double wedding, isn't it?"

Sully gazed at me, his expression almost daring me to say yes. My breath caught. I *wanted* to. I really did. How was that for commitment? No piddling waterfall when I took the plunge. When Beryl Blue jumped, she went all the way, right over Niagara Falls. But the idea of us getting hitched was nothing more than a lovely fantasy. We couldn't, case closed.

I shifted. Away from Sully.

"Just them," Sully said, turning to the JP, his voice tight. "Just them."

Mr. Holmes slipped his requested fee into his trousers pocket and began to read the familiar words. Peggy sobbed. Johnny looked glum. Sully and I stood side by side, not touching. I gazed solemnly at both men in uniform when the JP got to, "until death do you part."

I squeezed my handbag's strap. The Cack nestled inside, along with the photograph from last night. I couldn't think of Sully's fate on the battlefield and the future Glo stubbornly refused to give me clear info about. I had to focus on the now. I wanted him to have the chance at a long and hopefully happy life. Whether I was in it or not. *That* I wanted more than anything.

There was only way for that to happen—I had to save him from Jake.

THE BRIEF CEREMONY COMPLETE, the happy couple signed the register. And what do you know, Johnny's last name really was Smith. Mr. Holmes put his John Hancock on the marriage license and Peggy tucked that precious piece of paper into her purse with a giddy grin.

We motored back to Ma's to drop off the newlyweds, then picked up Marco and the others and headed toward Stretch's family farm.

"Looks like they're ripping up the old trolley lines to use for scrap metal," Sully said, as the jeep bounced over a stretch of rough pavement at the edge of town.

After that, we didn't speak, but when Sully shifted the jeep into a higher gear and sped up, he reached for me. I took his hand and held on tight.

Everything between us had changed since last night. I felt it. The gentle but firm pressure of his fingers on mine told me he felt it too. The men in the back seemed not to notice. Griff and Stan studied the scenery, what there was of it. We passed field after field, most stripped bare, some still studded with browning corn stalks. Marco, squashed between his pals, slept with his mouth open. He got an unexpected second breakfast from all the bugs flying in as the jeep sped along.

I kept an eye out for Jake. I tossed anxious glances behind us, looking for the Ford that had tried to run us down or some other car following us. I should have been looking ahead. Because when Sully took a sharp right and I realized where we were going, my heart dropped all the way to my toes.

My grandmother grew up on a farm on County Road, outside Ballard Springs. The Carter family raised cows and chickens and grew pumpkins and corn on a rugged thirty acres. What in my time was a development full of McMansions, had once been open land with a barn and a silo and a rambling old farmhouse at its heart. Just like every other farm in New England, and in the rest of the country.

"That's where the old folks lived, duckie," I remembered Grandma Blue saying when we'd go out for a Sunday drive on the outskirts of Ballard Springs. A spin around the countryside, windows down, even in winter because Grandma Blue was always hot, like a busted furnace.

The jeep turned off County Road and jounced along a long, dirt driveway. I shuddered so hard my teeth rattled. I was losing it. Literally. Black spots popped before my eyes. A million tiny pins danced across my scalp and I got so lightheaded I nearly toppled out of the jeep. Would have if Sully's solid grip didn't keep me in place.

"This is where Stretch lives?" I managed. "He lives at the Carter Farm?"

"Far as I know," Sully said. He released my hand, shoved the gear stick, and the jeep herked to a stop. Marco woke with a snort. The others tumbled out of the vehicle, but I didn't move. Sully didn't move either. He stared at me hard. "What's wrong?"

Wrong question. Should've asked what *wasn't* wrong. I mean, Carter farm. Where the old folks used to live. Where Grandma Blue grew up, in a white house, with a rooster weathervane on top of the barn.

Except... She was Minerva Carter then. And Stretch? Who was Stretch? My brain switched off the light and hid under the bedcovers. I did *not* want to know the answer to that question.

And then he stood by the jeep, all hundred-thirty pounds soaking wet of him, smiling down at me. Welcoming me. Stretch. Augustus Carter. Great Uncle Augie. Grandma Blue's brother.

Who died in the war.

18

Somehow, I got out of the car.

Two or three or forty dogs loped up. Border collies, barking and romping in excitement. The old folks crowded in behind Stretch. Hands were shaken, compliments exchanged. The dogs wound around my legs as they escorted us across the yard. Then I stood on the porch, in the hall, in the parlor. Someone took my coat, someone else thrust a glass of something into my hand. Sherry, maybe. Could've been poison for all I knew. Voices babbled around me, over me.

This had to be some kind of cruel joke. Glo, pranking me. Or I'd hallucinated the whole excruciating thing. I'd imagined Sully, Marco, Stretch. The cigarettes, the smell of lamb stew and potatoes, the dogs. Not real. None of it.

None of *them*. People long dead, people I'd only heard of in stories. Grandma Blue's father and mother, both leather-skinned and milk fat, looking much older than their forty-something years. Auntie Violet, the old maid, born the day the Civil War began, died the day World

War II ended, and shunted from relative to relative all the years in between. Will Gates, the farmhand who'd showed up on the doorstep one day in the Depression, got put to work, and never left.

Stretch came over to me, tugging a girl of about ten by the hand. All spindly legs and elbows, straight blond hair, pink-cheeks, and Sunday best pinafore.

Grandma Blue.

"Miss Blue," Augie-Stretch said, beaming. "This is my best girl, my sister Minerva."

Seemed like their mother had a liking for the classics. How else to explain great-grandmother Carter burdening her children with names like Augustus and Minerva in a world of Joeys and Ethels?

And really, the Blue family genes must've totally dominated the Carter ones in the DNA battle for supremacy when I was conceived. I didn't see a resemblance at all. Me, dark hair, dark eyes. Minerva, a blue-eyed towhead. Stretch too. Seemed I had more in common with hired hand Gates than any of my blood relatives.

Minerva clutched a copy of *Little Women* to her chest. Her favorite book. I wondered if this was her first time reading it. She stared up at me wide-eyed. Her mouth opened and closed, as if my very presence had robbed her of speech. I knew exactly how she felt.

"You...you look just like Rita Hayworth," she blurted finally.

Even if I could speak, I wouldn't have known how to respond to that. I didn't know how to respond to any of it. The room spun like a carousel, my heartbeat thumped in my ears, my throat had gone dry, and my stomach heaved. Sully watched me with a concerned scowl.

"Rita Hayworth's my favorite picture star," the girl who would be my grandmother said. "Do you have a favorite?"

Great-grandmother Carter came over and put her hands on her daughter's shoulders, gently massaging. "Minerva, stop pestering poor Beryl. Let her catch her breath. We'll have plenty of time to get acquainted and you can ask her all the questions you want later."

I covered my mouth to smother a sob. My great-grandmother had Grandma Blue's voice. And her smile, warm and tender. It was as if my grandmother stood in front of me, different yet exactly the same. My brain suddenly forgot how to work. So did my lungs and every other part of me. Except the tears. My eyes stung from unshed tears.

Sully had been eyeing me like he thought I'd explode. I had to get out of there or maybe I would explode. Or scream, or tear my hair out, or something. I couldn't stand it another second. I fled. Not quietly. The floorboards creaked madly as I bolted from the parlor and then the house. A chorus of surprised gasps and questions followed me.

Outside, I ran.

I lost my hair ribbon and my hair whipped around my face as I dashed across a corn field and into the woods. Sweat sprinkled my forehead and dripped down my back. My skirt hiked up and my delicate pumps slipped on pine needles. I stumbled over tree roots and got snagged on branches, but I kept on running. Away from the house, the barn, and Sully. Away from the old folks and 1943.

Running away, as only Beryl Blue knew how.

A long time later, I stopped. Had to, I could barely breathe. I bent over, palms slapped to my knees, hauling in great gulps of air. I had no idea where I was. Somewhere in the woods, surrounded by pines, standing on a carpet of pine needles and moss. Leaves and tree branches rustled behind me. I whirled around to see Sully rushing up to me.

"Beryl, what the hell?" he gasped, out of breath too. "You're crying."

"Of course I'm crying." I threw my handbag to the ground. "Why shouldn't I cry? I've been hanging on by a thread, trying to do what they want. Being with you, that's a bonus. But Stretch? And Grandma Blue, only she's just a kid and...I miss her so much."

Pain and heartache laced every word, followed by a new flood of tears. Sully drew me into his arms, and I let it all out. All the frustration and fear, the sorrow, the yearning, and the grief I hadn't let myself feel since my grandmother had left me. No, she hadn't *left* me. She'd died. Her leaving me hadn't been a choice at all.

Sully held me, murmuring comforting words that only made me cry some more, until finally, after what seemed like an hour, the waterfall slowed to a trickle then stopped altogether.

I pulled from Sully's embrace. "Your uniform's soaked." Well, just his jacket's shoulder, where my tears had left a small pond.

He shrugged and took a handkerchief from his breast

pocket. "Here, dry your tears and fix your face. After you're done, you're gonna tell me what happened back there. You're gonna tell me everything. And this time, I want you to tell me the truth."

I dabbed at my eyes and my cheeks, wiping away teardrops and what was left of my makeup. I looked up at him, at those wise, soul-piercing blue eyes. Eyes that said he hadn't believed a single word I'd said to him since I landed on top of him at that gas station two days ago.

I sighed. Why not tell all? This whole mission had gone to hell anyway, why not spill the beans about everything? "You're not going to believe this, Sully, but I'm from the future—"

I yelped as the tree branch above Sully's head exploded.

SPARKS SHOWERED DOWN, followed by bark and pine needles that plummeted like sky jumpers in freefall. I shoved Sully out of the way in the proverbial nick of time. The heavy branch snapped off the tree and pounded the ground where he'd been standing.

I gaped at the jagged, smoldering hunk of wood. Then I glared across the clearing, at Jake. Great. *That* asshole had joined the party. The cherry on today's sundae of suck. He crouched like a ninja, about twenty feet away. The Cack glinted in his hand.

Sully and I ducked behind the tree's thick trunk as Jake's weapon fired again. The blast crackled over our heads. Another branch crashed to the ground. I hurried to free my own weapon from my handbag. My hands shook but I managed to press *arm* this time. The powering whine cut through the air and pierced my skull. The button at the weapon's tip turned from red to green.

"Sully, get out of here." I peered through the smoke pouring from the tree's smoldering wounds and the blizzard of falling pine needles, trying to get a bead on Jake.

Sully braced his back against the trunk. "No," he said between gritted teeth. "I'm not leaving you."

The tree shuddered as third hot blast splintered its trunk. More smoke, and flame this time, the smell of a fireplace on a cold day. *Shit.* The tree had caught fire.

I grabbed Sully's arm. "Please go. This is between me and him."

But the big ox wouldn't cooperate. He planted his feet, an immovable force. "I'm not going anywhere without you. Not until you tell me what the hell's going on."

"Seriously? Now?" My eyes were spinning from panic and he wanted to have a chat. Another burst pinged the ground nearby, digging up a chunk of dirt. I cringed. "All right, you win. I'm not a spy, Sully. I'm from the future. So is that dingbat shooting at us. Only it's not *us* he's after, it's *you*, you gigantic, stubborn dope!"

His skeptical eyebrows shot heavenward.

I ground my teeth. "Think about it." I caught a flash of Jake's uniform through the smoke and aimed in its general direction. "The way I talk, the way I act. You noticed how strange it is. And the dancing? No one foxtrots where I'm from. I'm from the future. Jake's from the *future*. He wants to kill you. So, can we *please* leave now?"

A heartbeat. Two. Then Sully grinned. Actually grinned. At a time like this. Which meant he didn't believe me.

Another blast—did that thing ever run out of juice?— followed by laughter. Followed by a grating, "Might as well run away, Beryl. You can't stop me. You're too scared."

"You're the coward," I shouted. "He's unarmed!"

"You aren't."

Jake sounded closer. Sully growled and I followed his angry gaze toward a clump of tangled briars where Jake crouched.

"You don't have the testicles to kill me," he called.

First of all, testicles? The guy really sucked at trash talk. Secondly, I'd always hated that *Gee, you did something difficult or brave or courageous, you must have balls* thing. Because swinging a pair of sensitive doodads that shrink in cold water and yipe in agony at the slightest punch wasn't brave. Not in the least. A guy would hit the fainting couch and never get up if he had to take the tiniest bit of what women put up with every damn day.

"News flash, Jake. I'm not afraid of anything." So not true. Almost everything frightened me. Especially losing Sully. That terrified me beyond all reason. But no way would I clue my opponent into that little fact.

"Look, I'll make it easy for you." Jake stepped out from behind the bushes and into a small clearing between the pines, fully in the open. "Take your shot."

He spread his arms out. Sunlight cut through the branches overhead and kissed his handsome face. He looked for all the world like a martyr, ready to be fed to the lions.

Could be a trick. He still held the Cack. Probably was a trick, unless...

Did Jake have a death wish? Could that be what this drama was about? Suicide by time cop? I glanced down at my weapon. It hugged my hand like a needy child. Could I fire it? A tree limb lay at my feet, red-hot and smoldering. My insides twittered. If I pressed *kill*, the pulse would do that to Jake. Cut into his flesh and burn him from the inside out. Even with Sully's life on the line, could I actually do that?

Something flashed by me. Sully. Running. *Toward* the enemy. Damn it. In the split second I'd been wrestling with my conscience, Sgt. Hero had decided to take matters into his own hands.

Jake's expression morphed to terror as Sully charged him like the NFL's star linebacker. The men butted heads with an audible thwack. Jake flew backward and smacked into a tree. His weapon shot out of his hand and thumped to the ground.

I raced over to grab it. Jake lunged for it too, scrabbling on his hands and knees through the dirt and pine needles. Sully beat us both. He snatched it up. His hand curled around the Cack almost innately, as if he fired up the flat screen for Sunday Night Football. He scrutinized the device for a second then hit the arming button. A piercing squeal echoed through the woods. He pointed the weapon at Jake.

I stilled, terrified. Was Sully going to shoot?

I'd never find out. A roar, a blue flash and a rush of

wind, and Glo popped onto the scene. Two enormous guards dressed head to toe in gray flanked her. Each held rifle-sized versions of the Cack.

"Ah, shit," Jake spat, and sagged back against the tree. Clearly disappointed no one would be killing him today.

"I'll take that, Sergeant." Glo peeled the weapon from Sully's hand. He gaped, stunned, offering little resistance. She slipped the Cack into a holster on her hip then eyed one of the guards. "Rick? Extinguish that."

She tipped her head toward the burning tree and Rick stomped over, ripped a cylinder off his utility belt and doused the fire. They came prepared, these future people.

"We always leave the past as we found it," Glo said to me when the fire sputtered out. She skimmed the pine tree debris and broken branches on the ground. "Or as close to it as we can." She stepped over to Jake and her voice turned harsh. "Time's up. You're done."

He scrambled up, brushing pine needles from his uniform. "Glo, please. I need more—"

She hit him with a glare that shut him up fast. A bitter cold look. I could practically see the icicles shooting from her eyes. She jerked her head again, toward Jake this time, and her burly men took him into custody.

"I'm sorry, Beryl. I tried," Jake said as the wind whipped up and the time portal opened. He kept his ferocious gaze on me as the blue light flared and he disappeared into the swirling vortex.

I let out a slow breath. What a weird coda to the weirdest of all weird experiences. I had no time to digest. Glo turned to me, all business.

"Time for you to go too, Beryl."

That was it? I was done? All those threats, all that noise about having to kill Jake, and now I could just leave? I lasered in on Sully, who stared dazedly at the spot where Jake and the burly men had vaporized. My heart ached. Tears poked my eyes again. How could I leave him?

"I don't want to go," I said.

"You've *got* to." The hard, unyielding note in Glo's voice gave me the creeps. "Two minutes. Say goodbye."

She stepped discreetly away. I went to Sully. We stood looking at each other a bit awkwardly.

"Now I know why you wouldn't tell me the truth," he said finally, in shock.

"I know, right? Who'd believe it?"

He swallowed, glanced at Glo then back at me. "You're really from the future?"

"Uh huh, but I'm not from their future. I'm from..." I stopped. Explaining that would be too complicated. We didn't have enough time. I plucked pine needles off his tie and his jacket. "It's a long story."

His eyes searched mine. "Beryl..." He opened his mouth then closed it. His eyes held mine. He looked stunned. "Beryl, I can't—"

I put my finger against his lips. "I know. Don't even try to figure it out. It'll make your head spin." I took his hands and held them tight. "Sully, I've got to leave. Got to go back to my own time."

He nodded. Seemed about to say something, then thought better of it. "She knows, doesn't she?" He jerked his chin at Glo. "You must know too. Is it over soon? Do we...do we win?"

I glanced at Glo, a hundred percent certain she'd been eavesdropping. She didn't yell, "No spoilers!" so I went for it.

"Yes, Sully, we win." I squeezed his hands. "It's not over for a couple more years. It's messy and horrible and the things that happen on both sides are unforgivable. Unbelievable. But yes, we win."

He nodded, and I nodded back, glad he hadn't asked for more. Glad he hadn't asked about himself or his men. Or Stretch.

"One minute," Glo called over her shoulder.

I released his hands and put my arms around him. "Sully, I got drafted, like you, into a mission I didn't want. To protect you from that jackass. But it turned into something else, so much more. I couldn't help it. What I feel now, what I feel for you is...it's so... I guess what I'm trying to say is..." My shoulders sagged. I couldn't do it. Even after everything, I couldn't say those three fatal words. "Please, *please*, stop smoking. Will you do that for me?"

He gave me a lopsided grin that melted me right down to my toes. "You know what, Beryl Blue? You're a real piece of work."

Then he crushed me against him and kissed me so hard and so deep, I couldn't breathe. I sunk into his embrace, sank into his lips, willing him to hold me and kiss me for a long, long time. For forever.

"Time's up," Glo said. She had to say it three or four

times and shove her shoulder in between us before we parted.

I stepped back, my eyes locked on Sully. Glo wielded her Kicker and tapped the screen.

"Tell the fellas I said goodbye, and...and Godspeed."

Sully nodded, though I wasn't sure he could hear me. The wind had whipped up something fierce.

The sucking pull of the blue vortex squeezed my belly. Sully's image began to blur. From the tornado kicking in or the tears in my eyes, I couldn't be sure. Glo punched the final command and the soul-shaking swirl of the temporal tornado swallowed us up.

The last thing I saw was Sully, lifting his hand in farewell, before he dissolved into a million pixels and became a part of history.

19

I sat in a small office, in front of a sleek desk made of some unknown material, plastic maybe. Glo's office, circa 2130. Stark, white-painted walls, no prints or photos. Not exactly a cozy place. The only window, a teeny rectangle high in the wall, looked out into a narrow hallway.

Nothing cozy about the way I felt, either. Like Sarah Connor in *Terminator*, alone in the police captain's office, in the ominous calm before Arnold's menacing cyborg fulfilled his *I'll be back* promise.

In short, something seemed really, really wrong.

I didn't have any solid evidence or reason to think this, just felt it. Oh, and the fact that the office door had been locked from the outside.

After Glo and I had landed—smoother trip this time —she hustled me away too fast to get more than a glimpse of the time tourism operation spread across a warehouse-sized room. She pushed me past a toga-clad woman stepping into a compartment that looked like a miniature car-wash bay, then through a set of swinging doors and into a recovery room of sorts. It had a comfy looking sofa, a giant platter of food, and a shower with a dozen fragrant soaps and haircare products, customized heat settings, and a selection of pulsating water jets, all at voice command.

I'd dried myself with a fluffy towel worthy of a ten-grand a night hotel and discovered my 1940s clothes were gone. In their place, a plain, butt-hugging jumpsuit the color of blah. Okay, my dress and those snazzy pumps were pretty beat up and smelled like a fireplace after my run through the woods and Jake's wild tree-shooting spree, but my heart sank like a stone to find them gone.

Stark reality closed in. My journey had ended, with Sully in the past, while I was here.

And *why* was I here and not back in my library shelving books? I wanted to ask Glo, but I hadn't seen her. I'd only seen one person, a skittish young guy wearing a jumpsuit as blah as mine. He'd brought me to Glo's office after I'd freshened up and looked surprised to discover she'd stepped out.

He'd told me to wait and toddled off, locking me in. After that, nothing. Dead silence, except the occasional ping of the HVAC system that kept the office at a comfy sixty-eight degrees. Was it any wonder I feared the *Terminator* would burst through the door at any second and blow me away?

I distracted myself with a recon of Glo's desk. There were devices and tech doodads of all shapes, sizes, and colors, like Glo had hit a closeout sale at the Apple store. But no Kicker. Probably kept those suckers locked up after Jake had stolen one and used it to chase after Sully.

Happily, I saw paper hadn't completely gone out of style—several manila folders were tossed haphazardly on the desktop. I flipped one open to see dozens of newspaper clippings, Cuban missile crisis, post-WWII efforts to reclaim Nazi-pilfered art, a plot to assassinate Queen Victoria and more. They were stickied all over with handwritten notes. I thumbed through each file, looking for anything about Sully or me, but came up empty.

I went back to the electronics, an array of whippet-thin screens and touchpads, wondering if non-techie me had the slightest chance of hacking into any of them, when I heard footsteps thump-thumping down the hall-way. I darted to the window. It was high up and even on tiptoe, all I could see were the feathers atop a Three Musketeers-style hat bounce by.

"Sir? A moment," a voice called from down the hall. I straightened. I recognized Glo's voice, sounding worried.

I grabbed my chair. It snicked softly over the tiled floor as I rolled it to a spot below the window. I wobbled wildly when I climbed up onto the seat but managed to stand upright. I pressed my cheek to the windowpane and looked left.

Offices with closed doors lined both sides of the long hallway. D'Artagnan stopped at the one office with its door open at the end of the corridor. He peered inside. I couldn't see his face under that hat, but I did see Glo. She moved into the doorway and her attention whipped between D'Artagnan and another person inside the office.

They were arguing. I couldn't make out the words, but I'd heard enough muffled "discussions" through my foster homes' thin walls to know when people were having a Disagreement, with a capital *D*. From her tone, Glo didn't like what the man in the hat had to say. Not at all.

I caught a snatch of her response. "...not enough time...can't expect instant compliance..."

"It's Time Scope's directive," D'Artagnan said.

Glo replied with an angry, fly-swatting motion, shutting him down. I would've shouted a vigorous *You go, girl*, if I had the vaguest notion what was going on.

The lurker inside the office must've said something, because Glo and D'Artagnan snapped in that direction. Must've been something awful, because Glo spat, "God, no!"

And that's when she noticed my face pressed to the window. Her gaze snagged mine and she scowled. She motioned D'Artagnan inside the office and slammed the door. I pulled back, cold to the bone. I had the sick feeling they had been talking about me. And not in a good way.

I'd worked myself into a terrified snit by the time Glo entered the office a few minutes later.

She plopped down behind her desk and looked at me. "Sorry to keep you waiting. Please, sit."

She indicated the chair I'd rolled back to the desk, but I refused to sit. Too antsy, anxious, and angry. "Glo, what's going on? What were you and that Musketeer talking about?"

"Musketeer? Oh, you mean Daquan."

"Yeah, Daquan. You were talking about me, weren't you?"

"Everything isn't about you, Beryl." She opened one of the files on the desk and studied the clipping inside. Or pretended to. "We have hundreds of time-tourists every month. There's bound to be a problem and I have to deal with every single one of them. Gives me a headache." She flipped the file closed and touched her temples with her fingertips.

I felt kind of bad. Not *completely* remorseful, because that *Terminator* vibe came back. "Sorry to hear that." I rested my palms on the desk and bent down to look her in the eye. "But listen, I *know* you were talking about me."

She returned my gaze steadily. "Yes, we were talking about you."

I stood up straight. Honesty? From Glo, or *anyone* associated with this insane mission? Shocking. "So, what were you guys saying?"

She let out a gusty, long-suffering sigh. "That you failed."

"Why? Jake didn't kill Sul—" I snapped my mouth shut. I couldn't say his name. Could barely think it without choking up.

She gestured again for me to sit and this time I did.

"Beryl, you managed to stop Jake from killing the sergeant, I'll concede that. Actually, from what I gather, Sullivan stopped him." She huffed, frustrated. "But you didn't do as instructed."

"You really want Jake dead, huh? Isn't that a little

harsh? I mean, the man's not quite right. You know what he did before Sully tackled him? Before you showed up? He just stood there, taunting me, practically begging me to shoot him. I'm glad I didn't."

Glo worked her jaw angrily, reminding me of Sully. They were as different as two people could be, but they had the same jaw line. Solid, determined, utterly unbreakable.

"Jake was on my team for six years. He is, or was, my top extractor." She leaned forward, as if to make sure I heard every word. "Let me tell you, he's anything but insane. If he provoked you, he had a reason. Maybe to get you out in the open, distract you while he got Sullivan in his sights. I don't know. I *do* know he's thorough and focused. He doesn't make mistakes." She sat back in her chair and let out another sigh. "Just so you know, I don't want Jake dead. *He* does. He wants you to do it."

"Who, the Musketeer? Dustin?"

"Daquan. Jake was supposed to die. But you didn't follow through. And as a result, Sullivan learned about the mission, about us, about the company. You violated about fifty Time Scope directives and created more headaches for me."

"Well, you have your man, and Sully's still alive." My voice hitched. "Or was alive. Or whatever."

Glo tipped her head, looking like a curious parrot. "You really fell for that guy. Why didn't you tell him that?"

I frowned. "I *knew* you were eavesdropping before we left."

She lifted a shoulder, sort of an apologetic shrug.

"The man's heart was breaking. He was about to lose the woman he'd fallen for and you didn't say a word about how you felt."

"I was leaving. We'll never see each other again. If I poured out how I felt, it would've hurt him more."

"Hurt *him* more?"

I stilled. "Okay, hurt me. Hurt *me*."

She snorted. "You remind me of those time trippers who can't face their problems, so they run away into the past. We call them runners. You couldn't face how you felt about Sullivan, so you ran from it. You ran away from the farmhouse, and you ran from the mission. You're a runner, and I hate to say it, a coward."

Well slap me again, why don't you? "And you're a poor judge of character. Asking someone like *me* to do this job. Plus, you're a sneak. Why didn't you warn me about Stretch? I mean Augie. About my grandmother, and everyone else. That was a knife in the heart I could've

lived without."

"That couldn't be helped." She leaned forward again, and I thought I saw regret flash across her face. "I'm sorry, truly. But don't you realize what a gift that was? You had the chance to be with loved ones long gone, get to know people you only heard about in stories. It's rare that Time Scope allows a time tourist to knowingly mingle with their ancestors. You were face to face with your own past, and what did you do?"

I hadn't thought of it that way, being so totally freaked out at the time. And what *did* I do? What I always did. "I ran away," I said, my belly hot with shame and grief. "I wish I could have... You know Augie's going to die, don't you?"

"Yes, I know."

Her voice had tightened with emotion, and so did mine. "Glo, couldn't you just, with all your resources... You know?"

"No. We can't change the past. That's the rule."

"I don't care about rules. Augie's death hit Grandma Blue hard. I can't imagine what it did to his parents. Can't you bend your stupid rules just once?"

She shook her head. "Don't you think I'd go back and help my own ancestors if I could? They got the shit beat out of them for centuries. Time Scope has a lot of rules, but that one is *the* rule. Nobody, not you, not me, not Jake, not even our CEO can break it. Nobody can mess with fate. The timeline *cannot* be changed." She gazed at me, her expression softening. "I think you know that, deep down."

"I *know* it, but I don't like it." I took a breath. I had to shelve it all, before it crushed me. The emotion, the resentment, the anger. I shoved it up on the top shelf, out of reach. For now. "So, when am I going home?"

She tidied the folders on her desk. She looked small, fragile, and exhausted.

"There's a *lot* of paperwork after a mission like yours. A debriefing, post-mortem, etcetera, and so forth. Another thing that gives me a headache." She drew a heavy breath, sounding like her old self again, brusque and in command. "But it's got to be done."

I nodded. Learning that bureaucracy would still be a major pain in the butt a hundred years in the future was almost reassuring. "And then you'll send me home after that, right?"

"Yes, after that. Tomorrow. You can stay in one of our recovery suites tonight, then up with the sun, fill out a few forms, and off to your library you go."

"You'd better drop me at home. I've been gone for days and I'm sure my cat is pissed he hasn't been fed for so long." Angry, and no doubt plotting devious ways he could get back at me for leaving him alone. A real charmer, that feline.

Glo pushed a button on her desk and stood. "Don't worry, you'll find no time has passed since you've been gone." She came over and touched my arm. "If we send you back, it will be to the exact point in time where we both met." The door opened and the nervous young man who'd escorted me earlier stepped into the office. "Jacques? Take Beryl to Suite 603."

Jacques led me into a rabbit warren of softly lit, white-painted hallways. I'd never be able to find my way back to Glo's office if I wanted to. We stopped at a nondescript white door that swooshed open at his command. I couldn't help but smile at the *Star Trek*-ness of it all.

Jacques left but returned a short time later with a calorie and nutrition-controlled meal of greens and protein. I dined in my spacious, climate-controlled room, while a voice-controlled selection of classical music wafted out of unseen speakers. Even the amount of water in the toilet was regulated. All very tidy and energy and resource efficient if a bit antiseptic. And boring, since I couldn't find a single thing to read while I ate.

After dinner, I peeked through the dark curtains

covering the picture window, wondering if I'd see flying cars or Morlocks dragging their knuckles along the street or some other science fiction trope come true. Nothing but muted streetlights and the night-shrouded silhouettes of moving vehicles and tall buildings. Disappointing, to say the least. It's not every day a girl gets to travel forward in time. I should at least get a peep at what the future looked like before I went home.

I peeled off my blah jumpsuit and slipped into a pair of men's-style silk pajamas that had been laid out on the bed. I dropped onto the leather sofa and rubbed my eyes with my palms. Something had been tickling the back of my mind since I'd left Glo's office, something she'd said that got the *Terminator* theme music humming in my head again. I searched for it, but exhaustion had set in, and my drained brain refused to work properly. I couldn't remember what she'd said if my life depended on it.

Shaking it off, I turned my attention to what I discovered was a voice-activated television screen on the wall.

"Next," I said repeatedly as the TV flipped through a bazillion channels. After a while, I realized I was looking for a World War II documentary, hoping against hope I'd catch a glimpse of Sully's face in the black and white archival footage.

"Off," I said with a sigh. It didn't matter what I saw on the TV, anyway. All I *could* see was Sully's face. All I could hear was the volcano rumble of his voice, the caressing way he said my name. I hugged myself. I could still feel the way he'd touched me last night. Last night, and nearly two centuries ago, when he'd held me in his arms.

What had happened to him? Did he make it through

the war? If so, what did he do afterward? Did he ever think of me?

"I need a drink," I said out loud.

"Specify type," said a computer voice, which sounded suspiciously like Sigourney Weaver.

"Booze," I said.

"That does not compute."

I let out a bitter laugh. How could booze not compute? "Alcohol. Whiskey, vodka, beer, anything you got."

There was the briefest pause. I suspected she was translating. "Alcohol is not available without a prescription. Compliance is mandatory. There are carbonated beverages, juice, and H2O in the refrigeration unit."

Seriously? No way to get pie-eyed drunk and hopefully forget Sully and Stretch and that dull ache of loss in my heart?

I sighed. "Computer, you're a real piece of work."

"That does not compute."

A soft tap sounded on the door and the lights came up. "Jacques Comptois is at the door," the computer said.

Jacques jumped like a frightened rabbit when the door slid open. He held out a thin envelope. "Captain Reid asked me to bring you this. She thought you might like it."

The door whooshed shut. I slid the contents of the envelope out as I headed for the bed. A photograph. Not just *a* photograph, *the* photograph. I warmed up to Glo a smidge. The photo had been in my handbag, dropped and forgotten in the woods during the fight with Jake. Glo must've sent someone back for it.

I stared at the picture as I crawled into bed. Stared at Sully. Tears threatened. Two days. I'd only known him two days, less than forty-eight hours and yet I'd fallen in love with him. And I'd never told him.

Glo had called me a coward—and she was right.

20

I jerked awake at the sound of someone pounding on the door. The lights popped on and I squinted at a figure moving swiftly into the room.

"Captain Reid is at the door," the computer politely announced.

A little late, since Glo hovered over my bed. She held a khaki duffel bag in one hand, a scuffed pair of boots with laces dangling in the other. She dropped everything, grabbed a fistful of synthetic down comforter, and yanked it off me.

"Get up. He escaped."

I sat up. "What? Who?"

"Who do you think? *Jake*. He time-skipped again. He's gone to finish the job."

My heart slammed into my ribs. "Sully? Jake's gone back to kill him?" I scrambled out of bed and did a frantic search for some clothes. "How did he get away? How did he get the tech to jump through time?"

"We're trying to figure it out. Looks like he cold-cocked poor Jacques when he brought him a toothbrush." She sounded as pissed as she had every right to be. "Hurry and put these on."

She snatched up the duffel bag and threw it to me. I nearly toppled catching it. The thing weighed a ton.

"Why does Jake want to kill Sully so bad? You must've gotten *something* out of him by now." I yanked a bundle of clothing from the bag and dumped them on the bed. A World War II-era American GI's uniform jacket and trousers, a heavy, olive-drab wool coat, wool socks and mittens, a thick, knitted scarf, and a greenish wool union suit— woolen underwear, or long johns, as Grandma Blue had called them.

"We're closer to the truth," Glo said. "Signs are pointing to something Sullivan does after this day, the day Jake went to. That's what Jake wants to stop. Get dressed. There's not much time."

I stripped off my silky pajamas and scrambled into my unmentionables. I picked up the union suit. It felt scratchy as hell and looked twice as uncomfortable as the girdle Glo had forced on me. I flung it back on the bed and yanked on the trousers instead.

"You might regret not wearing that," Glo said. "It's cold where you're going."

"And where's that?" I stabbed my arm into the uniform shirt's sleeve then buttoned it with shaking fingers. "*When's* that?"

"Belgium. December sixteenth, 1944."

"December sixteenth? That's..." I let the rest hang, though it screamed in my head. The day the Battle of the

Bulge had begun. Two days before great-uncle Augie was killed.

"Your Sergeant Sullivan is about to be involved in that little skirmish."

"Skirmish? You're misremembering your history, Glo. The Bulge was a big, bloody battle."

"They're all bloody," she said flatly, and I wondered how many wars she'd seen. As a tourist, as a time cop, as a person who could only watch the carnage around her, unable to change history. Unable to break the rules. Frustrating times ten. Probably why she wanted so badly to stop Jake. That was something she could control.

Didn't explain why *I* had to be dragged into it but dragged into I'd been. I finished dressing, laced up the oversized boots, wound the scarf around my neck, and put on the coat.

I faced Glo, blinking the last vestige of sleep out of my eyes. "I'm ready."

More than ready. Three little words had shifted me into overdrive. Not *those* three words, though they were a big part of my motivation. Three other words—*Sully in danger*—had ratcheted up my heartbeat to marathon level. Made me desperate to jump back in time once more. I had to go back. I had to save him.

Glo led me back to the warehouse where I'd arrived earlier, a place she called the skip room. My boots clopped across the concrete floor, past dozens of those little car wash bay time machines lined up in three rows from one end of the cavernous room to the other. Glo steered me toward one on the end and tapped a million commands on her Kicker. The contraption's doors opened like a gaping mouth. I stepped inside. Barely big enough to fit a Mini Cooper, the interior smelled like a Mini Cooper, too, oily, with a whiff of new car smell.

Jacques ran up, out of breath and with a bump on his head the size of a melon. He handed me a Cack and a steel battle helmet. A steel pot, soldiers had called these things, though I wasn't sure which generation of GIs had given that nickname to the all-purpose helmet used to wash their socks, cook soup, and save their lives.

Glo snatched the Cack from me and inspected it before handing it back. "You remember how to use it, don't you?"

I dropped the weapon into my coat pocket. "Yeah, I read *Cack for Dummies*." A bad time for jokes, I knew, but she didn't even crack a ghost of a smile. Girl really needed to lighten up. "Wait, Glo, why can't you go get him? You know where he is and everything."

"To be honest, they won't let me. Look, Beryl, do the job, complete the mission, and then I'll tell you everything, I promise. Everything."

She slapped a button on the side of the machine, setting off all kinds of clanking, like Marley's ghost dragging his chains up Scrooge's front stairs.

"Don't waste time looking for Jake," she said. "Find the sergeant before he does. Protect Sullivan at all costs. We've pinpointed his location in a community meeting house at the center of the village. We'll land you close by." She paused a fraction and her face clouded over. "You know what to do if you see Jake."

My stomach flip-flopped uncontrollably, but I

managed a terse nod. I knew what to do. I had to finish the job. This time I had to kill Jake.

"And remember, Beryl, you can't tell anyone about the future. Not Sullivan, not your uncle. Not a word, no matter how much you want to."

I had a few choice words in response to that, but before I could let them rip, the door wings flapped shut, closing me in. I instantly discovered a new phobia. Claustrophobia. The sucking sound of a vacuum seal being set in place didn't help matters any. A creamy glow spread from somewhere—no light fixture that I could see—brightening the little room and revealing a cushioned door, walls, and ceiling.

Time machine, or padded cell? Definitely the latter. Anyone would have to be loopy to willingly walk into this coffin.

What happened next confirmed that thought. I braced for the wind and the blue tornado, but all I heard was a click, followed by more clanking. The light winked out. My body seized, as if someone applied defibrillator paddles directly to my forehead and cranked them to eleven. A thousand points of light swarmed around me. Inside me. An intense shaking scrambled my atoms, like a milkshake being savagely whipped, and everything went dark.

Seconds later, the vortex puked me out like a hairball, face first into the dirt. Or, rather, cobblestones. Damp, frigid cobblestones.

I jumped up, weapon at the ready. I didn't know what I expected. Jake standing there, his Cack trained on me? Maybe the German Army. I wanted it to be Sully. But the only things to greet me were an alley's cold stone walls and a skinny tabby cat Jenjen could take with one paw tied behind his back. I put my finger to my lips, as if a meow from this pathetic thing could carry more than two feet and alert the world to my presence.

I moved down the alley and stepped out into the village square. It looked like something out of a calendar, twelve quaint European scenes, one for each month. The setting sun peeked out from behind the spires of a stone church across the way. Bundled up pedestrians and a few GIs hurried along the sidewalk past gingerbread-style houses and shops. A distant airplane cut across the western sky and sparse traffic rumbled past—a farm truck, a car that had seen better days, and a couple of jeeps whose headlights swept along the shiny cobblestones.

I could've been in a smaller version of Ballard Springs circa World War II, except for the pall that hung over the place, as if the entire village held their breath, waiting for the other shoe to drop. That, and the smell. Didn't need to hear the chickens clucking or the cows gently mooing to know a lot of both were nearby.

I spotted what looked like a Belgian-style community center a few blocks away. I walked toward it as briskly as I could, hoping no one would bother me. In my helmet and baggy coat, I figured I could keep my identity as a woman secret from a distance, but up close and personal there'd be no doubt. I steered clear of other pedestrians and when more vehicles drove by, I ducked my head to hide my face.

I reached an intersection where several roads

converged around a patch of grass. I waited as another jeep roared by then, my heart thumping, I hurried across the street to my destination, a long, two-story stone building with arched windows and a pitched roof, a cross between a church and a castle.

I thought I'd been scared when Glo had abandoned me in Ballard Springs in 1943. Now I knew real fear. A bitter, deadly battle was about to break out nearby. I had to protect Sully at all costs. I had to kill a man. I was truly terrified. And truly cold. My nose had frozen, and my limbs were numb. I totally regretted not taking Glo's advice and wearing that woolen underwear.

I climbed stone steps worn smooth over centuries of use behind two scruffy-looking GIs. One of them tossed his cigarette over the stone banister. They both stamped mud-caked boots, then hustled into the building. I slipped my weapon into my coat pocket and followed them inside, passing through a dim foyer and into a spacious hall.

Heat radiated from a blaze crackling in a fireplace large enough to drive a minivan into. Even more heat wafted from all the men in the room. Dozens of them. Warming their hands by the fire and chatting or sitting on benches lined up in uneven rows. Reading, playing cards, scraping what looked like dog food out of tin bowls with tiny metal forks. Some men curled up on the floor, asleep, no doubt dreaming of home. Still more men leaned against the wall, listening to an old man in a beret play an accordion. His whiskered chin rested against his instrument, his eyes closed as if in prayer.

Most, almost all, had removed their jackets and rolled

up their sleeves. A few had peeled down to undershirts. That explained the male stink that permeated the air, nearly drowning the smells of the wood fire, burning wax from the candles in the brass chandeliers suspended from the high ceiling, and the smoke from a thousand cigarettes.

Staying in the shadows as much as I could, I circled the room, searching. I unwound my scarf and pulled off my mittens, shoving both into my coat pocket, but kept my helmet firmly in place. I hoped to delay being recognized as a woman as long as possible.

A white square of canvas had been stretched over one wall. A movie projector rested nearby on a wooden stand. A GI in a filthy shirt threaded film into the projector's take-up reel and turned a switch. The film went *ticka-ticka* through the gate, tinny music swelled, and *Top Hat*, with Fred Astaire and Ginger Rogers, flickered onto the makeshift movie screen.

A groan rippled across the room.

"Fucking Fred Astaire," grumbled a guy with his fist wrapped around a bottle. He drooped on the bench as if it took too much energy to sit up straight.

I hurried by him, scanning the crowd.

"I'm tellin' ya, television's gonna take off when the war's over. Put Hollywood out of business," said a soldier with bandages on both hands as I passed. The raucous singing of the group behind him nearly drowned him out. "Alouette," in English, with lyrics that would make a sailor blush.

"I'll toss in this bottle of cognac," I heard, swinging by a noisy group circled around a card game in the back.

"Cognac? I'm sick of that swill. I want good old American whiskey. You got any of that, Sanchez?"

I froze. I knew that voice. Marco. He squatted on the floor in his undershirt, his dog tags dangling over a big pile of money. Stretch sat on a bench nearby, writing a letter. My heart squeezed. Was he writing to Grandma Blue?

I flicked through the grubby faces, looking for Stan and Griff, when...

I saw him. A tall, redheaded man with his shirtsleeves rolled up, leaning against the wall. He watched the card game with mild interest. As if he sensed me there, he turned his head. Our gazes caught. My breath stopped. My heart did not. It pounded, soared, danced, leapt, all of those romantic gymnastics you read about in a novel.

Sully.

He blinked at me in disbelief for what seemed like an hour. I stared back. He looked older. Way older. It had only been, what, ten or twelve hours since I'd seen him? It'd been more than a year for him, but he looked as if ten years had passed. Ten rough years. His shoulders drooped, his shirt and trousers were rumpled, his boots muddy and scuffed, and deep lines etched his drawn face.

"Beryl?"

He pushed off the wall and moved toward me, slowly, as if I'd vanish if he moved too fast. He closed in. Touched my face tentatively, his hands rough and beaten. His fingers lightly trailed along my jaw.

"Goddamn," he breathed.

He took off my helmet, as gently as lifting a fragile egg, and dropped it to the floor with a dull *clank*. My hair cascaded down over my shoulders. He buried his hands in the tangled waves and searched my face.

"God. *Damn.*"

I smiled. "It's me, Sully—"

He shut me up with a kiss. *The* most exquisite kiss. It started slow, as if he'd forgotten how. Then his lips fully claimed mine. One hand cupped my head, the other slid around my waist and pressed against my lower back, bringing me against him, fitting me into place. My arms snaked around him, my pulse throbbing, burning with need. For him. We clung together, bonding, tasting, discovering one another anew, lost in our bliss for a long, long time.

We parted to cheers and hoots from the men who'd gathered around.

Sully scowled. Oh, how I loved that scowl. "Beryl, what in hell are you doing here?"

No chance to answer. Augie elbowed over. His thin, gloomy face broke into a sunny, if mystified, smile. Tears stung my eyes. I willed myself not to cry.

"Miss Blue." He held out his hand, but I knocked it aside and drew him into a hug, holding on so tight I probably bruised a couple of his ribs. Another hooting chorus.

"Give me some of that," Marco said, when I finally let Stretch go. He enveloped me in a hug and a liberal amount of body odor. He would've held on for the duration if Sully hadn't pried me loose.

"That's enough, Corporal." Sully's arm settled across my shoulders possessively.

"Aw, Sarge. I ain't had a real American dolly in my arms since we got here." He winked at me.

"Kiss her again!" someone shouted. The rest of the men took up the chant. *Kiss her again* bounced around the room, drowning out Fred and Ginger on the movie screen.

"Christ. Let's get out of here," Sully said. "I'm not giving a peep show to the whole First Infantry."

While I thought it best to scoot before a riot broke out, I preferred to remain here, with this big crowd for protection when Jake showed up. Because I knew he would show. But I didn't argue as Sully took my hand and hustled me out the back and into a roomy kitchen with a cast iron stove and huge pots hanging from hooks.

He stopped at the door to the outside and glanced toward a passageway across the kitchen. He tossed me a wicked grin.

"Come on." He took my hand and steered me toward the opening and a stone stairwell that curved downward into the shadows.

The lowering sun cut through the cellar's small windows, glimmering over chairs and music stands and other doodads littered across the stone floor. Colder than the Arctic, too, but it didn't stop us. We joined together in a scorching kiss the moment we reached the bottom step. No words, no questions, no sputtering explanations.

We tore at each other's clothing like two kids on Christmas morning, opening our gifts with frantic delight. He tugged off my overcoat and whisked my baggy shirt over my head. I plucked at the buttons on his trousers. He shoved a stack of chairs aside with his hip and spread my coat on the floor. Half-naked, we embraced, kissing again, and he lowered me down. A brief pause for the condom to make an appearance, and we were ready. I arched eagerly to meet him as his body covered mine and he entered me with a swift thrust that made me gasp with pleasure.

While Fred and Ginger tap danced above us, while soldiers argued and sang bawdy songs, and Marco gambled his way to a tidy fortune, we joined together as one.

Two people separated by time and war, grabbing a sweet moment of joy in the darkness.

WE STILL HAD our boots on. That made me giggle, and after he figured it out, Sully laughed too.

"Guess we were in a hurry," he said, tightening his arms around me.

I sighed, feeling warm and strangely at peace in this gloomy place, the farthest thing from peace. It wouldn't last. Real life would intrude. I already felt the cold again. We'd wrapped ourselves as best we could in my overcoat, but the furnace level heat of sex had begun to cool down.

"Your hair's so soft." He loosened his hold on me and ran a hand through my tangled waves. Then he touched the bruise on my cheek where Jake had smacked me with the Cack yesterday at the park. "Hasn't been long for you since you saw me, has it? Not as long as for me." He frowned, looking mystified. "I still don't get it. I know you tried to explain before you left, back then. Guess I'm thick. Even after seeing you disappear before my eyes, I only half-believed what you said. Tried to convince myself I was drunk or dreaming. The only thing real to me was you. Then, and now."

He shifted and leaned in to kiss me, this time soft and slow. He pulled back and sighed.

"You smell so nice, Beryl. Clean. I haven't smelled clean in a while. Haven't *been* clean."

"It's been bad, hasn't it?" I felt like a jerk asking that question. I *knew* it had been bad. And it would get even worse in the coming days. I was helpless to change that.

Sully grunted. "There's a reason we call First Infantry the big, dead one."

Words as sharp and quick as a knife to the heart. "Your men?"

I felt him brace. "We lost a lot. Too many. Stan got separated from us, sent to a repple depple for reassignment. God knows where he ended up. Griff lost a leg in September, went home to his sweetheart, lucky bastard. The others are still standing. Barely." He played with my hair again. It tickled against my shoulder. "It's been hurry up and wait, hurry up and wait, then boom, kablooey. Like the horror house at the carnival. Then we go back to hurry up and wait."

Anger fused with the bitter humor in his voice.

"We're bivouacked not far from here, waiting for orders to move out. You know, we've seen that damned Rogers and Astaire movie a dozen times. I swear, after the war, if I even *hear* a tap shoe, I'll force that hoofer to eat the whole thing."

I smiled and touched the dimple in his chin, all but buried under his soft, copper-shaded beard.

"Do you ever think about running away, Sully? Just taking off and hiding in a barn somewhere until, uh, around..." I searched my mental encyclopedia and came up with the day the war in Europe ended, the eighth of May 1945. But did I dare share that with him? Could that simple spoiler somehow cause a ripple that could change the whole timeline? I decided not to risk it. "Eh, sometime next spring?"

He shot me a dour look, like Grandma Blue when she went all stern on me. Like, how could I even think such a thing? Too polite to actually say it, he settled for, "The men need me, Beryl."

Of course, the men. I felt stupid again. He'd never leave them, never let them down.

Silence for a few moments. I ran my palm over his undershirt, feeling his hard chest and his heartbeat, no longer racing, now slow and steady. I stroked his upper arm, muscled, strong, and reliable. That's when I noticed the tattoo. I sat up and squinted to see clearer in the dying light. I traced the tattoo's outline of an impossibly curvaceous woman with flowing dark hair, winking pertly. Written on a ribbon that swirled around her legs were the words, *A real piece of work*.

"Nice tattoo." Was that busty babe supposed to be me? Wasn't sure whether to be flattered or insulted.

Sully reached over and dug something out of his shirt pocket. I tensed, thinking he reached for a cigarette and prepped for a lecture when he took out the photograph and showed it to me. The one of us at Jonesy's. Spider web cracks crisscrossed the picture's surface, and the edges were frayed, but I could still see the image clearly. He gazed at the photo fondly then flexed his bicep, making the tattoo babe do a hula.

"It's not a bad likeness," he said, eyeing me with a wicked grin.

I bent to kiss his cheek. "You *did* miss me, didn't you?"

"Damn right I did." He shoved the photo back into his pocket. "I thought I'd never see you again."

There, as simple as that. That broke my heart. But also snapped Jake back into my brain. The reason I'd been sent back to this moment. Sully tried to pull me down against him again, but I strong-armed him, hand on that steely chest.

"You weren't supposed to see me again," I said. "You know why I'm here."

He sat up with a put-upon sigh. "I doubt they dumped you here for a wall banger with me, nice as it was." His dogtags jingled as he grabbed his shirt off the floor and pushed his arms into the sleeves. "Who are you after? Too much to hope it's Hitler, so you can end this shit now."

I shook my head slowly. Sadly. "I wish, Sully. With all my heart. But it doesn't work that way. I know it's unfair, and I don't have the time to explain. The rules are firm. You can't change the past." For Stretch, for Sully, for anyone. Case closed. I felt hollow.

He growled in frustration but nodded. "It's that blue-eyed bastard again, isn't it?"

I started to dress. "Yeah. He escaped and he's back to get you."

"Escaped? How did he do that?"

I'd asked Glo the same question and hadn't gotten an even remotely satisfying answer. "Don't know. This time, I *have* to kill him."

"Isn't there enough killing to go around?" He stood and began the complicated process of fastening his trousers. "You future people are a hard race, Beryl, to dump so much on a girl. Why don't you let *me* kill him? One more is not gonna matter much."

Harsh, and the way he'd said that—as dead as the grave. "No, Sully. You've gone above and beyond. All of you have. I've got to stop him, or I can't go home. You see—"

He held up his hand. A change in tone in the hall above had alerted his soldier's ear. I noticed it too, after a moment. A stillness suddenly broken by muffled voices, hiked in alarm. Then movement and the sound of boots pounding toward the exits.

Sully scowled. "A fire?"

A boulder fell into my stomach. Not a fire. The word had gone out. The German offensive had begun. Church bells began to peal, a long, sad gong at first, then more rapid. Calling the men to arms.

"I've got to go." He kissed me. Fast, hard, devastating, like a lightning strike. And then he bolted, his footsteps pounding up the stairs.

"Sully, wait." I grabbed my coat and put it on as I chased after him.

The kitchen door had been flung wide, and so had the double doors into the main hall. I turned that way and stopped on the threshold, noticing they'd forgotten to turn off the projector. Fred and Ginger serenaded an empty room.

An empty room, except for two men.

I went numb. Jake held a pistol, pointed at Sully's chest.

21

Sully's hands were raised in surrender. The film flickered behind him. I dug the Cack from my coat pocket and stepped into the room.

"No, Beryl," Sully said in a strangled voice. His gaze snapped from me to Jake and back again. "His beef is with me. You run. Just run."

I shook my head. This had to end now. I palmed my weapon, felt it grip my hand. Sully crouched to attack, but Jake moved fast. He snatched a Cack from a holster with his free hand and aimed it at me. It whined, powering up.

"Make a move and she dies," he warned.

Sully and I exchanged glances. Jake stood maybe twenty feet away, arms at ninety degree angles, a deadly weapon trained on each of us. I felt as if I'd stepped into a Clint Eastwood movie with Jake as the killer punk with a gun. Did he feel lucky? Able to shoot both Sully and me before we could rush him? Were we foolish enough to test him?

Then Jake upped the stakes. He cocked the pistol's hammer.

Well, two could play at that game. I armed the Cack. Jake grinned at the sound of it booting up. I pointed the weapon at his heart.

"You won't do it," he said. "You can't. Last time, I gave you a target and you couldn't fire. You're a coward. Always have been."

Seemed like an awful lot of people had been calling me a coward lately. A trigger word that churned up every self-loathing thought I'd ever had. The negative waves I bathed myself in during the dark times. Sometimes even in the good times. Because the good times never lasted.

"You're a coward who runs away, Beryl. A coward nobody ever wanted. Except for him." Jake jerked his chin at Sully. "How will it feel to watch him die?"

Bang! I jumped. Jake's arm recoiled as the pistol exploded. The blast swallowed the peal of church bells and my shriek. A hole pinged the floorboards between Sully's feet. Big Red didn't even flinch.

"Next time, Beryl, straight to his heart." Jake cocked the hammer again.

There wasn't going to be a next time—I jammed the kill button and fired.

The Cack shuddered and turned bitter cold, but burned my skin, like dry ice. The surge of power electrified every hair on my body, making it stand on end. A pop and a hiss as the laser blasted its target. Jake howled and jerked back. Sparks shot from a hole the size of a silver dollar scorched into his uniform. His body twitched and seized. His eyes rolled back in his head. His limbs went as stiff as petrified wood. His weapons crashed to the floor.

And so did Jake.

———

AFTER THAT, everything flashed by in a blur.

Sully flew to my side. He pried the Cack from my hand, murmuring comforting words. A stiff wind and a burst of blue light and Glo appeared. She said something I barely heard and didn't care to hear. I watched dumbly as Glo's burly men bundled Jake's body in a bag and vanished. Bile rose in my throat.

I'd killed a man. Me, Beryl Blue, wannabe librarian. A murderer.

I trembled all over. My knees buckled, but Sully caught me. He found a bench and pulled me onto his lap. And then I cried. Call me weak, call me whatever, but I couldn't hold it back. Sully's strong arms cradled me as I sobbed and sobbed.

"It's okay," he said, again and again. Rocking me, consoling me. It took a long time for my tears to subside.

Glo approached, hands clasped behind her back, chewing her lip. "You did good, Beryl," she ventured.

Sully snorted and I glared at her. "No, I didn't."

"You did. He would've destroyed..." She narrowed her eyes at Sully, as if trying to decide how much to reveal. "A *lot* of things if he'd been able to finish the job. You stopped him."

"He wanted you to kill him," Sully said softly. "I've seen fellas like him. They stick their head up from a foxhole or draw fire with a lit cigarette. Like they think their number's up and want to make sure of it." He slipped his thumb under my chin and tipped my head up, his eyes boring into mine. "Beryl, that guy went around the bend a long time ago."

He was right. I glowered at Glo. It didn't matter what she'd claimed about Jake, the man had completely lost touch with reality. "I hope you and your precious Time Scope are happy."

Glo lifted a shoulder. "The timeline is secure. That's all that matters."

Sully eyebrowed her and she had the grace to look remorseful. The timeline had been secured. It didn't matter *how* it had been secured. Not at all. Making me do the unthinkable had just been collateral damage.

Sully brushed tears from my cheeks with a grubby thumb. "I won't say don't let it get to you because there's no way it won't. No damn way it won't."

The sounds of shouting and vehicles moving outside penetrated our grim bubble. Sully swiveled toward the door. "I'll stay here with you, if you want." He sounded agonized. "You need me."

I slid off his lap, teetering a bit on rubbery legs, but remained upright. "You've *got* to go, Sully. You're what this was all about. If Jake had killed you, then the future would've been upset and..." I faltered. There was an empty well where the rest of that thought should've been. My brain had stopped working. "Glo, you tell him."

She shot me a *seriously?* look, but I supposed she was still in remorse mode, because she sucked in a breath and let it all out. Or some of it, at least.

"You're going into a big battle, Sergeant. It's going to be bad. But you're going to help a lot of men through it. One man in particular. You save his life. That man's important to the future. Very important. If Jake had eliminated you, the ripple of that single act would have inextricably changed *everything*."

I took Sully's hands and gazed down at him on the bench. "Remember when you told me your men need you? You had no idea how right you were. I mean, how right you are. The future depends on *you*."

He looked a little stunned. I guess I would be too, having the fate of the world dumped on my shoulders like that.

"Mind telling me which of my men is the lucky fella?" he asked.

Glo didn't get a chance to answer—if she even would —because the front doors banged open, and several soldiers rushed in.

"Sarge, where in hell you been?" Marco cried. "We been looking for you. MPs are rounding up all the fellas. Hitler's boys broke through the line, and they need the Fighting First to clean up the mess. We got a jeep out front—"

He broke off, eyeing Glo, resplendent in her corporate issue blah-colored jumpsuit, a Kicker gripped in her hand. His expression of disbelief would've been comical if I felt like laughing. I doubted I'd ever laugh again.

The bench creaked as Sully stood. He towered over Marco, over Glo. Over me. My heart swelled. It wasn't just his height and broad-shouldered build, it was *him*. Sully, a man among men. A hero.

"Marco, get our gear," he said. "I'm on my way."

I found my helmet and picked it up. Sully gathered up his uniform jacket and overcoat from a bench. Glo and I rushed after him down the steps. The peal of the bells sounded louder, more urgent out here. Exhaust and gas fumes filled the frigid air. It also smelled as if snow was on the way.

I could barely keep up with the activity outside. The sleepy town had awakened. Soldiers piled into jeeps, trucks, even pony carts, all rolling east. Other vehicles went west, filled with civilians. A hay wagon jammed with people lumbered by. Children leaned over the edge and waved, calling for the GIs racing by to throw them chocolate. A man in the wagon clutched a mantle-top clock in his arms. A woman wearing a fox fur calmly gazed at her reflection in her compact mirror and straightened her hat.

The villagers, escaping. Or at least I hoped they would. Real people, real suffering. Glo's words to me earlier rang starkly in my mind. All wars were bloody. All wars sucked. From ancient times when men had hurled spears at each other, to dropping drones on an anonymous target today. War. Totally. Sucked.

As did knowing the future.

I watched Augie strap on his helmet. He grabbed a duffel bag and tossed it into a battle-scarred jeep splattered with mud, one tire nearly flat. I wanted desperately to warn him, to tell him to take care. Glo eyed me with a *don't do it* expression on her face. I gritted my teeth and nodded with great reluctance. It broke my heart, but I wouldn't breathe a word.

I shelved my pain and frustration and gave Augie a teary-eyed, stiff-upper-lip smile as he waved and climbed into the jeep. Marco followed, along with about a half dozen other guys.

Glo elbowed me and pointed to Marco.

"Seriously?" I said. "Marco? He's the one who influences all of history?"

She shook her head. "Ripples, Beryl. Corporal Santelli eventually procreates. He's the great-grandfather of a future president."

So, Marco the operator would spawn a politician. Why didn't that surprise me?

Sully finished barking out orders then swiveled toward us. "You'd better get out of here." He adjusted the rifle strap over his shoulder. "This is no place for a dame."

"No place for anyone, Sully. Here." I pulled my mittens out of my pocket and pushed them into his hands. I did the same with my scarf. "It's going to get colder. And supplies are going to be awful thin." I gave him my helmet then shed my overcoat and handed it over. "Take these too."

"Cripes, do I look like the corner laundry?" He grinned, sort of like his old self and my heart lightened. A smidge.

"Hey, Sarge! Get the lead out," Marco called from the jeep. He sat behind the wheel, gesturing for Big Red to get in.

Sully gazed at me, probably unaware that he cradled my overcoat in his arms like a baby. His expression darkened, going grimmer than grim. "You gonna be okay, Beryl?"

No. Never again would I be okay. "I'll manage, Sully. What about you?"

Marco revved the engine. Sully shot him a loathing look as he tossed the coat and everything else into the jeep. Well, onto someone in the jeep, since men filled every square inch.

He turned back to me. "I've got to go, sweetheart."

I stepped closer and Glo moved a few paces away, giving us some space. Sully took my hands. He brought them to his lips and kissed each of my fingers. His lips were soft and warm on my rapidly chilling skin.

"I don't want to say goodbye. I don't want to leave you," I said, whimpering like a child. I couldn't help it.

He patted his breast, where I knew the photograph was nestled in his shirt pocket. Next to his heart. "You won't leave me. You won't ever leave me. You'll be with me, always. Beryl. My Beryl." He kissed me, soft, sweet, short. Too short. "Thank you. I never thought I'd let myself love any girl. You woke me up."

I stroked his cheek. The corners of his eyes crinkled as he smiled. A smile like the sun breaking out after a bad storm. Every moment, everything I felt for him surged in my heart. I felt it, and I knew with certainty I had the courage to finally say it.

"I love you, Sully." And I could never see him again.

He crooked a finger under my chin. "You're a real piece of work, Beryl Blue."

I watched him climb into the jeep and it roared away. I waved, but he didn't look back.

"You told him how you feel." Glo took out her Kicker and powered it up. "I'm proud of you."

"You have a bad habit of eavesdropping."

"At least I heard something interesting this time." She tapped several keys, and a shroud of blue light began to wrap around us.

I stared after the jeep. It joined a mass of other vehicles clogging the road, rolling past soldiers on foot. "Tell me it was worth it, Glo. Jake...and everything. Tell me Sully lives. Tell me he makes it through the war." I couldn't help the pained catch in my voice.

"Yes, Beryl, he lives. He makes it," she said, her voice as gentle as a mother comforting her child.

I let out my breath and closed my eyes.

22

I lost my balance when I came in for the landing. I banged onto hands and knees, my palms scraping tile. My stomach heaved and I felt as if I was going to throw up. The blue light winked out and I cursed. Time Scope *really* had to work on reentry.

I stood, blinking rapidly as I took in my surroundings. We were in the library. Upstairs, on the mezzanine. Early in the day. I could tell by the sunlight streaming through the fanlight window over the entrance.

But when? What date?

My boots thumped the floor as I hurried to the bridge between the mezzanine and the reading room. The map table that had been there in 1943 was gone. I gripped the brass railing and looked down to the first floor. The audiobooks and DVDs were right where they ought to be, next to the teeny-tiny print newspapers and periodicals section. The imposing RFID exit sensors, theft protection a librarian of old could only dream of, stood between the checkout counter and the front door.

I darted to the other side of the bridge. Below, I spotted gray-haired Ida Pellerin asleep on a spongy red sofa in the children's section, hands folded in her lap. A muffled "Shazbot!" burst from the office in the back, the library director's go-to curse whenever his *World of Warcraft* game went sour.

I turned to Glo with a grin. "You did it. You brought me home."

She shushed me with the skill of a veteran librarian and led me the rest of the way down the bridge to the reading room. My boots left bits of Belgian dirt on the tile along the way.

"What time is it?" I asked in a whisper.

"An hour before we met," she whispered back. "You just went upstairs to the attic level."

That gave me a creepy feeling. A pins and needles feeling. There were two of me in this building? "What do I do? Wait an hour until I leave, then just go up there like nothing happened?"

"Not exactly." We stopped outside the reading room door. "What happens next depends on the answer you give me."

"Answer to what?" I tried not to sound testy, but really, I'd had it with Glo's cryptic comments and riddles.

"I want you to come work for me. Permanently."

What? "You want me to work for you? For good? I thought this mission was a one and done. Unless you mean you want me to shelve books. Do books even exist in your time? Paper books, I mean."

"If you'll keep quiet a minute, I'll tell you what I want."

She turned the doorknob. The heavy oak door swung

inward, and I followed her into the stuffy room. Oh, the trusting lamb, happily going to the slaughter.

The blinds were drawn, so she flipped the light switch. Rows of floor-to-ceiling bookshelves stuffed with thick old tomes and dusty almanacs filled most of the room, and at the center, a scuffed-up old mahogany conference table where our monthly book clubs met.

"Here's the thing," Glo said, closing the door. "I want you to work for me for selfish reasons. You'll be able to time skip in a way no other time cop can. Someone whose DNA hasn't been coded can be quite useful. You can work, I think in your time you call it under the radar? This mission has been a rough go, but you've proved yourself capable."

My head spun. "Wait, you're offering me a job in the future? You want me to be a *mercenary*?"

She pursed her lips in distaste. "For lack of a better word, yes."

"Why didn't you just come out and ask me?"

"I couldn't, until you passed the test."

I fumed, beyond annoyed. "Test?"

She nodded, grimmer than grim. "You had to prove yourself—"

"By killing *me*."

I screamed. Library rules be damned. I let out a shriek that shook the rafters as Jake Tyson sauntered out of the stacks.

I BLINKED. Several times. But Jake didn't go away. He still wore his uniform, and in the shadows of the bookshelves, he looked like the ghost of GI Joe. Pins and needles poked my brain again, and I thought for sure I'd faint.

I fell into the nearest chair. An old wooden thing, it creaked like a haunted house. "You're not dead," I managed finally. Oh-so-intelligently.

He dimpled. "No, Beryl, I'm not dead."

Dead man walking. *And* talking. "B-but how?"

"Your weapon was never programmed to kill, just stun." He put a hand to his chest, over the singed hole in his jacket. "Believe me, that was enough of a kick. Burns like hell."

I shook my head, disoriented. I couldn't deal with this. Not with him, not with any of it.

"The mission was a test," he said. "You had to *prove* you could kill me before Time Scope would let us extract you."

Okay, nothing made any sense now. "Extract me? Like a bad tooth?"

"Like someone we've chosen to work for us." Glo scowled like I should completely *get* this. "Extracting people from the past isn't something we do every day. It's exceedingly rare."

Jake jumped in. "We watch a candidate over time. Assess their skills. In some cases, enhance their skills. Don't think your taking karate was an accident."

"That was his idea," Glo said.

"Karate? Wait. What's happening? You want to... extract me, take me to your time, and put me to work. But why? And why me?" They exchanged glances. Troubled glances. "What? What is it? You two look constipated."

"She needs to know," Jake said.

Glo shook her head. "You already risked so much. Besides, knowing could be too much for her."

"As if flying into the past and thinking I killed a man isn't? Meeting my dead uncle and not being able to warn him? Having to leave Sully?" My voice had gone beyond shrill and into shouting territory at this point. Glo shushed me again and I shot her a glare. "I will *not* be quiet. Not until you tell me what's going on."

"Come on, Glo," Jake said. "She has every right to know."

He stared at her a long, uncomfortable time before she let out a world-on-her-shoulders sigh. A chair scraped the floor as Jake sat down next to me. I cringed away from him. He flinched and I flashed a sneer, glad my snub had bothered him.

His laser-blue eyes met mine, clear and open. "What do you remember about your parents? About how they died?"

I went glacial inside. "What's that got to do with anything?"

"It's got everything to do with everything, Beryl. I'm going to tell you something only Glo and I know. Something that happened long ago, when I first started working here. I was on a team. I went..." He paused, as if carefully choosing his words. "I went on a mission, chasing a time-skipper. A man named Oliver Bishop. There was a car. It caught fire. You were inside, with your parents. I know this because I saw you. I was there when they were killed. I took you out of the car."

"You?" I could barely hear my own voice. "You were the guy who rescued me? How... Wait, did you say they were killed? I thought it was an accident."

"No. It was Bishop. He torched your family's car. I don't know how. Maybe it was a Cack or some other weapon. After that, he skipped. Vanished into time. He's still out there. He's the reason why Time Scope instituted the DNA mapping. We had other security protocols in place, but now, no one steps into a Temporal Displacement Catalyzer without a complete DNA map."

"Bishop," I said. "He's still out there? You lost him?"

Jake sagged, as if every ounce of energy had been sapped from his body. "I did. It was my failure. I take full responsibility. For your parents. And for you."

My parents, killed. Murdered. By a man from the future. More pins and needles stabbed my brain. "But... why did he do it?"

"I don't know." He exchanged glances with Glo again. "We don't know."

Why did I get the sick feeling they did know? And that they were still lying to me.

"I think your parents got in the way of something," Jake said. "Something Bishop wanted. Don't think I haven't been searching for the answer or searching for him ever since. I regret not catching that son of a slug, every day of my life."

His eyes sparked anger. Anger surged within me, too. All my life I'd thought their deaths had been an accident. A stupid accident. "Can't you just...go back and stop him?"

I said, close to bawling again. I pinched my thighs to keep from letting the tears out.

"You know he can't," Glo said flatly. "Nobody can. It's history now."

"Beryl." He rested his palm on the arm of my chair. Close, but not touching. "That's why we need *you*. Someone who can help us *stop* runners before they can wreak havoc across history, like he did. We selected you for extraction because of what happened. I've kept an eye on you since that night. I've watched you, trying to keep you safe."

"You did a damn lousy job of it." I swiped at the tears that wet my cheeks. Big fail on the not crying thing. You'd think I wouldn't have a single teardrop left in me at this point. "If I come work for you, will I be able to look for Bishop?"

Jake straightened. "Does this mean you will? You'll join us?"

I lifted a shoulder, wanting him to sweat it out a little. "I don't know. Do *you* want me to?" And by *you*, I decidedly didn't mean him. I looked straight at Glo. She headed up the whole security shebang, didn't she?

She nodded. "I can use you. You're tough. You're an okay fighter. You proved yourself. And you make me laugh."

That was breaking news, since I'd never seen Glo crack a smile, much less laugh.

I looked back at Jake. "Okay, what's in the fine print? I'm cynical enough to know there's got to be a catch to this amazing job offer. What aren't you telling me?"

"It's...complicated," he said.

"Don't give me that crap. No more lies. I'm toting a bucket of lies courtesy of your century. It's full to overflowing. I can't handle another lie. Why me? What aren't you telling me?"

Glo pinned me with an icy look. "In less than an hour you're going to fall off that ladder upstairs."

"And you sort of catch me," I said warily.

She shook her head slowly. "If we return you to your timeline, you fall. No one catches you. You hit your head and..."

"And *what*?" I gripped the chair arms so tightly I thought they would snap off.

Jake eyed me like a doctor about to tell me I had cancer. A diagnosis he had no choice but to share, despite being so very, very sorry about it. The pins and needles in my head became knives and pokers. Razor sharp knives and scorching pokers.

He took a breath to speak, and I imagined a drum roll and a smarmy TV host saying, *and, the number one reason we chose Beryl Blue for extraction is...*

"You die, Beryl," Jake said. "It's that simple. You die."

23

Forget sharp knives and hot pokers. A tent pole seemed to shoot straight into my heart and out the other side.

I looked to Glo, remembering that moment in her office when she'd said something like, "If we send you home..." *If.* I remembered her threat when she'd abandoned me in 1943—if I didn't kill Jake, I wouldn't live to see tomorrow. Not a lie, the bald truth.

She nodded, her scowl fiercer than I'd ever seen it. "That's the truth, Beryl. You fall, hit your head, and *pffft.* The end."

"Stop it, Glo." Jake snapped her an ugly look. I mean, *ugly.* He tipped toward me. He smelled like that village in Belgium, like a soldier, and I missed Sully with a palpable ache. "Occasionally, we find someone in history, someone whose timeline ends. Abruptly. We pluck them out of time and offer them a job. The people we usually extract are ex-military, well-trained. But you were different. Difficult."

"Damned difficult," Glo put in, earning another glower from Jake.

"I don't understand," I said, mostly because I'd stopped paying attention after *you die.*

"Beryl." Jake spoke softly, tenderly. "We had to go through a lot of hoops to get you here. We had to be sure you could do the job before extracting you. Make sure you could think on your feet, that you'd keep your mouth shut about the future, even when you learned about your uncle. We had to make sure you could..." He touched his uniform jacket and the singed hole over his heart. "You know. We came up with a plan to test you—"

"*He* came up with a plan," Glo said. "Went to bat for you when Time Scope's top brass were against it. They couldn't see what you had to offer us, beyond the anonymous tracking."

"I knew you had *everything* to offer," Jake said. "You're valuable to us."

His hand closed over mine. I thought about pulling away but didn't. His palm was warm, his grip firm, like an anchor. His eyes had a darkness that reminded me of Sully. A lived-it look. He'd seen it all.

He'd seen my parents die.

"I don't want to lose you, Beryl. I was too late to save your parents, too late to stop Bishop. I don't want to let you down, too. We need you."

I stiffened, not used to hearing words like that. Who needed Beryl Blue? Certainly no one in my current time period, except maybe my library colleagues and Jenjen. Partially my fault. After Grandma Blue had died, I'd pulled away and shut down, determined not to get close to—or need—anyone ever again. As a result, no one needed me.

"Tell her about Daquan's ultimatum," Glo said. "About if she failed her test mission."

"I'm getting to that," he said over his shoulder, then looked back at me. "This was the deal. We put you to the test. You had to kill me. We sent you to a time of uncertainty and upheaval to pump up your emotions and keep you on your toes. Matched you up with Sullivan, hoping you'd get close enough to him to want to protect him. I...I did my best to push you two together. If you failed the test, our instructions were to send you home. If you refuse extraction, our instructions are the same. We send you back here, to the library. Where you die in exactly..." He squinted up at the old clock on the wall, as a man from a fully digital world would squint at the face of an analog clock. "Thirty-six minutes."

Good people, those Time Scope powers that be. You don't do what they want, they cut you loose. From thirty thousand feet.

"Join us, Beryl," he said. "You'll be our secret weapon."

I rest my case, your honor, apparently, because with an encouraging hand squeeze, he sat back and waited. Glo crossed her arms over her chest, waiting too.

Now it was up to me. For the first time in my life, I had control of my destiny. I'd been shuffled from foster home to foster home with no say. Sent to a therapist because Judge Moreno had ordered it. I had no choice but to go to college. Oh, I was glad I did, but I'd been pushed into it by my caseworker, who dangled that college fund Grandma Blue had thoughtfully banked for me by saving every penny in overtime pay she'd earned working as a nurse. Even me taking karate and flying back in time and pretend-killing a man had been orchestrated by someone else.

In fact, the only thing I'd ever done on my own was to fall in love with Sully.

My gaze ping-ponged back and forth between my new best friends. Glo watched me with her usual scowl. Jake eyed me like he'd just popped the question and desperately hoped for a yes.

Well, damn, what else could I say *but* yes?

"Gee, let's think about this." I held out my hands palms up as if weighing plums, each rotting and covered with fruit flies. "One hand, break my neck and die. Other hand, play time cop for you two and probably die anyway. Guess I'll go with the still breathing option."

Glo let out her breath. Jake dimpled at me, nodding like an idiot.

I stood. "Now, if you'll excuse me, I have to go throw up."

I RAN from the room to the mezzanine bathroom. I didn't care if my clopping boots woke Ida from her nap or interrupted George's mid-morning gaming break. I had to get away from Jake and Glo. No, not away from them, away from *it*. Reality. Unreality, really.

I splashed cold water on my face and stared at my reflection. I looked tired and grubby, but still me, the same me who'd trudged upstairs to the attic to shelve some books what seemed like decades ago. It had only been three days. Three days that shook my world.

A squawk of ancient door hinges and Glo came inside. She leaned against the baby changing station and fixed her gaze on me.

"You okay?" she asked, looking genuinely concerned.

"Maybe. Well, no, but I'll live." I snorted, realizing what I'd just said. "Oh, maybe I won't live, if I don't take your shitty deal."

"It'll take a while to digest everything."

"Understatement." I tore half a dozen paper towels from the dispenser. The last one got stuck and ripped, the end sticking out of the holder like a tongue. "It's going to take a long, *long* time to digest this bad meal."

I turned back to the mirror, avoiding my own angry eyes. I wet the paper towels and started to scrub Belgium off my face. I wiped away the past, and Sully.

I froze at a sudden thought. "Glo, you caught me when I fell off the ladder. If I said no to the deal, how would you un-catch me?"

"The Kicker. I'd send myself a message to abort the intervention."

"Like temporal texting? But you said you can't change the past. You already caught me so how can you—"

"Don't. You'll twist your brain into knots trying to figure it out. Your timeline was at an end. That's the history. We'd have to let it play out."

I started scrubbing again, twice as hard. "What happens? To the me in my time, I mean."

"You disappear. We empty your bank accounts, buy a

bus ticket, make a few purchases on your credit cards. Then...the trail goes cold."

"You make people think I ran away?" For some reason that angered me more than anything else.

"Wouldn't be the first time," she said softly.

Ooh, throwing shade at a time like this. "You really need to work on your people skills."

She snorted. "That seems to be Jake's job where you're concerned."

I spun around to face her. "So, I wasn't imagining things. He's...into me? He *likes* me?"

She drew herself up. "It was inevitable, I guess. He felt responsible for what happened to your parents. Responsible for *you*. He saw what you went through over the years. There was something about a beautiful, unattainable young woman, a woman who'd lost everything, who struggled to survive. He let his feelings get the best of him."

My stomach rolled. "Yeah, well, that woman doesn't exist. He'll find that out when he gets to know me. Soon he'll be all, Beryl Blue? Hate that chick."

"Doubtful. Not after what he went through to get you here. Highly unethical, totally against every rule in the book. But that's Jake." She shifted. "Don't tell him I let that slip, okay? He doesn't want you to know. He doesn't want it influencing your feelings toward him in any way."

"You guys made me hate him, remember? *He* made me hate him."

"We had to do whatever it took to save you."

I rolled my eyes at that, the tag line to a terrible movie. "Well, Jake doesn't stand a chance, anyway. In case you haven't noticed, I'm kind of hung up on someone else. Thanks for that, by the way. Matching me up with a guy who lived and died long ago."

My heart squeezed. Something else to digest. Sully was probably gone in my time, long gone in Glo's. He'd lived his life. Without me.

I wadded up the wet paper towels and flung them into the trash barrel. "Why Sully? Why send me to him?" Not just send me to him, they'd *thrown* me at him.

Glo paused a long time before answering. "We had to find someone compatible. Someone as tough as you. Someone you'd come to care for enough to do the job."

She sounded ashamed of herself, and rightly so. Both of them should be, toying with our emotions like that. Not so much messing with me. I'd be all right, but what their little temporal game had done to Sully made me burn. I'd left him in the past with a broken heart and thinking I'd killed a man.

"Was any of it true, then?" I asked. "Was Sully really important? To history, I mean."

"Mostly. After a fashion, as my Nana Reid would say." Her expression softened. "You're not the only one with a wise old grandmother, you know. Your sergeant saves Corporal Santelli. In fact, Sullivan helps lots of folks in the war. And after. He becomes a cop."

A cop. Why didn't that surprise me? "Tell me, did he find someone? Did he fall in love, have a family?"

Glo looked down at her hands, clasped in front of her. Evasive, or sparing my feelings?

"On second thought, don't tell me." I mean, if Sully married a glamour queen pinup girl after the war and had a dozen kids, well, good for him. But really, did I want to know that? "Just tell me that he was happy."

"He was." She spoke slowly, as if choosing her words with care. "He was happy because he had you, Beryl. Just a minute in time, but that was enough."

I nodded, glad to hear that. Heartbroken, but glad.

"Now, it's time to go," she said. "We need to get you settled in our time. Your training starts in the morning. Are you ready?"

Uh, no. I doubted I'd ever be ready. But I wasn't going to run away, not this time. Not ever again. I nodded and Glo opened the door.

I followed her out, into my new life.

EPILOGUE

SIX MONTHS LATER - 2130

The melancholy strings of "I'll be Seeing You" faded, and my apartment's communications interface segued into another heartbreaking song, "It's Been a Long, Long Time," without a pause.

I pulled the ring off the fourth Budweiser of the contraband six pack I'd smuggled back from 1977. The ankle I'd irritated chasing after that roller boogie time runner earlier today had stopped throbbing. Or maybe the alcohol in my system had dulled the pain. Whatever, I couldn't feel the ache anymore.

At least not in my ankle. The ache in my heart? That would take a lot longer to heal.

Before I'd left Sully in the past, he'd asked if I'd be okay. At the time, I'd thought no, never again. So, it surprised me to discover after a while that I kind of was. Things weren't so bad here in Futureworld. Sure, corporations still made obscene profits and there were still homeless people. But most everyone had health care and major strides had been taken to alleviate the impact of climate change, so progress had been made. And much to my surprise, I liked my job, in spite of the danger. I guess I enjoyed the rush.

In my downtime, Beryl Blue, Time Cop became Beryl Blue, Librarian. Yup, no longer a wannabe. Jake had made that happen. When I discovered that libraries with real books with spines and ink and both hard and paperback covers still existed in this future world, I demanded to be taken to one, *stat*. Jake had gone above and beyond, and fixed it so I could work part time in the city's west district branch.

So yeah, when not chasing temporal runners, I spent a couple hours a week happily shushing people, grousing about the library director, and craftily avoiding shelving books, though to be honest, most shelving had been automated decades ago. I even wore my hair in a bun once in a while.

My new life was the best of all possible worlds, except... Except Sully wasn't in it.

I still held the photograph in my hand. I gazed longingly at my redhead, the only thing missing from my new life. I missed him. Mourned him. It would take a hell of a lot more time for *that* to be okay.

A pleasant chime, like an ice cream truck heading my way, sounded overhead. "Jake Tyson is at the door," my apartment's computer voice announced.

Jake? It had been six months since I'd become a time cop, assigned to his team, and he'd never stopped by my place. Not once. I'd think he had no idea where I lived if I didn't know that he knew everything that went on at Time Scope.

He'd always been polite but distant whenever we interacted, whether during my training, debriefing after missions, or at company gatherings. Sometimes I thought Glo's claim that he had a thing for me had been a joke, except for those rare, unguarded moments when I caught him watching me, a wistful look on his face. Like the boy at the school dance yearning to ask the cheerleader to cut a rug, but too afraid to speak. A tongue-tied situation I approved of wholeheartedly.

So, Jake coming here was a big effing deal. My curiosity was duly piqued.

"Let him in," I said, standing up and trying to blink away the beer-induced fuzziness in my brain. I tested my ankle before putting weight on my right leg and turned as the door whooshed open. Jake stepped over the threshold.

"What are you doing here?" I blurted. It may have been six months but the permafrost between us had thawed only a fraction. I made sure of it.

He gave me a nice display of those dimples and I scowled. I didn't want to like him, not one bit.

"Just wanted to say good work today. As usual, you brought the perp in with no injuries, no ripples in the timeline."

I accepted his kudos with a nod. I didn't get a lot of *atta-girls* in my old life. Kind of nice to get praise now, even if I suspected the motives of the guy doing the praising.

He strode toward me, his movements fluid, his muscles flexing under his snug khakis, his simple black T-shirt hugging finely honed pecs. He got close enough for me to catch his scent, clean and correct, nothing scruffy about him. I held up my hand for him to stop, hoping he wouldn't get a snootful of the beer fumes coming off me.

"Here's a dossier for your next job," he said, holding out a small square of plastic. "Seattle, 1997. Some jerk wreaks havoc at a Starbucks."

Jenjen roused himself from the sofa and wound around my visitor's ankles.

"Shoo, get away from him." I nudged that traitorous feline with my foot. I didn't even want my cat to like Jake, though he'd arranged for Jenjen to time trip here. And if I never again see a cat hucked out of the temporal vortex, claws out and howling, it'll be too soon.

I reached for the dossier as if Jake had cooties, then slipped it into my pocket. Feigning indifference, though the assignment intrigued the hell out of me. I'd never been to Seattle. I wondered if Starbucks had served Oreo Frappuccinos in 1997.

"What's up, Jake? You could've sent that to me remotely. You didn't have to haul all the way to the west side to give it to me."

His gaze drifted around the small apartment, taking in the bare walls, the tidy, generic furniture, and the books on the kitchen counter—H. G. Wells' *The Time Machine*, a manga history of the 21st century that gave me the shudders, and a WWII-set romance I wished the author had consulted me on. He shifted, eyeing the beer cans on the table next to my chair with a frown.

"I wanted to see how your ankle's doing," he said, looking back at me. "I've seen you limping the last few days." Did I detect a bit of sheepishness in that admission? That he'd been watching me? He hurried on. "I want to be sure you're A-1 before we send you out on another job." He turned as if to go then swiveled back. "Oh, and we got a ping on Bishop."

That swept the beer cobwebs out of my brain like a broom on fast forward. "Really? Awesome. Where is he? *When* is he?"

"It's only a ping, Beryl. No confirmation. Just thought you should know."

"When?" I repeated.

"Seventeenth century." He frowned, still not a good look for him. "Disappointed? Hoping it'd be 1946 or '47? A mission where you could go back, maybe accidentally on purpose bump into Sullivan? That's what you're hoping for, isn't it? Going somewhere close to him." He seemed to stagger after dropping that, like he'd been holding the accusation in for a long time.

I gave a reluctant nod. Oh, I wanted to find Oliver Bishop. Wanted to make him pay for what he'd done to my mother and father. That's why I'd been so cautious during extractions, so reluctant to use my weapon on time runners. I wanted Bishop to be my first kill. After I beat a confession out of him. After he told me why he'd murdered my parents.

But Jake had hit the nail on its painful head. I hoped to see Sully again. *Ached* to see him. I'd resisted looking him up on the myriad search engines available to me in this century. I couldn't bear to stumble across his marriage announcement. Or his death notice. But that didn't stop me from hoping I'd *see* him one more time.

Every new assignment that came my way I wished would take me to the late-1940s—and Sully.

I shrugged. "Can't blame a girl for trying."

Jake went all serious. "Give it up, Beryl. You're never going anywhere near that time period, not if I can help it."

It clicked then. How could I be so dense? Six months on the job and I'd never gotten an assignment in the postwar era. Was Jake that jealous? That petty?

"What?" I said. "Have you been deliberately keeping me away from Sully?"

"Damn right I have." Jake's gaze slid to the photograph, still in my hand. "You need to move on. He's gone. He's in the past. It's time you accepted it and moved forward, instead of pining for a ghost."

I flinched. Harsh words, but true. Hadn't I just been thinking that myself?

"Beryl, you've got to stop wallowing in self-pity and open your eyes. There's a big world out there with lots of vibrant people in it. Grieving's normal, but you have to make the effort to move on."

I returned Jake's stare. His breathing had ratcheted up during his little speech, and his cheeks were flushed. His black hair spiked at comical angles.

Deep down, I knew he was right. I should close the book on Sully. Our story had ended. Not a happy ending, more like bittersweet. But all the plot threads were wrapped up. Except one, and I couldn't let that go. I mean, how could I put Sully to rest, put the past in the past and move on, if there was the slightest chance we might meet again? If only for a brief, breathless moment?

"I miss him, Jake." There, I said it. Every bit of naked emotion I felt poured out in those simple words. "I miss him every day. And I barely got to say goodbye. To him and Stretch and Grandma Blue. I feel so...so *empty*. How do I get over that?"

"You don't. You don't get over it. You just get used to it."

His eyes flashed and I gasped. Selfish, selfish me. Jake had lost someone, too.

"And I'm sorry, Beryl, but you should be glad I'm doing this."

The sudden steel in his voice alerted me. "What does *that* mean?"

No answer, just silence. He looked super uncomfortable. If he wore a tie, he'd be tugging at the knot right now.

"Jake, why did you choose to send me to 1943? Why'd you push me into Sully's path?"

I'd asked those questions, a lot, and always got the same answer. Sully and I were compatible, the war years were a time of heightened emotion that would keep me on my toes, and on and on. A lot of unsatisfactory rhetoric had spilled from Jake and Glo the last six months. Now I wanted the truth.

"Tell me the *real* reason this time. And don't you dare with that *it's complicated* stuff."

He scraped his fingers through his hair and let out a capitulating sigh. "All right. I'll tell you. We wanted to find someone to match your strengths. Someone selfless. Someone who'd go all the way for you." He looked me straight in the eye. "Even die for you."

My heart stuttered. This is what he and Glo had held

back, what all those meaningful glances they'd been exchanging had been about. "Why wouldn't you tell me that?"

"I didn't tell you because I've tracked him, followed his postwar timeline. It's full of ripples and fuzzy as hell. The only clear thing I've seen is you, meeting Sullivan again. Not sure when, but it'll happen. And, Beryl, you'd better hope you don't run into him for a long time."

My whole body filled with dread. "Because?"

Jake's expression darkened and he held up both hands, palms up. I knew what that meant, but I made him say it.

"Because, when the two of you meet, Sullivan's time-line will end."

The world turned dark. Even Jenjen went still and quiet. I could hear the blood rushing in my ears.

"You see?" Jake said gently. "That's Sullivan's fate. That's why I've been keeping you from that time period."

How's that for a joke? The thing I wanted most, to see Sully again, to be in his arms once more, was the thing I had to hope against with all my heart. I felt as if a bottom-less pit opened before me, and I teetered on the edge.

"But there's got to be a way around it," I said. "I mean, after everything we went through, everything you and Time Scope threw at me and Sully. We can't just let him di—" I cut off. I couldn't say the word. Could barely think it.

"Beryl..." Jake reached for me, then seemed to think better of it and stepped back. "I hate how much this hurts you. But the timeline can't be changed. You'll meet again, and when you do, he'll die. It *can't* be prevented. The only thing I can do is delay the inevitable. If I could fix it, I would. You know that."

I gazed into those pretty, pretty eyes and the ice wall I'd built between us cracked a little. I *did* know that. He and Sully were alike in a lot of ways. Both good men. Both caring, selfless men who wanted to protect me. But Jake differed in one important way. Sully would've told me the truth from the start. No matter how much it hurt.

Jake suddenly smiled. A weird thing to do at a time like this. "I have an idea. It won't change Sullivan's fate, but it'll give you a chance to say goodbye. Maybe ease the sting of loss. Get some closure, as they said in your era."

I brightened a little. "What do you have in mind?"

A DAY LATER, I stepped into the gaping mouth of a time transport bay. The doors clanked shut and a swirling blue vortex kicked up. In seconds, the machine tossed me out onto a bed of pine needles. I scrambled up, brushed off my skirt, and started through the trees toward Carter farm. The old folks, lamb stew, and Sunday dinner waited for me there.

And so did Sully.

I spotted a flash of copper hair through the tree branches and headed toward it. My heart swelled to see Sully where I'd left him in 1943, in the woods near Stretch's house, on a beautiful October day. He sat with his back against a tree trunk, a lit cigarette in his hand.

"*What* did I tell you about smoking?" I said when I got close enough.

He jumped, startled, then broke out in a broad grin. My stomach spun like an out of control washing machine. His face, so young, so open, so much less feral than the Sully I'd seen in Belgium in 1944. The Sully I *would* see, more than a year from this moment.

"See what happens when you're not here to nag me?" He stubbed the cigarette out on the tree trunk and flicked it away. "What happened? You only just left."

Ah. The beauty of time travel. "Lo-o-ong story. It's classified. Suffice to say, everything's all set. For now." He nodded, though he still looked confused. I tipped my head. "Sully, why are you still here? Why didn't you go back to the farmhouse?"

"Not hungry." He aimed another grin my way. "Truth? I had to sit down, after everything that happened. All that ish kabibble about the future. Those weapons, those folks, coming out of thin air. You, disappearing like a ghost. I had to..." He trailed off with a shrug.

"You had to take a second to wrap your brain around it?" I finished. Welcome to the club. "I can try my best to explain the logistics of popping around in time." Like how this moment had already happened for him when I saw him in Belgium, but not for me. "But thinking about it will just give you a monster headache. My best advice? Don't even try to figure it out."

I held out my hand to help him up. He stood, fluid and easy, like a panther. A large, redheaded panther. He kept hold of my hand, lacing his fingers with mine.

"I was hoping you'd come back," he said, like a kid who got what he'd wished for when he blew out his birthday candles.

I got the gift I wanted, too. A big, shiny present all tied up in a bow from Jake.

"I can give you an afternoon," Jake had said. "A chance to see him, and the others, your family, one last time. You can finish that meal. Try not to think about what happens next, to Private Carter or to Sergeant Sullivan. Try not to think about anything. Take the time to appreciate the now. Maybe that'll help you let him go."

A gift of the now. I had to focus on that. Sully was supposed to die, two years after the war, or three or four, I didn't know when. I only knew that sometime after the war, Big Red's timeline would end. He'd die protecting me. Fate had decreed it, and unless I could somehow kick fate's ass and change Sully's future, I had to do my best to stay away from him. For as long as possible.

But I had today. This peaceful fall afternoon, these precious hours. I took it all in, took him in, with every sense. Imprinted the memories down deep. Determined to treasure each touch and smile, every blink and heartbeat of this man. I'd never felt like this before. I knew I'd never feel like this again. I felt it now, though, this moment, and that was enough. It had to be.

He gazed down at me, our eyes locked, and that eyebrow flicked upward. "You look different. You *are* different."

What clued him in? The fact I no longer had a bruise on my cheek? Or that I was slightly older and a skosh leaner after six months on the time cop job? Or just me, who'd changed in so many ways since that fateful day I'd toppled off that ladder in the library and into Sully's life?

"That's another long story, Sergeant, guaranteed to

make your head spin." I smiled into his eyes, feeling light and giddy. "But let's go back to the farmhouse and eat first. I'm starving."

Grinning, he took my hand and held it tight. "You know something, Beryl Blue? You're a real piece of work."

I laughed. "Sully, have you ever thought about getting a tattoo?"

---

*THANK YOU FOR READING **BERYL BLUE, TIME COP**! I HOPE YOU ENJOYED BERYL AND SULLY'S ADVENTURE IN TIME. IF YOU DID, PLEASE HELP OTHERS FIND THEIR STORY BY LEAVING A REVIEW.*

AND DON'T FORGET TO SIGN UP FOR MY NEWSLETTER FOR THE LATEST NEWS ON THE NEXT BOOKS IN THE BERYL BLUE, TIME COP SERIES AS WELL AS MY OTHER STORIES, PLUS EXCLUSIVE CONTENT, FREE BOOKS, AND ALL KINDS OF OTHER GOODIES.

JUST STOP BY MY WEBSITE TO JOIN THE FUN!

WWW.JANETRAYESTEVENS.COM

BERYL & SULLY'S STORY CONTINUES IN...

IT'S BEEN A LONG, LONG TIME

Some days, it just doesn't pay to get out of your century...

It's been two years since Beryl Blue left her bossy, sexy sergeant behind in 1943. Though her heart still hurts, she's moved on with her new life as a time cop in the year 2132. But fate isn't done teasing her or Sully yet. The discovery of an old suitcase leads Beryl to 1946 on a hunt for the man who killed her parents—and straight into Sully's arms.

A dead body, a jewel heist, Sully's prickly new girl-friend, and secrets from Beryl's past all come into play as she struggles to catch a time traveling thief, evade a killer, and keep her beloved Sully from falling victim to his destiny.

Coming Spring 2022!

OTHER BOOKS BY JANET RAYE STEVENS

Cole for Christmas

An event planner getting over a bad breakup, a chef who was left at the altar. Recruited to save a Christmas Eve wedding during a blizzard, the last thing on their minds is new romance—but the mistletoe has other plans.

A Moment After Dark – a WWII paranormal mystery

Addie sees the future with a simple touch. A valuable gift in a time of war. Will a determined federal agent get to her before the enemy does?

ABOUT THE AUTHOR

Meet author Janet Raye Stevens – mom, reader, tea-drinker (okay, tea guzzler), and teller of hilarious and sometimes totally true tales. Derringer Award finalist and winner of RWA's Golden Heart® and Daphne du Maurier awards, Janet writes mystery, time travel, paranormal, and the occasional Christmas romance, all with humor, heart, and a dash of intrigue. She lives in New England with her husband, who's practically perfect in every way, and their two sons, both geniuses and good-looking to boot.

www.janetrayestevens.com